Maybe the Horse Did It

Sanford Champlin IV

OTHER BOOKS BY SANFORD CHAMPLIN

My Friend Donny

Maybe...
The Horse Did It?

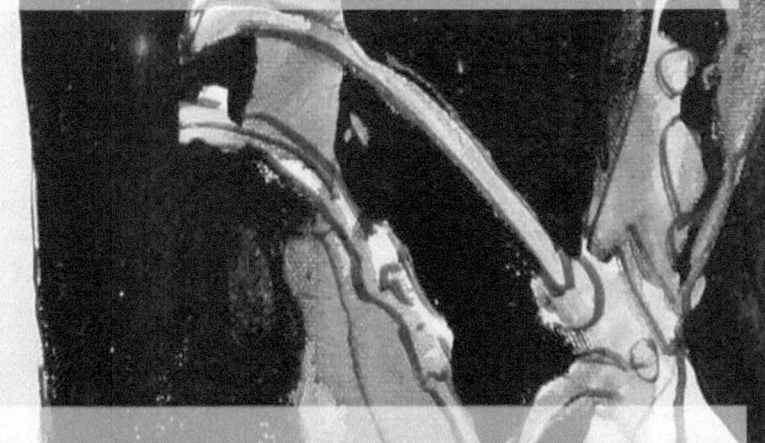

Sanford Champlin IV

Second Print Edition 2018 Dark Ink Press

ISBN-13 **978-0-9984801-8-3**
ISBN 0-9984801-8-5

Cover design by John Gray Esq.

Printed in the United States of America

*To my wife and kids,
who put up with me
through this process.*

*And to Janet Durham,
the teacher who opened
my eyes to the wonderful
world of reading.*

Chapter 1

"Oh hell no," Sam Nickles said as he opened the front door of his home to go to work.

It was a quarter to seven in the morning, and it was already over 90 degrees. The heat and the humidity smacked him in the face, like walking into a brightly-lit sauna.

"I can't do this," he said to himself as he walked back into the house, pulling off his gun belt and shirt.

"What are you doing?" Lilly, Sam's wife, asked as she walked into the living room.

"I can't do this vest today. I just stepped outside for a second and already have sweat running down the crack of my ass," Sam said, pulling off his bulletproof vest. That made him feel cooler and lighter.

As Sam was putting the body armor back in the closet, Lilly said, "I know it's hot, but…"

Lilly stopped as he looked at her. He said, "Don't worry, I got my tactical vest in the car. I'll put it on if I get a hot call." But, she would worry; Lilly always worried.

Sam put his uniform shirt back on and reached for his gun belt, thinking, "I can't wait for the day I don't have to put this crap on anymore."

Sam moaned as he felt the pain in his lower back. Sam had been on the McCrackin's Bluff Police Department for twenty-seven years, doing what he had wanted to do since he was a kid, but now it was starting to wear hard on him. At fifty-four years old, Sam had been a cop for half of his life. His youth and his lifestyle were catching up with him. He was overweight from eating junk food on weird shifts. Sam's joints ached from the wear and tear of all the "fun stuff" he did when he was young, but the things that he did then helped to keep him alive as a cop.

Spending his childhood in the woods playing, hiking and camping, Sam had started shooting when his dad gave him his first BB gun at five years old. He'd received his first real gun, a .22 caliber Marlin Bolt action on his 9th birthday. There were many birthdays and guns after that and Sam kept all of them. Sam knew the basics of tracking and trapping; he could start a fire with flint and steel, among other survival skills. Hunting and shooting became second nature to him, be it a handgun, rifle or shotgun. Sam could pick up practically any gun, and be proficient with it in minutes. This natural ability led him to become the police department's firearms instructor. He hadn't hunted in years. He said to others that he didn't have time, but actually didn't have the heart for it.

As a kid, Sam climbed anything he could find a hand and foot hold in, never thinking about getting back down. He had always made it down, but not always without some scars to remind him of his mistakes. He and his friends would ride bicycles to Shawnee National Forest; they would camp overnight and spend the day rock climbing at the Garden of the Gods. Sam loved the Garden of the Gods, a sandstone outcropping whose rock formations like the Camel's Head and Devil's Smokestacks offered great climbing and rappelling challenges. "The Gods," as all the kids in the area called them, were surrounded by a large thick forest that in the fall was full of colorful orange, yellow and red foliage and bright green pine trees. In his teen years, Sam learned to rappel from these rocks and do rope rescues. With his friends, Sam spent many a night sleeping under the stars by a roaring fire, telling stories. They would pretend to be Wild West pioneers, like a lot of young boys did in that era.

In school Sam was a daydreamer, not a star student by any means. He hated English and math, but loved history and art. In junior and senior high school, Sam was on the wrestling team, and he was pretty good, his short stout frame giving him a lot of power. But, his real love was boxing. He and his father, who had boxed in the U.S. Army, would spar quite a bit when he was a teenager. Sam wanted to box competitively, but there was not any organized boxing in their area. Boxing and wrestling were a lot of help in his martial arts classes in college, and he had loved to compete. These activities were excellent training for police work, but not as much as being a bouncer in the bars. While in college, working as a bouncer, Sam got some real lessons in fighting. He had the broken nose and scars to prove it!

Sam walked into the bathroom where Lilly was getting ready for work. After a quick kiss and a, "Love you, have a good day," he turned and headed out the door. It was typical summer day in the mid-west: high temperatures, and high humidity. Sam hated it. The NOAA weather site on the internet had called for a chance of thunderstorms, but there were no signs of it now. There was not a cloud in the sky and a blazing sun beat down on his black and white Crown Victoria police cruiser. Sam opened the car door, reached in and turned the key on. The air conditioner kicked in, but he waited a minute to let it start cooling off before getting into the car.

Sam waved at Harry Rose who was walking by with his Bassett Hound, Saggy. "The older Harry gets, the more he looks like Saggy, with those drooping jaws," Sam laughed to himself.

Plopping himself into the seat of the patrol car, he thinks to himself, "I need to get rid of some of this gut, it's probably causing some of the constant aches in my lower back. He stretched and tried to get comfortable in the cruisers seat.

Sam turned on his police radio and signed in "City-4, (Sam's Call Number) on duty."

Dispatch responded immediately, giving him a call of a 10-90 (business alarm) at Bub's, a local hardware store on Main Street. Sam rolled his eyes and sighed, "Geesh… can't these people figure out how to turn an alarm off?"

Not even given a chance to start his duty log, he put the cruiser in reverse and backed out of his driveway, headed for Bub's. Sam hurried to the store which is just a few blocks away, as everything is in McCracken's Bluff, a small town of 6,000 people. He didn't even bother to turn on his lights or siren, the streets were clear.

Sam hated the sound of the siren and didn't use it unless it was absolutely necessary. For some reason, it just grated his nerves like fingernails scraping a chalkboard. To him, the siren was just a call for nosey people to come and look at what is happening. Sam thought the worst event was when the town had their Homecoming parade, and all the police and volunteer fire departments led the parade with sirens blaring. Even though it only lasted about 10 minutes, Sam always ended up with a headache. Sam thought people should never used a siren on an alarm call anyway. If it was a real break-in, it just told the burglars that you were coming. The idea, for the police, was to catch the criminals- not to run them off.

Dawn Pearl, Sam's partner, advised him she was leaving her home across town. As Sam arrived, he noticed Bub's pick-up truck in the parking lot. Sam looked around cautiously and informed her that the owner was there, and all looked ok, and that she can probably disregard the call. Sam knew this wasn't a proper tactical move, but he knew his beat, and at that time of day, he was sure it was a false alarm and he didn't need back-up.

As he walked up, nearing the front of the store, he saw no one else moving. Looking into the business, Sam could see really well through the big windows at the front of the hardware store. Bub was back behind the counter in the middle of the building. With a puzzled look on his face, Sam entered the front door. Half way down the aisle, Sam realized that Bub was up on top of the counter. By the expression on his face, Bub looked as if he had seen the devil, himself. Now, Sam was small in comparison to Bub. Bub was 6'5" and every bit of 450 pounds, very round with a Howdy Doody face. Now seeing him up on that counter shaking, made Sam smile.

"What in the hell is going on Bub?" Sam asked. Bub just pointed to the floor. Looking down, Sam laughed out loud.

Chapter 2

"Really?" Sam said. He was no fan of the slithering reptiles, but since his son, Jeb, had snakes as pets for several years, he got used to handling them. The snakes would get out of their tanks way too often for Sam liking. His favorite place, Shawnee National Forest, was full of them, some poisonous and some not. The Forest Service there even shuts down a road every year for the snake migration. It was really creepy- thousands maybe millions of snakes moving to their summer home. Sam and some friends went one year to watch. Once was enough for Sam.

The worst encounter Sam had ever had with a snake was while rappelling near the Camel Rock. That day, he had stopped half way down a 120-foot drop. It was a beautiful view up there, so Sam thought that he would take a couple of pictures. As he was tying himself off, Sam heard a noise coming from the rocks. When he looked, he was eye to eye with a timber rattler hiding in the cervices. It was probably a small one, but right then, to Sam, it looked to be a 10-foot-long monster snake. Sam pulled out the knot, pushed out and loosened his grip on the rope. He dropped the rest of the way down with just one kick, falling fast, but controlling the stop right on the ground. Everyone was impressed with Sam's death-defying feat until he told them why. After that, they then went and looked for a new spot to tie off their ropes, and checked for surprises. Sam learned his snakes well, at least the ones to watch out for; the ones with triangular heads and stubby tails were poisonous.

This was not a big poisonous snake on the floor of Bub's hardware. It was only a foot-long rat snake curled up in the center of the aisle. Sam reached over and grabbed a broom, pinned the snake down, snatched the by the end of its tail and carried it out of the store. Sam took it to a grassy spot across the parking lot, and let it go.

"Did ya kill it?" Bub asked as Sam came back into the store.

"Noooo," Sam said, shaking his head, "It wasn't going to hurt anyone. It might have gotten rid of a few of those mice in your basement."

Sam smiled as he watched Bub trying to roll off of the counter, thinking, "How in the hell did he get all of himself up there in the first place?" Bub was shaking, saying how much he hated snakes and how that one had snuck up on him.

Sam started to ask Bub how he got up there, when dispatch called, checking to see if all was ok. "Intruder apprehended, given a warning and thrown in the grass," Sam said, smiling, Sam knew that answer would just bring up questions at dispatch.

Sam turned back to Bub, who was trying to get the alarm system to reset. "I'm sorry, Sam, I walked in to turn off the alarm and that thing scared the shit out of me," he said while pushing the buttons frantically, still shaken. "I couldn't get to the alarm panel or the phone."

Sam stepped in and asked Bub for his code and reset the alarm. "But, Bub… how did you get up there?" Sam asked.

Bub turned around and looked at the counter and just stared at it for a minute, then said, "I haven't a clue, Sam."

Sam laughed! Then he asked, "Bub, you have a whole store of things you could have killed that snake with. Why didn't you just grab an axe and whack it?"

"Those things are fast," Bub said, lumbering back to the front of the store.

Standing at the front of the business, not ready to leave as he was enjoying the cold air, Sam told dispatch he was available. Dispatch responded saying, "Signal 8 (Meet) with City 7 (Dawn), an accident at the corner of 2nd and Mill Street."

"Clear dispatch," Sam replied. Then he said, "Well, Bub, it looks like it's going to be one of those days. Go next door and get a cup of coffee and settle down." As Sam got back into his car, he saw Bub locking up and going to Purple Lotus Café.

Sam wished he had left his car running. It would take a few minutes for it to cool down again, and his shaved head was already beaded with sweat, running down his forehead into his eyes. As he drove to the accident, he heard his partner, Dawn Pearl, arriving on the scene. She told dispatch that there were no injuries, and they could disregard the ambulance, but let Sam know she needed him for traffic control. By then Sam was only a few blocks away, and he advised dispatch he was arriving.

Shaking his head, Sam noticed cars backed up as he got to the scene. These were mostly rubberneckers wanting to see what was going on. They could have easily gone around the block, but no- small town busy bodies!

Dawn was already getting the information from drivers for the report, so Sam started clearing the traffic out of the way so the tow trucks could get in. Looking over at Dawn, Sam saw another familiar face. It was Sherrie Hall, a classmate that he had dated a few times, but after graduation had moved to Boston and gone to law school. It had been years since he had seen her, but had always wondered about her. Sam smiled, for she had not changed much- older now, but maybe even prettier. Sherrie was a tall, long-legged, red-head, with shining green eyes that could look right through you. She always had a very classy way about her and was smart, 4.0 smart. Sam was not sure why they hit it off, but they had had some good times together.

After she had got done talking with Dawn, Sherrie walked towards Sam, calling his name.

"Sam… Hey, Sam, I guess you never got away from here, huh?" she asked.

'Well … you know…are you okay? Sam asked.

"Oh, I wasn't in the accident, I'm just a witness," she replied

"Good! Well, how have you been? It's been a long time," Sam asked.

"I'm good," she said, but only half smiling. "Mom is sick, and I came back to help out with her. And I guess you have probably heard I got a divorce a couple months back. I needed some time away from the city."

"No I hadn't heard, but sorry, if there is…." Sam stammered.

"Stop," she said waving her hand, "It's no big deal, life goes on!" Then, she flashed that big smile that always seemed to brighten up things.

Talking to Sherri, Sam took his attention off of the traffic and a car almost hit them. After yelling at the driver, Sam told Sherrie she should probably get out of the road, and that he hoped they could catch up while she was in town.

She said, "You can bet we will!" as she turned and walked off. Sam smiled, as he always enjoyed watching her walk away.

After the accident, Dawn and Sam met up at the Randy's for a cup of coffee, or in Dawn's case a bottle of herbal tea. They talked and laughed about the incident at Bub's Hardware.

"You should have seen him, Dawn, it was the funniest thing," Sam said while trying to hold back the laughter. "Bub, up on top of that counter, on his knees, his hands pumping up and down, face fire engine red, mouth moving but nothing coming out. I wish I had one of those body cams, it would have gone viral on YouTube."

"How did he get up there? I mean…he's not very spry," Dawn asked.

"I don't have the slightest idea. I can't even picture it, but I bet it was funny!"

"That snake wasn't even a foot long and about as big around as my pinky, but you would have thought it was a boa constrictor… I bet Bub is telling everyone it was thislong and as big around as his arm," Sam said, holding his arms all the way out, almost hitting a customer with his coffee cup.

Before they left, Dawn told Sam about a warrant that was going to be issued for Joe Kerchak, a guy Sam knew well and had arrested several times. "Joe beat up a guy last night at The Fuwalda. He took off before our guys arrived at the bar. They looked for him all night but couldn't find him."

"How did you hear about the warrant?" Sam asked.

"Oh… uh… Jason called me while I was driving over here. He wanted me to pick it up at his office," Dawn stammered. "He has other paperwork to go to the station, too."

"Damn, he's up and in the office, early," Sam said.

12

"Yeah… I guess, he must be busy," Dawn replied.

Sam didn't say anything but thought it strange. It was just past 8:00 am and the District Attorney's Office was seldom ever open before 9:00 am, and why would Jason be calling Dawn directly, not dispatch?

Chapter 3

His partner for the last six years, Dawn was eleven years younger than Sam- a tall, wisp of a woman, but with a determination to make it in an otherwise all-male police department. Sam liked working with her. She did her job well and didn't back off from anyone.

They had been at Randy's for a bit when Dawn looked at her watch and said she needed to go. She had to take her six-year-old daughter, Brit, to the pool for swim lessons. They talked about meeting up for lunch, but knowing that probably was not going to happen the way this day had been going so far.

Only 8:20 and two calls already, it looked to be a busy day. Then, Sam got a call of a theft that had occurred on Willow Street. "Number three," Sam thought to himself.

While en-route Sam heard Dawn get a call to go to the Prosecutor's Office. Sam arrived at 410 Willow Street, and saw Gracie Allen standing in the yard pacing back and forth. As he got out of his car she unloaded on him, yelling "How come a person can't leave something unguarded for a minute without someone stealing it, what's this world coming to?!"

Trying to calm her down, Sam asked, "What happened?"

Gracie said, "I went to the grocery store early to beat the heat, and when I got home I was taking the bags into the house. I came back out to get the rest of groceries and found a bag scattered on the ground." They walked around the other side of her car, and there was a plastic grocery bag on the ground about 10 feet from the car with some of the groceries scattered around.

Sam asked, "Do you know what was taken?"

Gracie said, "I'm not sure yet. I didn't want to touch anything, I want fingerprints taken." Sam started walking around the house to see if he could find anything else.

Then he saw Monte, Gracie's German Shepard, munching on a large beef roast.

"Another case solved, maybe I should take paw prints," Sam said as he pointed out Monte to Gracie. Gracie just stood there, mouth agape, as Sam walked back to his car shaking his head, and told dispatch he was done with the call.

Sam had left the car running, and it was cool as he got in, he sat back and enjoyed the air conditioner. He had not even had a chance to start his daily log for the day, so he got a new form from his clipboard and put down the information from the past calls. Sam thought about going out to the Town Park to, "run some radar" under the big trees that overhung the road, but that didn't work out. Dispatch called him and told him to report to the station to meet with the chief. "Oh, joy," Sam thought as he pulled away.

Sam was only a few blocks to the station but was in no hurry to get there. The new Chief of Police, Seth Wallow, was twenty-eight years old and only a four-year veteran of the department. Sam had known Seth since he was a kid, even arresting him once for being a minor in possession of alcohol, but that didn't go anywhere because Seth's Grandfather was mayor at the time. Sam was Seth's field training officer when Seth first got on the Police Department. Sam did not see much fire in this kid, then or now. Sam didn't dislike Seth but never felt he had paid his dues.

The McCracken's Bluff Police Station was in the old Town Hall building that was over a hundred years old. All of the other town offices had moved into the new facility across the town square except for the police and fire departments. The young officers hated the station and thought it was old, dusty and drafty. Sam thought it had charm and style. The building was built in 1841, a two-story brick with old lathe and plaster walls and magnificent oak woodwork. A huge safe that had been constructed into the building for the town treasury and records was always a conversation piece. It had an outer door that was opened by a combination lock and an inner door that had a key lock. The outside door was never completely closed because no one had known the combination for years. The chief kept the keys to the inner door because the evidence was stored in there. Inside the outer door were taped old newspaper clipping of local historical events, all yellowed with age.

The fire department used the back of the building and the upstairs. They still had an old brass pole from when the sleeping quarters were upstairs. After the remodeling, the sleeping rooms were now on the ground level, and the pole was just decoration, though Sam remembered when he was a kid, hanging around the station, getting to slide down it, and thought it was so cool. Back then, the police and fire departments were dispatched out of that building, and Sam would spend many a rainy afternoon sitting in the dispatch room listing to the calls, and to the stories the police and firemen told while sitting around the station. Sam even ate many a meal there; the firemen's chili was the best. That was one of the places Sam learned to cook.

Sam pulled into the parking lot out front of the station. He sat there for a few minutes, rolled the windows of the car up, enjoyed the air conditioning and listened to the end of Hotel California on the radio- it's just one of those songs you can't end half way through.

Song over, Sam walked into the office and stopped to say hi to Winnie, the department secretary, at the front desk. Winnie's desk was where the dispatcher sat years ago. Back then, it was an open counter Safety concerns changed that. Now, it was enclosed with glass and a small hole to talk through and a slot for papers. Winnie or whoever was at the desk would have to buzz the door for the officers in to get from the lobby to the offices in the back.

As Sam came in, Winnie told him about the midnight shift's arrest of Clifford Duggs. She said that that he was drunk, wrecked his bicycle. When Officers Fogerty and Clifford got there, he had fought them as usual. They finally got him in the car, but he kicked Fogerty in the forehead with his big work boot, leaving a waffle-print bruise. Sam laughed, he remembered the numerous times that he had arrested Duggs. Clifford was one crazy drunk.

Just as Winnie was telling Sam that the Chief was not in a good mood, Seth Wallow walked in the door, saying, "Where the hell have you been, Nickles!?"

"Out in the car, working," Sam replied.

Wallow went on some tirade on not checking in or checking the day basket, and the case and patrol boards.

Sam just listened and shrugged, saying, "You wanted to see me?"

Chapter 4

Wallow looked at Sam like he wanted to jump his ass, but the look on Sam's face told him it would probably not be a good time.

"Yeah," Wallow said, "The sheriff called me, and they need some help from your tactical boys for a raid on a meth lab." Wallow went on to tell Sam that the Sheriff's Department had been working to get a warrant on Tommy Little's house and finally got the probable cause for an arrest and search warrant. Wallow said, "The sheriff wanted you and the other officers to meet at the jail at 2 am."

Sam asked the chief, "Who do you want me to get? And, should I take off early so not to go into overtime?" Wallow replied as he walked away, "Sam, just get it done, I don't have time to mess with it." Sam said sarcastically, "Okey dokey, Smoky!" Then turned to Winnie and asked, "You heard that right?" Winnie just smiled, nodded and winked.

"My tactical boys?" Sam thought to himself.

He started and ran the multi-department entry team for 16 years, but gave it up a few years back, to make his wife, Lilly happy. He passed the job to Deputy Kent Phillips. Phillips was 28 years old, and had 5 years on the sheriff's department and 6 years in the Marines. Phillips was street smart and as Sam had many years ago, loved the entry team detail. In fact, Phillips liked to use one of Sam's favorite lines: "Kicking in doors of drug dealers is the next best thing to sex!" It was an adrenalin rush, and as much as Sam tried to get away from it, for Lilly's sake, the excitement kept calling him back.

Winnie asked Sam if he wanted her to contact the other officers. Sam thanked her and gave her a list of who to call, and asked her to let him know how many she got. As he was leaving, he told Winnie he would talk to Dawn to see if she would want to help. Tommy Little had some on and off girlfriends, and it was always good to have a female officer. Sam knew Dawn would complain that they only called her when women were involved. Besides Sam's old partner, Murphy Dam, Dawn would be his next choice to have his back. Sam knew Murphy was on his last couple days of vacation, and didn't think he was back in town yet.

As Sam got back into his car, he heard Dawn arriving at a call. He didn't hear her being dispatched, so he asked what she had, and she replied saying that she was just picking up some statements for the State Attorney's office. Sam knew he needed to talk to Dawn, so he drove to the address and waited outside for her. As Sam had known she would, Dawn complained about the detail for 10 minutes, but agreed to go, saying, "No reason to be at home!" Sam didn't ask but knew something didn't sound right.

Most of the rest of the day went along pretty quiet, except for Sam having to scold a couple boys on bicycles who had come out of an alley without looking, and Sam almost hit them. Sam gave them a couple of Bicycle Safety coloring books he had in his trunk and sent them on their way.

Just about 10 minutes till 3:00, Winnie called Sam and told him that she had 4 officers that would be there and had left a message for 2 others. As he was driving home, Sam heard Assistant Chief Kenny McDollin sign on duty. Kenny said he was clear on the message, bringing the number to 7, counting himself. McDollin was the next officer hired by McCracken's Bluff 5 years after Sam. Like Sam, McDollin had an Associate's Degree from Vincennes University in Law Enforcement. Kenny had always worked hard and was a good cop; he deserved the Assistant Chief's Job. He was an excellent choice for the job, being he was detailed orientated and worked well with the other officers. Even at his age, Kenny could probably out run any officer on the department, and at 6'4" seemed like mostly legs and loved to run. He would run 5K's whenever he got a chance and usually came in among the top 10. Kenny's blond hair and tan with a lanky build that made him look more like a California surfer than a mid-west cop.

When Sam got home, he got his tactical gear together to check everything. He knew with these types of details you never knew what you were going to get into. Doing an equipment check, Sam looked at the date on his tactical vest. "Hmmm, over 5 years, that's not good," Sam said to himself.

He checked his favorite Ruger P-89, 9mm pistol that he kept in the holster in the front of his TAC vest, along with 3 extra magazines. Sam had had this gun for years, and it always felt just right in his hand, even more than his department issue Glock .45 that he's carried daily. He checked that Glock, its extra magazines, and just in case his little Ruger LCP .380 caliber pocket rocket. There were flex cuffs, and four pairs of steel handcuffs, his knife, some paracord, a wedge in the vest cover. He also got out his leather and lead slapper, which wasn't used much anymore, and carried mostly out of habit. He got his black BDU's out of the closet and grabbed his ballistic helmet that he knew he probably would not wear.

It was 5:00 pm and he thought he should get some rest, but he knew sleep would not come easy, and Lilly would be home soon. As Sam sat on the couch, Lilly walked in.

She looked at the pile of equipment, and said, "Sam!"

Lilly was Sam's second wife, and they had only been married 4 years. Sam had turned over the Tactical Team about a year after they got married, to the delight of Lilly. She never got used to Sam going out in the middle of the night on that kind of detail. She knew when he got dressed in the black stuff, she would not sleep until she heard from him that they were done. Nothing else was said between them about it, they both knew how the other felt. Sam kicked back in the recliner, listening to the news, and asked her to wake him before she went to bed or about midnight.

Sam did fall asleep; the heat must have taken the energy out of him. It was about 11:30 pm when he woke up. He had some time to kill, so Sam went to his office and sat at his computer desk. Sitting there Sam checked out the weather, then his Facebook and Twitter accounts. He saw on Facebook another brother in blue had been killed in Florida. "Damn," he said to himself. "That makes five this month."

He typed a little message, sending prayers to the fallen officer's department, friends and family." Sam had personally known three officers killed in the line of duty over the years, this always made him more aware of the dangers of his job. This also made him think of the officers that he knew, who had taken their own lives. Suicide was such a waste, so many could have been prevented. Sam had known five officers that committed suicide over the last several years. He was aware that departments lose more officers, every year, to the stress of the job than to the bad guys.

Lilly came in and said good night, bringing Sam back out of his thoughts. He gave her a kiss and a long hug, then started to get ready. Sam looked up and watched as Lilly walked down the hall to the bedroom in her robe. She still had a wicked figure that moved like a cat as she walked. Sam smiled.

"She's something else!" he whispered to himself.

"This is not going to be fun," he thought. "Midnight and still almost 80 degrees and 88% humidity."

Sam would wait till after the briefing to put on his tactical vest, trying to stay comfortable for as long as possible, knowing that he probably would not have time to go home and change after the raid so he would be in the sweaty black BDU's all day. Looking at the clock, he saw that had plenty of time, so he got dressed slowly, watching the news. Sam followed politics, but lately, he couldn't stomach the unconstitutional way things were being done in Washington. Sam always remembered the oath of office he took to protect the Constitution and the laws of his country, and he believed in that oath.

The news got depressing, so flipping through the channels Sam found an old Andy Griffith re-run, this would give him a laugh. He was smiling as he thought of the wisdom of Andy Taylor and the way he always handled people. In the show Andy hardly every wore a gun, but Sam bet that Andy had a pocket rocket hidden somewhere, and thought how funny Barney would react if Andy would suddenly pull it out and shoot it. Sam chuckled, amusing himself.

When he was finished getting dressed it was almost 1:00 am. Sam thought he might as well go- better to be early. In his patrol car going through town, there was hardly anyone else moving around, which was a good thing. Sam used to love to work the midnight shift, nothing was better than the peacefulness of the freshly fallen snow covered streets after midnight. He wished it was cold, now. Sam drove the side streets, avoiding being seen and getting up the public's curiosity about why so many cops were moving around this time of the morning.

The sheriff's department was just outside of town, and there were already a few cars there parked around the back of the jail. Sam noticed the black 1956 Cadillac sedan that Aaron Peeks drove slowly drive by as he was turning into the lot.

Sam thought, "That car and Aaron give me the creeps; wonder what he's doing out this time of night."

A few of the officers were outside talking, smoking, joking around and telling stories, as Sam got out of his car and walked in. One of the young officers said, "Hey look, the old man is here." Sam shot him a look, and the rookie shut up. Sam went on to the jail, hearing the other officers razzing the kid.

Inside the conference room, Sam saw Deputy Kent Phillips at the whiteboard drawing a sketch of the area and the layout of the property to be searched. "Hey Sam, glad you're here, do you know this place?"

Sam told Kent that he had been there before He had been backing up some deputies up on a domestic violence call. "It's a tactical nightmare, a long dirt driveway, a hill you can't see over and several out buildings."

As they talked the sheriff, Larry Dickens walked up and was listening to the plan. They asked if he was going to go on the raid, and Dickens said, "Uh...No... I'm going to stay out and answer the routine calls, my deputies working the shift are going on the raid, but I will be close in case you need me. It's good for the young guys to get some experience."

Sam thought, "Then what am I doing here?!" Dickens walked away.

Larry Dickens became Sheriff by a fluke and some good luck for him. Dickens had worked as a jailer for the former Sheriff Harold Hanover. He and Harold never got along, and when Hanover got a complaint from a female inmate about sexual harassment by Dickens, he gave Dickens a choice of quitting or being fired. Dickens resigned as a jailer but came back by running for Sheriff against Hanover in the next election. Hanover was well-liked in Callsworth County and had a lot of family and friends there, so the election should have been a shoe-in for him. As fate had it, Sheriff

Hanover had a heart attack and died just 4 days before the election. Things being normal, the party might have picked someone else in his stead, but when Hanover died he happened to be in the apartment of a woman. The woman he was with was, in fact, the one who had filed the complaint against Dickens. The scandal went rampant, and Dickens won the election.

Dickens had no real police experience and was not very competent as an administrator. On the plus side, he did know how to schmooze people and was smart enough to let the deputies do their job. Dickens would answer calls occasionally, but usually got there after other deputies had arrived, and never actually arrested anyone. He spent most of his day at different coffee shops talking to his buddies. All of this was ok with Sam. He always hoped that Dickens would never get into a shooting situation. Sam had never seen anyone, let alone a cop, that was as inept with guns as Dickens was. Dickens was not afraid of weapons. He just could not hit anything. When Sam was a firearms instructor, it always had to take extra time to get Dickens qualified. It seemed like he just couldn't line up his sights. Sam tried everything. Sam had asked Dickens several times to get his eyes checked, but he claimed to have 20/20 vision.

"Oh well," Sam thought. "Dickens will be out of our way tonight, which would be good, and we will not have to watch out for him."

Kent and Sam sketched out the plan. First, the officers would drive their patrol cars to a church parking lot. This was about a half mile from Tommy Little's house, then everyone would be getting into two pickup trucks that were owned by a couple of deputies. The trucks would be good because all the officers could get out quickly, then move in different directions if need be. Information had it that only Tommy and his girlfriend Angie should be at the property. Tommy was only known to have one weapon, a shotgun, that he kept by his front door, but he did have some surveillance cameras pointing all around the house. Sam had never had trouble dealing with Tommy before, but he was real deep into meth and had been tweaking for several days so he could be very unpredictable.

Kent called everyone together and had them sign the log sheet for the record. Sheriff's Department Detective John Buckman was keeping the records since it was his case, and he would be doing the majority of the paperwork. There was a total of twenty officers at the briefing. They were told that the target was Tommy Little's house at 2771 Deerhead Lane. Kent described the property and what the issues were. He told them that they believed there would be an active meth lab, and said for everyone to be careful and remember the inhalation and explosion risk. Kent asked who was familiar with the property; only Sam and one other McCracken's Bluff officer said they were, as well as all 8 deputies who were there.

Meth, or methamphetamines, had become a huge problem in southern Illinois or the mid-west in general. The formula for "cooking" the meth was called the Nazi method because it was used by Hitler's regime during World War II to keep his troop awake and going for days. Anhydrous ammonia was one of the harder chemicals to acquire in the formula, but it was readily available in the mid-west because farmers used it as a fertilizer on their crops. Large tanks were stored all over the place, and the meth cookers would sneak in at night and steal what they needed. This caused a problem in itself- several times had the thieves had a hose or tank blow out, and the anhydrous ammonia would burn them and sometimes kill them.

Methamphetamine labs, themselves, are dangerous, using several flammable or explosive chemicals. Since most illegal cookers don't use many safety precautions, the labs would often catch fire and burn down the house, barn, car, or where ever it was being cooked. Unfortunately, the fire would also often burn up the evidence needed to charge the cooker with manufacturing. Sam knew from the cookers he had arrested in the past that most were not capable of cooking a good batch of Hamburger Helper, let alone be safe with the chemicals they were using.

The worst of all was the grip meth took on the users. Sam had been around drug addicts since his time in college, and he had never seen a drug take over lives of people the way meth does. He had been through the different waves of drugs. Cocaine, heroin and LSD were all bad, but it seemed that once they got into meth, it completely controlled them, and the need to get more meth would make them do anything. Sam once worked a case where a mother was pimping out her 12-year-old daughter to other users and dealers to get the drug. She was a hardcore user, shooting it up. She had even got her daughter hooked on meth by lacing marijuana with it. People lost jobs, spouses, savings, and their lives over meth.

The ten officers who knew the property would do the actual entries. There would be two teams, including one for the residence, which was an old trailer. It had a standard floor plan, a living room, kitchen at the front entrance, a long hallway with a couple of rooms off to the right side, and the main bedroom at the back. The only other exit door was near the rear of the hall. The second team was to secure the outbuildings, which were mainly big barns with a lot of junk!

Kent asked, "Sam will you take the house team?

Sam said, "Sure."

As soon as he did, McCracken Officer Brandon Teasdale said, "I'll be Sam's second, I've been in that trailer."

Sam just sighed and shook his head. Kent would take the second team, which Sam thought that would be good, mainly because of the number of buildings so they would have to move fast. Sam chose the rest of his team, and Kent gave the perimeter officers their locations. The last thing Kent told the team, from what he had learned from Sam, was, "Remember that the best-made plans never work. Keep your eyes open, think tactical, and keep with your partner."

The perimeter team was deciding on their weapons: some with shotguns and others with AR-15's, according to who was qualified. They were everyone else's extra eyes and covered the entry teams or acted on what would happen outside the main points. They had to be sharp. It was going to be dark, confusing, and anything could happen.

Sam's team decided on how to stack up for the entry. Sam would take the lead and breach the door. He passed on the battering ram; Sam liked to use his foot to kick the door in. He then would cover Teasdale- he would be the second man in. This made Sam a little nervous. Brandon Teasdale was young: 24 years old, and had 2 years on the department. He had the makings of a good officer but was sometimes a livewire. Sam didn't want him to get hurt.

The next 2 deputies in would clear the first room, while Sam and Teasdale covered them. Then, they would go to the next room as the next deputies covered them and so on. The last officers in would cover their backs.

Sam knew that Teasdale had been on raids before, but never on the direct entry team. Sam pulled him aside and told him as soon as he kicked the door, he was to roll into the left and cover the others. When the room was cleared, Teasdale was to follow Sam. The last thing Sam said to Teasdale was, "Whatever you do, stay with me and don't shoot me. I will shoot you back." Sam said it jokingly, but it was in the back of his mind.

Kent's team stated that they were all ready; they had a detached garage, a barn and a small travel trailer they had to clear. As they would clear each one, a perimeter team would come up to secure it.

Kent again said, "We are not sure of how many people will be there, and what they would be doing, so everyone needs to be ready for anything!"

As they walked out to their cars, Sam talked to Dawn, he wished she was his back up, but she said she didn't know the place. Dawn was going to be on the perimeter, with a shotgun. Sam knew she hated shotguns because of the kick, but she could shoot them well and she wasn't qualified with the Ar-15.

Sam joked with her, "If Teasdale accidentally shoots me, you should "accidentally" shoot him."

She smiled and said, "Not a problem." They laughed and high-fived, as they walked to their own cars.

Chapter 5

It was about a 10-minute drive to the church. It could have been quicker, but the direct approach would have taken them right by Tommy's driveway, so the team took a long way around. When they got to the church, everyone did the final weapons and equipment check. They all made sure their cell phones were silent and then loaded quietly into the pick-ups. The perimeter teams loaded first and went closest to the cab. Sam had 2 teams of city officers in his truck, Dawn being in one of the teams. Kent had 3 perimeter teams with him: 3 deputies, 2 state troopers and a Conservation Officer. Most all the officers were experienced, with Teasdale being the youngest, but Sam did not have a good feeling about this.

As the pickups started moving, Sam noticed sweat rolling down his back. It was so hot, his tactical vest felt like a massive heating pad on his chest. Sam had worn the same black bandana covering his head for as long as he could remember. It was his good luck charm, as were his pocket knife and lighter that his dad had told him to carry at all times. Sam's father instilled in him that these were essential survival tools of life. Back in those days, the bandana was red, the knife smaller, but the lighter always had been a Zippo. Sam still deemed them all necessary. Sam adjusted the bandana down to keep the sweat out of his eyes.

As they traveled down the gravel road sitting on the tailgate, Sam's feet occasionally dragged the gravel like they would when he was a teenager in the back of his dad's pickup. Sam could feel his heart beat harder. This was the time he liked best: all of his senses were heightened, nerves on edge, kind of like foreplay. A big grin came to his face as he looked around at the others in the truck and they unknowingly smiled back, Teasdale giving him the thumbs up and a big smile with his eyes wide open! Sam could only chuckle and shake his head.

Moving down the gravel road, Sam could taste the dust in his mouth, he felt it up in his nose; he snorted, trying to clear it. Clouds were moving and the moon was peeking out now and then. It was not a full moon, but if it stayed out as they arrived it might help them to see better. But then that works both ways- the bad guys could see better, too.

The pickups turned into Tommy Little's driveway, which was hidden by a grove of trees, some of the low-hanging, small limbs were slapping the officers in the head as they went down the lane. As they cleared the trees going into the open field, the trucks picked up speed, knowing that they had to be quick to keep the element of surprise. When they topped the hill and could first see the trailer, and "The Plan" suddenly went to hell!

Everybody started quietly talking.

"There's a bonfire."

"A whole bunch of people, maybe twenty."

"They are having a party!"

"Oh great," Sam, thought But then, he could hear the group around the fire yelling "Party," as the trucks approached.

So, Sam yelled back, "Party, woo hooo!" and the rest of the officers joined in. The partiers were oblivious that their night was going to turn really bad, really fast.

The two trucks pulled in as the party-goers watched, but could not see who was coming to "party" with them because of the bright headlights in their eyes.

Sam told Teasdale, "Just stay with me!" Sam knew that with all the people outside the whole team would not be able to stay together, and there was no time to make a new plan. He and Teasdale would cut off the trailer so no one could get inside it to get the only weapon they knew was there: the shotgun by the front door.

It wasn't until the officers started bailing out of the trucks that the group partying around the bonfire realized that it was the cops. Suddenly, there was a lot of noise, officers yelling, "Police! Stop, let me see your hands, don't run!"

The suspects were yelling to each other about ways to get away. Most everyone who could started to run towards the barn or the woods. A few never made it away from the fire before someone on the team caught them, mostly because they were too stoned to realize what was happening. Sam and Teasdale were the only ones who went towards the trailer and just after covering a few steps, they noticed Tommy Little running towards the trailer too.

"Oh hell no, you don't!" Sam said. He wasn't about to let Tommy get to that shotgun. Sam knew there was chaos at the fire and people running. But he was focused on Tommy, who was several yards ahead of him. Tommy jumped on the porch but got slowed down while opening the screen door to the trailer. Sam almost got a hold of him as he was going through the doorway, but Tommy turned quickly towards the hallway. Sam could see the butt of the shotgun by the door but decided to get Tommy first. His lungs were already bursting, but Sam kicked it in and ran harder. They ran hard down that long skinny hallway, bouncing on the walls as they did. Tommy slowed down trying to go into one of the small bedrooms. Sam, not slowing, stepped on Tommy's lower leg, driving him to the ground. His momentum would not allow Sam to stop and he ran right over Tommy, stepping on his back as he passed over him. Sam then slammed into the rear wall of the trailer at a full run. When Sam turned around, he saw Teasdale take a flying leap onto Tommy's back, trying to get an arm. Tommy was trying to get back up with Teasdale riding his back.

Sam thought, "Good boy," while Teasdale was trying to get Tommy under control.

Sam kicked Tommy's arms out, and then dropped a knee onto Tommy's upper back. Teasdale told Tommy to give it up, while grabbing his arm. Tommy finally realized it was over, quit fighting, and Teasdale cuffed him up, smiling all the time.

Sam and Teasdale pulled Tommy up and walked him to the front door. Tommy was pissed, saying, "I'll get you mother fuckers, you can't do this to me, you better watch your back." Sam got up in Tommy's face, squinted his eyes, and set his jaw, and just looked at Tommy eye to eye and said, "Really?"

This seemed to unnerve Tommy, and he got quiet. Sam told Teasdale, "Get this piece of crap out of my sight." Teasdale took Tommy to the group of prisoners that the others had cuffed and were sitting by the fire.

Once outside, there was still the sound of other officers yelling for people to stop. Some officers were walking up with people they had caught.

Kent Phillips had re-assigned some of the perimeter team to watch the suspects they had, and others to keep covering the officers who were still out. Sam could hear four-wheelers going away in the distance, and figured that was how most of the people got to the party, since there were only a couple of cars there. Sam reached down, and unloaded the shotgun that had been sitting by the door. Looking at the shells, he thought, "Hmmm deer slugs, ouch!"

Sam yelled to Kent, asking if someone could come stand by the trailer. Kent told him everyone was busy; he had already sent Teasdale out with a Deputy to check the small Travel Trailer that they hadn't had a chance to get to yet. Kent asked Sam, "Can you stay there for a few minutes?"

Sam replied "No problem!" He was still trying to catch his breath, thinking to himself, "I am getting too old for this shit." But then smiled, this was going to be an impressive bust!

It wasn't long when everyone started to come back in, and a head count was taken. No officers were hurt, and only a few of the suspects had some bruises and scrapes through the whole thing. Twelve men and four women were sitting by the fire all had been handcuffed and searched. The officers thought two or three got away. One was on a four-wheeler and had a passenger, but the Conservation Officer, Marvin Paul, did a flying tackle and knocked him off the back of the four-wheeler. The driver never looked back, gunned it and kept on going. So much for friendship.

Jason McDollin and Willy Fogerty said that they had chased Joe Kerchak into the woods south of the trailer, and when he came to the creek he had just kept running, bailing off of that 20-foot drop.

McDollin said, "We were lucky that our flashlights were on him when we saw him fall, if not both of us would have run off of the cliff, too."

Fogerty said, "I thought that we would find him at the bottom, in the creek, all broken up. But when we got there, he was already climbing up the other side. He was limping, but that was the last we saw of him."

Both said they could positively identify him and would get a warrant for him the next day. Sam said, "That would make two warrants, in two days for Joe, but that's Joe."

Sam wrote a quick text message to tell Lilly all was ok. Phillips called the sheriff and asked for the jail bus to transport the prisoners. That's when Teasdale ran up excitedly, saying, "Sam, you guys need to come look, this is so cool!"

Sam, annoyed, said, "What?" Teasdale just said, "You and Kent needed to see this." Then he ran back to the travel trailer. Sam asked one of the officers at the bonfire to watch the front of the trailer. Then, he and Kent walked back to where Teasdale and Deputy Mike Oldam were.

"Is Lilly ok?" Kent asked.

Sam told him, "Yeah, she will be able to sleep now."

"I need to call Donna, too." Kent said, and pointed at Teasdale, "The kid gets a little excited, doesn't he?"

Sam replied, "Yeah, but he did ok."

Looking inside the travel trailer, Sam and Kent looked at one another, and both said "Wow." Just at a quick look, they could see the trailer was full of guns. There were AK-47, Mini –14's, AR-15's, shotguns of all sorts, and a few handguns that were lying out in the open, Sam noticed 2 Desert Eagles. It was crazy, there were stacks of gun cases of all sizes. They could not even have guessed how many.

"We're going to be here awhile," Kent said, and called the sheriff back and asked for a couple more trucks. Teasdale and Oldam were told to stay with the trailer, and not to play with anything.

A large working lab was found in the barn, and it was secured to wait for the State Police's lab clean up team. Everyone at the party was holding some sort of drugs- either pills, marijuana or meth. After an NCIC (National Crime Information Center) check, several of them were found to already have outstanding warrants for their arrest. When the van got there, all of the arrestees would be loaded up and taken to the jail to be booked in.

"This is going to be a paperwork nightmare," Kent told Detective John Buckman, "and we haven't even gone through the trailer yet."

Buckman asked, "Sam what did you see in the house trailer?"

Sam said, "We were a little busy. I didn't see any other people, but I did see the shotgun by the door, and a pile of dishes on the kitchen counter. There was some stuff in the back bedroom that might be interesting, looked like some glassware."

It was 4:30 am and Buckman, Kent and Sam did a walkthrough of the trailer. In the kitchen, as they first walked in the door, there were pistols in three of the drawers. In the living room, there was a .45 under the cushions at each end of the couch, and a 12-gauge shotgun under it. There was a sawed-off shotgun in the bathroom. In the bedroom there were three shotguns under the bed and an Uzi with 6 magazines under the pillows. Found buried under dirty clothes in the bedroom closet were cases of different types of ammo. It looked like Tommy was either going to start a war, or was dealing in guns too.

The living room had three large flat-screen TVs hooked up to ten cameras that covered all of the outbuilding and the road. The best part was that they were recording, so the investigators would be able to tell who had been there. The recording could also show how the drugs were distributed. They thought this should be an interesting interview, if they get a chance to talk to him, but that he would probably lawyer up.

For the team, the best was yet to come. In one of the small bedrooms, there was more meth than any of the officers had ever seen. The bedroom was a processing room with scales, cutting material, little baggies, packaged with different amounts. They all went outside, and Sam watched door again, while Buckman went and got his camera, and put on some protective gear. While standing there looking at the inside of the trailer, it was a mess of stacks dirty dishes, food left out, trash all over, beer cans stacked in the corner.

Sam thought, "If you're tweaked on meth and up for days on end, and you have all that energy, why can you just clean up your house little?" Sam could never understand the appeal of being doped up all the time.

Larry Dickens, the sheriff, showed up in his pick-up with a jailer in the bus, and they loaded the prisoners up, and couple of deputies rode with him to the jail. Several of the officers got back into the other pick-ups to shuttle their cars to the scene. Sam rode along to get his cruiser. It would not be long before he would have to go on regular duty. When Sam got back to his car, reaching into the car to start it up, then he took off his tactical vest, opened the trunk and secured his gear inside. Climbing back into the car, Sam sat for a moment and noticed how wet his shirt was from sweat. The air conditioner hit it and almost gave him a chill, it felt so good! He took his time driving back to Tommy's- enjoying the air conditioner, listening to Sweet Emotion on the radio.

While driving, he went over what had transpired in the night. It was now almost 5:30 am, and the sun was coming up; the sky had a few clouds that were starting to shine from the rising sun. Thinking his part of paperwork should not be too bad, maybe a couple of hours, Sam was just glad he was not logging in all the evidence; the detectives and the lab people would do that. The drive was over way too soon.

As he pulls up to the trailer, Sam noticed the sheriff and several deputies setting up a display of all the guns. The weapons were placed onto tarps on the ground to be photographed. Sam knew that this was for a photo-op for when the news got there. The sheriff told Sam that the TV stations had been contacted, and were on their way, so they needed to get everything out.

Sam said, "Kent told me he wanted to take the time to get everything properly logged and photographed- shouldn't you have waited?"

Sam then looked up and saw Clifford Duggs coming out of the travel trailer with several gun cases.

Sam said, "How did he get here?"

Sheriff Dickens replied, "I brought him from the jail, He's got a strong back and a weak mind."

"Really?" Sam replied, shaking his head. Then, he walked away.

Poor Clifford,- you could tell he was hung over, only being arrested for public intoxication the night before. Clifford Duggs was not an idiot. Yeah, he had problems, like alcoholism, a speech impediment, and a bad temper, but he got a bad start in life. Clifford was the product of incest, his father was his grandfather, and his sister his mother. He did have a learning

43

disability, so he was raised in a state hospital until budget cuts turned him and his other family members out to fend for themselves. Living on his own made him sharper that a lot of people realized. Clifford grew a garden, raised chickens, and did odd jobs for people that most others would not do. Most did not see it. In fact, most people tried to take advantage of him. If they would have just taken the time to talk to Clifford, they would have known he was no dummy.

A few of the lab team had arrived and were suiting up in their protective gear to take apart the lab in the barn. This was not a little personal meth cook. This guy had some good equipment and a lot of chemicals, including anhydrous ammonia, ether, packs of lithium batteries and boxes upon boxes of Sudafed- many in blister packs, but also several 500-count bottles. The scary thing was, many chemicals make it very dangerous to breathe and cause an explosive risk.

Sam walked over to Kent and Buckman who were coordinating things and keeping logs of all the coming and going. "Wasn't quite what we expected was it, Sam?" Buckman asked.

"Is it ever?" Sam replied.

While they were talking, Teasdale ran up with a big grin on his face, and large gun in his hand. "This is what I need," he said, he was holding a Barrett .50 caliber sniper rifle and a .50 AE Desert Eagle handgun.

"No you don't… and take them back," Sam said.

Teasdale frowned and walked away, kicking the ground like a scolded little boy.

"Make sure he doesn't get away with those," Sam joked with Kent, "I have to go on shift soon, and I won't be able to babysit him."

Kent said, "I think we are ready to let several of the guys go, but I wanted to know if you were going to stay for the press release."

"I don't think so," said Sam, "I'll leave that to the brass."

"Well then, "Kent asked, "Could run some evidence bags back out here, I didn't think I'd need this many."

"No problem," Sam replied.

Sam looked around for Dawn to check on her before he left, he could not locate her. He asked John Buckman if he knew where she was. Buckman looked at the log and said, "She left a little before 4:00 am. Dawn told me that all the females were gone, and she had a call she needed to take care of."

"A call?" Sam questioned, "Why didn't midnight shift take care of it?"

Buckman just shrugged and said, "I don't know, but she seemed like she was in a hurry."

Back in the car, Sam jotted down a few note while cooling off, he would get to writing the report after going on shift. Listening to the morning news as he drove back into town, it was now 7:00 am, so Sam signed onto regular patrol. He said, "City 4 (Sam's call number) to Dispatch I'm 10-41 (On

Duty).” Heading towards the station, he called the Purple Lotus Café and asked if they could make him a couple of sausage and egg sandwiches, and said he would pick them up in a few minutes.

On the radio, Sam heard the newscast of the bust. He thought to himself, “That was quick.” Dawn then signed on to duty. This made Sam feel better, he would find out what happened to her later.

As Sam was going inside the station to grab some evidence bags, Chief Wallow stopped him. Sam could tell he was mad!

“Where the hell have you been?!” Wallow screamed.

“Again, with the, where have I been…” Sam said. “I’ve been where you told me to be.”

“Why didn’t you call me, the news has been calling all morning, and where am I?” Wallow rattled. “I’m here, clueless.”

Sam smiled, and just said, “Yep.”

Wallow asked, “Why didn’t you call me”?

Sam retorted, “You told me to handle it, you didn’t have time.” Sam got the evidence bags and walked out the door, smiling and winked at Winnie. He could hear Wallow still screaming from the parking lot.

Sam stopped by the Purple Lotus and grabbed the sandwiches, and as he was walking out, he bumped into Sherrie Hall and her sister, who were going in.

“Join us for breakfast, Sam,” she asked, and smiled.

Sam apologized, saying, "I wish I could, but I'm a little busy."

She huffed "I will catch you, yet!" Sam walked to his car, thinking...

As Sam started his cruiser, *Sherry*, by Frankie Valli and the Four Seasons was playing.

"That's too weird," Sam thought to himself, but it made him smile and he sung along in his best falsetto voice.

When Sam got back to the scene, the news was already there. The sheriff had finished with the interviews and was strutting around schmoozing the news people. Kent said, "You would have thought he did everything all by himself."

Sam told Kent that Wallow was pissed. "He's not happy he was not informed of what happened."

"We'll blame it on the sheriff," Kent said, and they both laughed.

Sam walked around for a few minutes. He watched Clifford Duggs and a couple of others load the guns into the pick-up. Teasdale was looking at the Barrett .50 cal., again.

"What would you do with that?" Sam asked. Teasdale went into a tirade on why the department needed a sniper, and why he should be the one to do it. "Just make sure that thing gets in the truck," Sam said.

Sheriff Dickens walked up and told them they were ready to go. Teasdale put the gun back in the case with the look of an abused puppy. There were one hundred and fifty-seven guns in the Travel trailer, and that was not counting the ones in the main trailer- everything from .22 rifles and pistols to 6 full auto MP5 machine guns. The guns were a great extra, with the drugs and lab, Tommy would probably never get out of jail!

Ready to leave, Sam saw Kent and congratulated him on a good operation. He told him if he needed anything else to call him.

Kent said, "Thanks, but it was a team effort." They both watched as the sheriff drove out with Clifford Duggs in the passenger seat.

"Idiot," Kent said.

Sam questioned, "Clifford?"

Kent just said, "No."

Sam thought he had better get back into town; it was a quarter till eight and Dawn had been there all by herself. He couldn't figure out why she had left right after the female prisoners got loaded into the van. As he pulled out, Sam unwrapped one of the sandwiches, going down the drive. He ate it while driving on Deerhead Lane.

When he was about two miles from the scene, Sam saw Sheriff Dickens and Clifford Duggs, standing outside of the sheriff's truck, which was pulled over to the side of the road.

Sam stopped and asked if all was ok. The sheriff, who was looking in the bed of the truck looked up startled and said, "No, no, the load just shifted, Clifford didn't tie it down like I told him to."

Clifford walked over to Sam's car, and said: "Hey Tam, how are ya?"

Clifford had a problem with S's and other parts of speech, but Sam had known him long enough to understand. In fact, a new officer was no longer a rookie when they could "speak Clifford."

Sam was eating his sandwich as Clifford was watching intently, Sam asked: "Are you hungry Cliff?"

"Yeah," he said. "Toot me too fast to get brckfas!" Sam handed Cliff the other sandwich and drove off.

Looking down the road, Sam saw two figures ahead, he thought it could be a couple of the ones they didn't catch the night before. But as he got closer, he saw it was two young boys, Alex Gear and J.J. Jay. They both had .22 rifles over their shoulders, and Sam stopped to talk to them. "Hi, Officer Sam," J.J. said.

"What's up, guys?" asked Sam.

"Just going to get a little practice in before squirrel season next month," Alex replied.

"That sounds good, I haven't had any squirrel for a long time," stated Sam.

"If we do good, we'll bring ya some, Sam. Hey, are you going to have a range day this year? I loved shooting that AR-15," J.J. asked.

"Yeah, the 25th of August, would you two like to help me set up the range?" Sam asked.

Both boys got excited and said that would be fun.

"Ok, it's a date, but listen, don't go too far up this road, there are a lot of officers working up there, so don't get in their way," Sam told them.

"Don't worry, Sam, we won't," Alex said.

As Sam drove off, he could see the boys standing in the road talking in his rearview mirror, he thought how much he like working with the kids in town.

Once in town, Sam called Dawn on the radio, and they met up at the city park. Sitting under the trees in their cars, they talked about the night's activities and laughed about the chief being mad. Sam could tell that Dawn's mind was elsewhere. Just as he asked what was wrong, she got a call from dispatch, telling her to go to the prosecutor's office.

Sam said, "Are you his delivery boy, uh, girl?" She just smiled nervously and drove off.

Sam sat there for a while and working on his log, it was 9:16 am. Sam was enjoying the air conditioning, and listened to Little Deuce Coupe on the radio. He thought maybe he could go by home and change his shirt. The one he was wearing had been soaked in sweat all night and didn't smell very well. Sam put the car in drive, but before the car started moving, dispatch was calling him.

"Dispatch to City-4." The radio chimed.

"City-4" Replied Sam.

Dispatch said, "Go to Jefferson Elementary School, there is a stray horse in the playground."

"A horse," Sam thought to himself. "What is it with these animals lately?"

"Clear, dispatch," Sam answered.

When Sam arrived, looking for the horse, he drove around to the back of the school through the grass to the playground. The school yard was deserted except for Fred Long, a maintenance man, and a beautiful quarter horse. Stopping the car, Sam thought to himself that he had seen the horse somewhere before, but could not remember where.

"It's just been hanging around here, eating grass, but I didn't know what to do with it," Fred said, walking towards Sam.

They both walked over to the horse, and Sam grabbed the reigns and looked at the saddle. "That doesn't look good," Sam said to Fred. There was blood on Sam's hands from the reins, blood on the saddle and on the mane of the horse- a lot of blood.

Sam called dispatch for an ambulance. He didn't know for who, but thought someone was going to need one. He also asked for the animal control officer to meet him there, and dispatch advised they would be en route.

Sam asked, "Fred, can you watch the horse?" Fred nodded his head yes, stunned by the blood. As Sam tied the horse to the monkey bars, Sam said to Fred, "Don't let anyone come in this area unless they ask me first."

"Ok, Sam," Fred yelled, as he picked up his mop bucket and walked towards a spigot on the wall of the school. "Can I get it some water?"

"Sure," Sam replied, with his thoughts elsewhere.

"Sam, I'll have to go to the spigot on the side of the building, someone has broken the handle off of this one." Fred said. Sam just waved back at Fred as he started to walk away.

Sam could see blood drops on the ground and began to follow them. He called dispatch on his radio and asked the time he got there so he could log it on his report.

Dispatch replied, "Time notified 0807, the time arrived 0811." Sam wrote the times in his notebook along with where everything was when he arrived.

Due to the hot summer and lack of rain, most of the grass was brown and dry, the blood drops stood out in the hot sun. Sam walked north towards the woods, there was a field about 200 yards wide, then an oil tank battery before the stand of trees. The blood drops went due north in a straight line towards the tank battery, and Sam followed them.

About a hundred and fifty yards in, Sam noticed something lying in the grass. There was a dip in the ground, that why he didn't see the object from the school yard. Sam quickened his pace, and when he got close, Sam could see it was a person.

As Sam ran up, he looked at the body, as it lay crumpled in a large pool of blood, upon seeing the face, Sam thought to himself, "Oh hell no!

Chapter 6

Jason Kelly was the kind of State's Attorney that police officers liked: still young, experienced, aggressive and willing to go the extra mile, all the while keeping people's rights in mind. Jason was 48, and had never married, having focused on his career. Jason had worked as Deputy State's Attorney in Chicago for several years. He returned to Callsworth County and McCracken's Bluff when he heard that the former State's Attorney was not going to run again. The drug and violence problems that were occurring in his hometown made him want to come back and do what he could to help. Jason won the election easily, due to his record in Chicago, but also because of his friendly, easygoing manner. This would be the kind of case he would thrive on, but instead, he was lying crumpled on the ground in a pool of blood.

After years of police work, Sam knew dead, but it did not stop him from sticking his hand in the blood-soaked neck of Jason Kelly, to try to find a pulse. Sam really liked Jason and hoped he could find some sign of life. But, Sam knew with the amount of blood, ashen skin, and the lifeless eyes that Jason was dead. The siren alerted Sam to the ambulance approaching, and he waved them to stay at a distance, not to get into the crime scene. Sam hoped they could run a strip and catch something of a heartbeat. Sam took a few quick pictures with his phone before the paramedics moved anything, and told them to be careful where they stepped.

Sam called Dispatch on his cell and told them to call the coroner, the chief, Dawn, and Murphy Dam. Mary Beth, the dispatcher, reminded Sam that Murphy was on vacation, but Sam told her that he was back in town.

Murphy had texted Sam around midnight, saying they were almost home and checking to see how things were going. Sam said, "Just call him and tell him I need him here, he will understand."

Sam said, "Don't put anything over the air; contact them by cell phone. I don't want a media circus out here as we are trying to work.

Mary Beth asked, "Sam, what's going on?"

He just said, "I'll tell you later when I know more." Sam thought to himself, the less people who know right now, the better. Thinking it over, he also told her to contact the sheriff's department and their detective, and the State Police Crime Scene Unit. Sam knew you can't get too much help on something like this. Mary Beth knew Sam didn't get too excited about much. This must be big and she wanted to do the best that she could, so she listened carefully to Sam.

Sam looked down at the medics as they were running a strip and shook their head, "Damn," he thought. At first examination of the body, Sam was not sure of where the blood had come from, but when the medics wiped some of the blood off, Sam saw a nearly 3-inch slit in Jason's neck.

Nita, one of the medics said, "It looks like someone cut his throat, Sam, the common carotid was severed, he probably bled out in minutes."

Sam told them, "The coroner is on his way, remember to pick up everything that you brought and nothing you didn't."

The medics quietly got their gear together and went back to the ambulance. They were saddened and very careful because they also knew Jason well. They had worked with him, and it was a loss for all of them. Sam asked them to stay in the ambulance, and watch the body so he could walk back to the school, to get control over the scene.

As Sam walked back to the playground, he got out his notepad out of his shirt pocket and started a list of everyone who was coming and going, he would get the times from dispatch later. The animal control officer had arrived, whom everyone called Furry because he had more hair than most of the animals he caught. Sam asked Furry just to keep an eye on the horse. The evidence technicians would probably want to look at it, so don't touch it if you can keep from it. Furry asked if he could get it some water. Sam pointed to the bucket that Fred had brought, but it was empty, the horse must have been out for a while and thirsty.

While talking with Fred, Sam asked what he had seen. Fred said, "Sam, I had just saw the horse through the school window, and called 911, by the time I got out here, you were arriving. I didn't even notice the blood until you said something about it."

Sam thanked Fred for watching over everything, and asked if he could hang close in case he need him.

Fred asked, "Can I go back inside the school? I have work to do."

Sam said, "Yeah sure, I'll find you if I need to." Sam asked, "Oh wait, did you see anyone around this morning?"

Fred thought for a minute, "Yeah the newspaper guy, I can't think of his name."

"Hmmm," Sam thought, "Bobby Ellis?"

"Yeah, Sam, that's him," Fred said excitedly.

Sam knew Bobby well and didn't like him. Sam thought Bobby only had the morning paper route to do a little window peeping. So far it had been hard to catch him. Since he started passing the papers at 3 am, he always had an excuse to be out in people's yards that early in the morning.

As Sam and Fred were talking, Fuzzy walked back up and asked Fred where another water spigot was, he said that the handle was broken off of the one by the air conditioner units. Fred said, "I know, the damn Kids! They are always tearing up something around here! Last week it was plastic forks stuck all over the playground, took me two hours to pull them all of the damn things out." Fred explained to Fuzzy that there was another spigot around the corner of the building, by the maintenance room door. Fuzzy walked off with his bucket, and Fred went inside.

Dawn Pearl drove up in her patrol car, and Sam walked towards her, she asked, "Sam, what in the world is going on?" As Dawn started to get out of her cruiser, she looked over at the horse and suddenly got nervous, saying, "Isn't that…"

"It's Jason…Jason Kelly's. It looks like he's been murdered."

The color ran out of Dawn's face, her knees seemed to go out from under her as she sat back down in the seat of the patrol car. Sam could see her eyes welling up with tears as she just stared straight ahead.

All this made sense to him now- the several meetings at the prosecutor's office and the comments about home. "Oh hell no," Sam thought.

"What's going on, Dawn?" he inquired.

She just looked off into space. Sam closed Dawn's door and went around to sit down in the passenger's seat, moving a book lying there. The book was "10 Stupid Things Couple Do to Mess up their Relationships" by Laura Schlesinger.

"Shit," he mumbled under his breath, and threw it in the back seat.

"What's going on, Dawn?" Sam asked again.

It took her a minute to speak but finally said that she had known Jason since high school and they had dated some back then. Sam knew there was more so he just listened.

"We started seeing each other a couple months ago. Things at home aren't good, and he was lonely and..." Dawn stopped, wiping tears from her eyes, "I just saw him a few..."

Sam stopped her and said, "Ok, that's enough for now, but you need to stay away from here!"

"But I want to see him!" she cried.

"Oh no, you don't!" Sam told her, "Not like this, and not now. You know you will have to be questioned later, and you can't get involved in the investigation. We will take care of this, trust me!"

Sam talked to Dawn for a few minutes trying to calm her down, then he called dispatch and asked for a couple off-duty officers to be called out and to tell them to get there ASAP. Sam said she should go home or to the office and he would cover for her until he talked to the chief or Murphy.

"Oh God, not Murphy!" She started to cry again.

"You know he will have to talk to you," replied Sam.

Dawn thought to herself, "Murphy is gonna love this."

Sam was good friends with Murphy and with Dawn, but they could not get along with each other at all. Dawn didn't like Murphy's cocky manner and believed he thought women were beneath him. Murphy thought Dawn took advantage of being a woman. They generally just didn't like each other, but usually put up with one other because of the job.

One time, a year or so back, Sam got in the middle of an argument between Murphy and Dawn, in the office lobby. They were arguing over the way Murphy had critiqued a report Dawn had written. Sam got them quieted down, then he told them both the reason they could not get along was that they were both just alike. They were hard-headed, set in their ways, never backed off, and always thought they were right!

Both of them started yelling at him, both complaining they were not like that. Sam just walked away, smiling and shaking his head. As he drove out of the station parking lot, he could still hear them yelling at him. Neither of them spoke to Sam for a week after that, but he knew, and so did they, that he was right. They both got over it with Sam, but still didn't like each other. But Sam knew, when push came to shove, they would back each other up because they were both good cops.

At the school, before Sam got out of the car, he asked Dawn if she was ok to drive. She nodded yes. She then said she would go to the station and talk to Winnie. Sam thought that would be ok, for now.

"Just be careful what you say, and avoid the chief," Sam reminded her.

Not knowing what else to do, Sam patted her on the hand, gave her a smile and got out of the car. Before he closed the door, he noticed Chief Wallow driving up.

"Dawn, go out around the other way, I will handle this." As she drove off Sam wished he could stay with her. She looked heartbroken.

Chief Seth Wallow pulled in quickly and threw up dust as he stopped, jumping out of the car yelling at Sam, "Nickles, what in the hell is going on!"

"Jason Kelly is dead," Sam told him, and Wallow stopped in his tracks.

"What are we going to do?" Wallow asked.

Sam thought, "We? I'm doing it, but you probably won't do anything but ask stupid questions." Knowing this was not the time to argue, Sam explained, "I have help coming: the coroner, investigators, other officers." He further explained, "So far the only people who know so far are Dawn, the paramedics, and us.

"Where did Dawn go? I saw her leave." questioned Wallow.

Sam said, "I sent her to check on something for me."

Sam thought, "That's all he needs to know right now."

Sam handed Wallow the notebook, telling him he needs to log in everyone who comes and goes, and the times, saying, "Don't let anyone back there that doesn't need to be on the scene." Sam turned and walked back to the scene. Wallow didn't say anything. Murders were not a common thing in McCracken's Bluff, and Wallow had never worked on one. Sam had only worked a couple, and his mind was reeling, what he needed to do, who to contact- Dawn, Jason's family? All problems he was thinking of how to handle.

Murphy Dam was the first to arrive, he knew if Sam asked for help it had to be bad. Murphy had just grabbed his gun, badge and shown up in jeans and an old Aerosmith t-shirt.

Murphy Dam had been an officer in the department about a year when Sam got hired on. They were about the same age and had some of the same interests, like shooting and good whiskey, except Murphy's idea of camping was staying at a Holiday Inn. Sam and Murphy took to each other right away and were even partnered up for several years. Clark George, who preceded Wallow as Chief of Police, never knew what was going to be in the day basket after Nickles and Murphy worked a shift together, but they got stuff done. Where Sam was big and bald, Murphy was a small guy, not tiny, but only 5'7 about 165 pounds. Murphy had this full head of coal black hair that he was always combing, and a crooked smile that gave him a certain cockiness.

Murphy got out of his car and walked up to Wallow and asked: "What's going on, Chief?" Wallow just shook his head saying "Ask Sam, all I know is Jason Kelly is dead."

"Jason, dead?" Murphy said. He looked at his watch and signed into the scene. Murphy went back towards his car, telling Sam to wait up. Sam kept on walking, waving for Murphy to come on.

Murphy grabbed his backpack out of his patrol car and took off after Sam. When he caught up just a few yards from Jason's body, Sam filled Murphy in on what he knew so far.

Sam said, "The scene is going to go on further because the blood seemed to go on further north." Then, he stopped and grabbed Murphy by the arm, "Dawn has been seeing Jason. She is real upset. I got her out of here, and I haven't told Wallow."

"You know I will have to interview her," Murphy mentioned, knowingly.

Sam said to Murphy, "I told that her that, but can you use a little tact?"

Murphy replied, "Sam! I may be an asshole, but I'm not a complete prick." Sam chuckled and shook his head.

Sam was pointing out the blood trail, which Murphy had already noticed, and walked around as Murphy walked up. Sam explained that horse had blood all over it and the saddle.

Murphy looked at Sam and said, "Horse?"

Turning, he saw it and stared with a perplexed look on his face.

Sam pointed back towards the horse that was still standing near the school. He explained how he found it and followed the blood trail to

Jason's body. It seemed funny to Sam that Murphy, as detail-orientated he was, missed a horse!

Murphy asked, "Do you know if Jason rode through here a lot?"

Sam said, "I've never seen him here, but don't know." While they were talking, they noticed the corner, B.J Peeks, talking to Chief Wallow. Murphy waved to him to come up, but warned him not to disturb the scene.

Murphy got his camera out of his backpack. Starting to take pictures and examining the body, the first thing Murphy said was, "Looks like he's been cut, by a big knife, a very big knife."

They both looked at each other and said "Joe!"

Joe Kerchak, 6'4 280 pounds of pure orneriness, with a bushy head of blond hair and a half-toothed smile. Joe was one of those guys that just could not stay out of trouble. Sam and Murphy had arrested him many times over the last few years. Joe was not just big, but could be downright mean, and loved knives.

Joe was brought up rough. His dad was in prison for murder. His mother, a full-blooded Apache, was mean in her own right. She raised 4 boys all by herself. She would yell and wallop those boys over the slightest thing, but it didn't seem to help. Joe was the youngest and has spent a lot of time in jail. Jack, the second, got killed in a bar fight, and Hawk, the oldest, was in prison for rape. The only one that turned out good was Sky. Sky Kerchak was born blind, his mother raised him to fend for himself, and he did. He was taught to read Braille by a local preacher, but the only Braille book he owned was the Bible. Sky became a minister and moved to North Dakota to pastor on a reservation.

Several years ago, Sam had stopped Joe for doing donuts in his car at the park, tearing up the grass on the softball field. Joe was just 18 at the time, but already had a hell of a bad attitude.

Sam finally got Joe stopped that night, and could tell that he had been drinking. When Sam started to cuff Joe up, he swung around and tried to hit Sam. Sam ducked the punch, and they went to the ground, the battle was on. They rolled around in the field, Sam trying to get his walkie out, guarding his gun. Joe had managed to get his hand on the butt of Sam's Ruger once, but Sam swung his forearm down knocking Joe's hand away. Finally, Sam got Joe into a full Nelson, not a recommended hold, because you can break someone's neck with it, but at this point, it was a life or death situation for Sam. After a few minutes of pressure, and not being able to breathe, Joe finally gave up. Sam figured they had been fighting for a good 5 minutes. He was almost out of energy. Sam got Joe in cuffs, being Joe's size it took 2 sets. Sam was so worn-out, he just sat on Joe's back, covered with mud and blood. He called for back-up, but everyone was busy, so after a rest, he fought to get Joe in the car.

As bad as that was, it gave some mutual respect between the two of them, and Joe never gave Sam much trouble after that. In fact, would give him some information from time to time.

Still, Joe could handle himself in a fight, and he loved knives, all kinds of knives. He always carried an enormous Bowie knife, and he was even known to have a sword or two in his house or car. Joe also had no love for Jason Kelly. In fact, Joe blamed Jason for his girlfriend running off. Jason had put Joe in jail for domestic abuse and got her in a domestic violence shelter that helped her move out of state. That was just a few months ago, when Jason Kelly gave Joe 60 days for domestic violence battery. Joe threatened to kick Jason's ass when he got out.

Standing by Jason's body, Sam was telling Murphy about the drug raid the night before and that Joe had gotten away into the woods just a couple miles north of there. Sam pointed out to the area where Tommy Little's place was, and said that Joe could have hidden in the woods overnight and ambushed Jason.

Murphy said, "Well there is suspect number one, who else do we have?" Sam told Murphy about what Fred Long had said about seeing Bobby Ellis passing papers.

"Well, Ellis is a little peeping weasel, but to kill someone, I don't know, Sam. But, we will check him up anyway," Murphy concluded.

Sam reminded Murphy about Ellis stabbing his ex-wife several years ago, Murphy said, "I completely had forgotten about that."

"Ok, anyone else besides Dawn?" Murphy asked, saying "Not that she is a suspect, but someone I need to talk to." Sam feelings, in this case, were getting worse by the minute.

People were arriving at the scene quickly, many of them hurried out of curiosity, due to the way they were called out with no explanation. Murphy told Wallow to hold everyone up at the school. B.J. Peeks walked up, in his usual manner, spouting out, half joking around like he usually did, until he saw who the body was.

"Shit, that ain't good," B.J. said. It was the first time Sam or Murphy had seen that kind of reaction from B.J. seeing a body in the years that they had known him.

B.J. Peeks was no stranger to dead bodies. He had been County Coroner as long as Sam could remember, and his family had owned Peek's Funeral home for 4 generations. B.J. was working in the embalming room before starting high school and was now 69 years old. Away from the funeral home, B.J. was loud and boisterous, unlike what you think of as a funeral director, but was very caring and personal with the families he dealt with. B.J.'s son, Aaron, was doing more at the funeral home now, which was a good thing. Several times in the last year, Sam or one of the other officers would have to go to Fuwalda Bar and pick B.J. up and take him home after he had too much to drink.

B.J. was sober today, and he asked Murphy if he should call Aaron to bring the hearse. He would need to take the body to the medical examiner's office, the nearest one being in Harrisburg, in Saline County. Murphy thought that this would be a good idea, so not to tie the ambulance up any longer.

Murphy told B.J., "Tell Aaron to come on, but there is no hurry because there's a lot to be done at the scene yet."

Sam thought, "That Aaron gives me the creeps. He's a strange one."

Murphy told the paramedics they could go, but to leave a copy of their reports at the station and to back out the way they came in not, to disturb any more of the scene.

While Murphy and B.J. discussed the scene, Sam pointed out that it probably went further north, but didn't know how far or wide. They walked around a bit, and Murphy called Sheriff's Detective Reb Main to bring up his truck. Reb would have, in his Suburban, a better camera, marking cones, and flags, evidence bags, paint or whatever they needed.

Sam and Murphy looked closer at the scene. They could barely see the horseshoe prints in the hard dirt. What they had observed was where the horse had come through the field by the trampled grass. They could see other paths, to the North, crossing the horse's path.

Before they moved anything, everything needed to be videotaped and photographed. Sam and Murphy both took pictures. Sam took some of the pictures with his phone as they walked to the place they had Reb pull into.

Reb got out of the truck and looked over at the body, he asked inquisitively, "Did he get thrown from his horse?"

Sam and Murphy, shaking their heads said at the same time, "Looks like he's been murdered."

"WOW, I just talked to him early this morning, he called me…" Reb said, stopping when he looked at B.J. "…about a case he wanted me to work on." Sam and Murphy both got the hint that what Reb needed to say something, but it couldn't be said around B.J.

Murphy asked Reb if he could start taking pictures and mark the scene while he and Sam followed the blood trail. Reb said "Got it." As he looked over at the other side of the Suburban he told Johnny Hazzard to help him get the equipment. Neither Sam nor Murphy even noticed Deputy Hazzard standing there. He was a quiet kid, a rookie on the Sheriff's Department, but had all the makings of a good cop.

Johnny Hazzard had gone to college to study forensic science and graduated at the top of his class at Iowa State University. While he was in school, he went on a ride-along program and now just wanted to be on the street. When asked why he chose Callsworth County, he had just said, "It was the first place that offered me a job." No one expected Hazzard to stick around long before moving to a larger department, but they thought for now, his education may come in real handy!

Leaving Reb, Johnny, and B.J. at the body, Sam and Murphy slowly started walking north to follow the blood trail, when Chief Wallow called Sam on his cell phone. Wallow asked, "Are you going to keep me here on this log sheet all day?"

"Uh, that's up to you." said Sam, "You're the chief, if you want to do something else give it to one of the young officers, but tell them to keep everyone out."

"Do you need me up there?" Wallow eagerly asked,

"Only if you want to testify later." Sam knew this would throw him off.

"Uh well, I do have other things I need to be doing, call me if you need me." Wallow stammered. Sam just smiled at Murphy, and they went about at the job at hand.

It was a slow process: walk a bit, check anything they found on the ground, photograph all the blood droppings, and when they came to a path crossing the horse's path they would investigate where it went. Some of the paths looked like deer tracks, other like four-wheelers had been through there. At about 60 yards south of the oil tanks both of them stopped, there was a lot more blood at this point, and it went out in a larger pattern. Splatters and squirts were everywhere. Sam said to Murphy "Looks like the horse stopped here for a bit, more hoof prints overlapping each other, and the grass is bent over in a wider area, not a straight path."

"Yeah, I think we have found our murder scene!" Murphy said looking north, "I don't see any more blood past here." They took several pictures, marked a Camel cigarette butt that looked like it had been there for quite a while, and a fresh chewing gum wrapper, Blackjack Gum.

"This is really weird, Sam," Murphy said with a shrug. "There are no other paths, footprints, or places to hide and ambush someone within 50 feet of here, doesn't make sense." They talked about different scenarios, someone lying in the grass? But there were no impressions, and the grass was not really that long. Was someone following Jason on horseback? They could not say for sure if all the horseshoe prints were from the same horse. Was someone riding double with Jason, or even following him right behind him on foot? The ground was very hard, and though you could see hoof prints, a shoe print from a person may not show up.

While Murphy was working at the scene, Sam asked if it would be ok if he went on and followed the path towards the oil tanks. Murphy said, "Yeah, ok, just mark and photograph anything you find."

Sam followed the path, not seeing anything out of place except the hoof prints. When Sam got to the oil tanks he lost the trail, it went right up to a large concrete pad that had a rack with several lengths of drilling pipes stored on it. It looked like there had been more equipment stored on the pad, but it had been taken out. All that was left was some rust stains.

Sam thought maybe if he climbed the stairs that went to the top of the tanks, he could see where the path went on to. His phone rang just as he started up the stairs. "Ouch, damn," Sam said out loud, looking at his hand, there was a 3" cut in the middle of his hand, bleeding. "Shit, they should fix that." Sam answered his phone with his left hand, aggravated he said "Yeah, who is it?"

"Sam, it's me, Reb, you ok?" Reb asked.

"Yeah, I just cut…never mind, whatchya need?" Sam said.

"Who wiped the blood from Jason's neck?" Reb asked.

"I stuck my fingers in it and felt it, but the paramedics wiped the blood off. Why?" Sam told Reb while trying to hold his phone with his shoulder and get his bandana out of his back pocket.

"There could be trace evidence in that blood, I need to get those sterile pads back… Uh, don't worry about it, I'll call them and ask them to come back, they probably haven't had time to throw them away yet." Reb said.

"Good catch, all of that education is paying off," Sam said.

Sam put his phone in his shirt pocket, looked at a broken piece on the metal handrail that was jagged and sharp, got the bandana out of his back pocket and wrapped it around his right hand. Sam made a mental note to tell Murphy about the blood that he had dripped onto the ground while on the phone. Sam didn't want Murphy to find it and think it was evidence. Sam, for sure, didn't want his DNA accidently found at the scene of a murder. Looking at his hand he thought of his of his dad, and what he had taught Sam as a kid, the bandana always came in handy for many things, including as an instant bandage.

As Sam got up to the top of the tanks and he could see what looked like the horse path that went behind the tanks and through the woods. From this vantage point, he could also see the whole field really well. Sam could see all kinds of paths in the area, but one really caught his attention. It looked to be a set of four-wheeler tracks that looped just west of where Murphy was bent over taking pictures. The path came or went, from the west to a place just about 15 yards from the horse trail and made a wide U-turn and went out the same direction. The suspect could have ridden up on a four-wheeler, killed Jason, and rode off, but it seemed to be on the wrong side. This would still interest Murphy.

Sam came down from the tank and after taking several pictures, he almost put his hand down on the jagged railing but caught himself before getting cut again. He turned and walked behind the tanks and picked up the trail again. The hoof prints went into the woods through a small, almost waterless creek and up the other side. He went through more trees and came out on a gravel road. Sam walked both ways on Deerhead Lane, but the tracks disappeared, probably due to vehicles traveling up and down the road. "Damn," he thought.

Sam started back to where Murphy was, to tell him what he found. Looking around for the oil tanks, Sam could not see through the trees to find his way back. He walked back down the road and finally found the narrow path he has used. While climbing up out of the creek, Sam slipped on the mud. As he was getting back up, with his hands and pants covered with mud, he thought, "Damn, can this day get any worse?"

Walking back to where he left Murphy, Sam couldn't help to think that he has missed something. He walked slowly and took pictures, from an entirely different angle. Sam looked across the field and saw that the school yard was getting full of other police vehicles. Then he heard the radio crack, it was Chief Wallow's voice, and it said, "Dispatch City 1 will be done at the scene of the 10-0 (Code for Dead Body) and en route to the station".

"Oh, hell no, he didn't put that over the air," Sam thought. Sam hoped that the media didn't pick it up on their scanners. "This day just does keep getting worse," Sam thought. "Oh well," Sam decided, "We'll just tell them they will have to talk to the Chief for any information."

As Sam walked up to Murphy, he asked, "Did you hear that?"

"Yep," Murphy said just shaking his head, "Let's get back to B.J. and Reb, to see if they can at least get the body away from here before the news arrives. Using those telephoto lenses, they will be able to find out who the body is even way back at the school."

Walking back to the where the body was, both Murphy and Sam took more pictures of the blood drops, "It sure looks like that was where he was attacked, there is a large blood splatter pattern. We'll need to get the State Police Crime Scene Investigators to look at it. I think he's a blood splatter expert," Murphy said.

"They've been called but it will be a little while until they get here," Sam told him.

Murphy looked at Sam's hand, and blood dripping from the bandana and asked, "What the hell happened to you?"

"Oh, I cut myself on the damn rail on the oil tanks, I was going to tell you because there is blood there too. Sorry, for bleeding in your scene, Murph," Sam replied.

Murphy nodded and put it down in his notes. Murphy looked up from his notepad, stopped and looked around, then told Sam, "Look where we are, this is actually going to be a County case, we're out of the city limits."

Both of them smiled. It was true, the murder scene was actually about 30 yards out of the city limits, they could tell by an old fence line from the property next to the school. Where the horse was found, on school property, was in the city limits, but the murder didn't take place there. Even with this, they both knew, with this kind of case, everyone was going to have to work together!

As they walked up, B.J. said, "Well, I think we have everything I'll need. We took a few photographs, videotaped some, bagged and tagged what I needed. So now I'm going to call Aaron to come up, load the body and get it into the cooler. He has been in the heat long enough that's for sure."

"That's good," Murphy said, continuing with, "I expect the media will be arriving before long and I want to keep the ID of Jason under wraps for a while, next of kin still needs to be notified."

It was already 10:55 am and with everything going on Sam hadn't really noticed how hot and thirsty he was! Sam told Murphy he was going to walk back to the school to get some water, and asked if he wanted some. Murphy just nodded and kept talking to B.J., Murphy asked B.J. if he knew next of kin.

B.J was shaking his head thinking, then said, "Both of Jason's parents are dead. He has a sister, I think she moved to California. I don't believe he has any other relatives that live close."

Murphy thought that was probably good, the longer they could keep this quiet, the easier on the investigation. Murphy told B.J., "I bet Sam will know, he was close to the family."

Growing up in McCracken's Bluff, Sam knew just about everyone in town, who they were related to and being a police officer, a lot of their secrets. Sam knew Jason's father well, he met him shortly after they had moved to "The Bluffs," during the last oil boom when Sam was a kid. Thomas Kelly, Jason's father, was a bear of a man, he had the biggest hands Sam had ever seen, that even seemed bigger when Sam was a boy of twelve. Thomas had started out as a roughneck with the oil company, but worked his way up over the years and ended up running the drilling operations.

Sam's and Thomas Kelly's first meeting was not so great. Sam and some other neighborhood kids were playing sandlot baseball at Wabash Park. That day Sam got what was probably the best hit he had ever made. The crack of the bat told everyone it was going to be a home run, and as everyone stopped and watched the ball sail overhead. Sam stood still, shocked, himself, as the ball climbed over everyone's head. Sam also eyed a shiny new Corvette as it pulled up and park on the street at the end of the park. Sam's mouth gaped open as the ball dropped, right through the hood of the 'vette. He just stood there unable to move, as all the other kids ran.

Thomas Kelly got out of his car, and Sam thought he was a giant. Kelly looked at the hole in the hood, opened it, and retrieved the ball. Sam still stood there shaking as this monster of a man walked towards him. As Thomas Kelly got near, he got a big smile on his face and said, "Nice hit kid," then tossed the ball to Sam.

Sam stuttered, "I…I'll pay for the damages, sir."

"Don't worry about it kid, a little fiberglass and some paint, and it will be as good as new. What's your name?" Kelly asked, holding his hand out to Sam.

Shaking Thomas Kelly's hand, Sam said "Sam Nickles, Sir."

"Well, not running tells me a lot about you, Sam," Kelly said.

Sam replied, "I was so scared. I couldn't get my legs to move." Thomas Kelly let out a big laugh, and from that time he and Sam were good friends.

Sam would often stop by the Kelly house and play with Jason even though Jason was a lot younger. But Sam actually stopped to talk to "Bear," as Sam always called him. After the death of his own parents, the saddest day in Sam's life was the passing of Thomas "Bear" Kelly, and his wife. They were both killed in a car accident, hit by a drunk driver while on vacation in Colorado. Sam often got a lump in his throat when he drove by the Kelly place on the outskirts of town, remembering the good times he had there.

Jason lived there now; he and his sister kept the place after their parents died. They held on to it partially because their parents loved it so much, but also because it was a beautiful 30-acre ranch, they had several horses that they both loved to ride. Both Jason and Jenna lived there on and off after their parents' death and when they were going to college. Jason had moved back in full time when he returned to McCracken's Bluff to run for State's Attorney.

Sam got back to the school's playground and asked if anyone had any water. But everyone had come so quick, no one stopped to get anything to drink. Sam asked Willy Fogerty to run to Randy's and get some water, cokes, and several cups of ice and charge them to the police department.

Fogerty said, "Shouldn't I ask the Chief first?"

"Do what you want, or listen, I'll take the blame. I'm already on Wallow's bad side, but these guys are going to need something to drink," Sam said looking at Willy. This was the first time he had noticed the waffle print on his forehead, from Clifford Duggs' boot.

Sam laughed, and turned towards his car, with Willy just asking, "What?"

Sam got into the trunk of his car and got 3 bottles of water that he tried to keep in there just for an occasion like this. They would not be cold, but they were wet and would cut the dust in his mouth. He drank one of the bottles on the way back to Murphy's location. As he got to him, he heard dispatch give Dawn a call of keys locked in a car. Looking at Murphy, he told dispatch he would take that call and show him 10-8 (complete) from this call.

"I need to get back on the street, and check on Dawn to see how she is doing." Sam said, then continued, "You got plenty of help now, the State's Crime Scene Investigation Unit should be here soon. Is it ok with you, Murph?"

Murphy said, "I've got it."

They both watched as B.J. and Aaron loaded the stretcher into the hearse and closed the door. Aaron looked at them with that ghoulish grin he always seemed to have. Murphy reminded them to back out so not to disturb the scene.

He told Sam, "I'll need your reports as soon as possible, and if you talk to Dawn be careful what you ask her.'

Murphy looked up from taking pictures, pointing at Sam saying, "She needs to go home, tell Wallow she needs to take a leave of absence, but be available so I can talk to her."

Sam said he understood and would take care of it.

As Sam walked away thinking, "These last 12 hours have been a nightmare." So far he hadn't gotten the first word down on paper from the drug raid or this case. He stopped, realizing he was still holding the water bottles. He yelled at Murphy, when he looked up Sam threw both remaining bottles to him.

Murphy yelled, "Wait!"

Sam stopped.

"Do you know how to get in touch with Jason's next of kin?" Murphy asked.

"I am pretty sure I have Jenna's number at home, I'll check," Sam said.

Murphy looked at Sam and said, "Someone needs to notify her."

"Ok... I got it, I will make sure I get in touch with her, at least she knows me," Sam replied, but thinking, "I hate making those calls."

Chapter 7

Sam signed out of the scene, walked to and got in his car. He noticed that his shirt was sweat-soaked and he cringed, as he could smell himself. Sam was really hoping that he could slide home and change clothes soon. Enjoying the cold air as he drove to Rosie's Beauty Salon, Sam felt refreshed. Arriving he saw Dottie Como waiting nervously outside in the heat, with her car parked backward, on a yellow line. "No time to worry about that," Sam said to himself.

As he pulled up and got out, Sam noticed the car was running, and he told Dottie to go back inside, it was too hot for her to be out in this heat. Dottie, who was every bit of 80, said: "What about Manfred?"

Sam looked in the car, looking out at him was Manfred, her dachshund, standing on the armrest.

"I just pulled in to drop off a check and left the car running," Dotty nervously said. "Manfred must have stepped on the door lock, dang these new-fangled cars!"

Sam again told Dottie to stand inside the door where it was cool, and he would get it. Sam got the door wedged open with the inflator, and when he stuck the rod in to push the door lock, but Manfred attacked it. Every time Sam would just about get on the button, the dog would grab the rod again and pull it away. The battle went on for about 10 minutes, and Sam had to keep wiping the sweat from his glasses.

Sam looked up from the window of the car and noticed J.J. Jay was walking towards him. Sam asked J.J., "Will you bang on the window on the other side to get the dogs attention?"

J.J. started making faces and knocked on the glass, and when he did, Manfred turned and barked at him leaving Sam to hit the unlock button. J.J. was laughing and thought this was a great game, but when the door was opened Sam told him, "Thanks J.J., you can stop now."

While getting his tools together, Sam asked J.J., "How did your target practice go earlier?"

J.J. said "We stayed for a little bit, shot a few tin cans, but then heard some others shooting nearby, and we decided to leave. It was getting hot, so we went to Randy's to get a Coke and just hang out in the store where it was cool and play the old Pac Man game."

Sam told J.J., "Next time you're at Randy's, get yourself a Coke on me. Just tell Randy, I said so. Thanks for your help." J.J. said thanks and ran off.

Dottie came out and thanked Sam, and told him to wait as she was digging in her purse.

Sam shook his head and said, "No Ma'am we can't take any money."

Dottie insisted, handing Sam a shiny new dime.

Sam looked at the dime, looked a Dottie and laughed to himself. Then, he took the dime and said thank you, with a smile!

When Sam got back in the car, he cleaned his glasses again, wrote in his daily log and noted about the dime with a smile. He wanted to check on Dawn, so he drove to the station.

As he arrived, Chief Wallow was coming out. "Sam this thing is going crazy; the press is calling me every five minutes," the Chief said nervously.

Sam said, "Just tell them to call the Sheriff, it is actually in his jurisdiction, the end of the playgrounds is the City Limits."

Wallow smiled, "Great, that what I will do, let Dickens handle them!"

Sam reminded him, "Don't release any names because we haven't contacted the next of kin."

Wallow said, "Duh, I know that, but what was up with Dawn?" Sam explained the best he could that Dawn and Jason were very close, and he should give her some time off. Wallow told Sam that they were too short-handed with vacations and all. He didn't know how he could cover the shifts.

Sam said to him, "I've worked alone a lot over the years, I'll take care of day shift."

Wallow said, "I guess it would be ok, you go ahead and tell her, I've got to go meet with the Mayor."

Sam said he would, thinking, "Well, maybe Seth Wallow is not all that bad!"

Sam walked in the office, and Winnie pointed to the investigator's room across the hall, saying, "She came in and just went straight in there."

Sam knocked on the door, and Dawn's weak voice said, "come in."

Sam opened the door, and Dawn looked up, and half smiled, "Sam, it's you, I thought it was Wallow or Murphy. Sam, what am I going to do, Jason texted me last night during the raid, he said..."

Sam told her, "Stop! Dawn, you have to listen to me, you cannot say anything right now.... you need to go home, I got Wallow to give you some time off... wait for Murphy or me to call. I will see if I can sit in on the interview if you like, but we cannot do this now."

She looked at him with tears in her eyes, and said, "You don't think I did it, do you, Sam?"

"Of course not," Sam said to here trying to reassure her, "But we cannot even give a hint of a cover up, if we do it by the book, it will be ok." He told her to go home, and would bring some food by later.

"Is Greg home?" Sam asked.

Dawn started to cry again. "No Sam..." She barely got out. "I haven't seen him since yesterday morning, and he won't answer my calls, I think he knows something, Sam!" Sam thought, oh great another suspect. They started to walk out and Sam gave a signal, for just a minute, to Winnie as they left. Winnie had that, "what the hell is going on" look on her face.

Sam asked Dawn, "Do you have anyone that can stay with you?" Shaking her head, she said she wanted to be alone. As they got to Dawn's car, she said, "Sam, I know you are trying to quit smoking, but you do have a cigarette hidden, somewhere don't you?"

"Dawn," Sam commented, "You haven't smoked in years."

"I just want one for the ride home," Dawn said.

Sam got into his car, got one out of the glove box, gave it to her and lit it. Sam watched her drive off and lit one up himself and thought, "Yep, quit smoking. Oh, hell no, not today."

Chapter 8

As he took the last few puffs from his cigarette, Sam looked at his watch. It was already 1:25 pm. As he turned to go back into the station, he noticed a TV van heading towards the scene. Sam was glad he wasn't there; he never did like the limelight or, in particular, cameras.

When he walked into the station, Winnie looked as if she was going to pee her pants. She had been waiting so long to find out what was happening. While explaining to Winnie that Jason was dead, Winnie blurted out that she knew something was going on with them two. Sam asked her why she thought that. Winnie explained, "I noticed that Dawn would always get to the station early, grabbed the overnight paperwork and head to Jason's office. Then, if she could, she would stay for a long time."

Sam said, "Being at the office is pretty innocent."

Winnie also told of the time a couple weeks back, she said, "I was driving out Cotton Mill Road where Jason lives, and I saw Dawn jogging.

That wasn't unusual, but that day I passed her almost in front of Jason's house, and when I looked in my rearview mirror, she was gone."

"You think she went into Jason's," Sam concluded.

Winnie said bluntly, "I don't blame her, with that asshole of a husband she has, she should have got rid of him a long time ago!"

While Sam was talking to Winnie, he had sat down in a big office chair. While Winnie was on the phone, Sam nodded off until the chair rocked back quickly, and jolted him back to life. Sam told Winnie that Murphy would have to talk to her, and she got nervous and said: "Oh God, I hope I didn't say anything wrong."

Sam patted her on the shoulder and said, "Everything will be ok."

Going back out to his car, Sam thought about the reports that need to be done. He almost turned around and went back in to get them done, but he was so tired he decided he would finish out the last hour of his shift, go home and get a nap and then work on them at home. He could always get one of the evening or midnight shift guys to come by and pick them up. That way they would still be there by morning when the chief came in.

As Sam was driving around, killing time, he swung through the town park.

At the other end of the loop road, he saw someone running across the park. "Shit, that's Joe," Sam said out loud. He floored the accelerator pedal and sped to the other end of the park. As he did, Joe disappeared behind a barn that sat just little ways outside the park, but there was a short fence between them. Sam quickly looped around and went out the park's exit, and drove to the barn. Sam advised dispatch where he was, and that he was getting out of the car because he had seen Joe Kerchak. Sam looked all around, checking the barn, but found no signs of Joe. The barn was all padlocked up from the outside so no one could have gotten in. Sam radioed for everyone to disregard that; the subject got away. After driving around the area and searching every place he could think of, Sam figured Joe had escaped.

"Hmmm," Sam thought to himself, "Joe must know we want him, I hope he doesn't leave town. Damn, I wish I hadn't lost him!"

Sam heard Teasdale and McDollin sign on duty for the evening shift, with a sigh, Sam signed off duty. As he drove the last few blocks to home, he thought. "What a day!"

He was so glad to get into the house, it almost felt cold as he walked in. All he wanted was to take a shower and get into his recliner. Taking off his gun belt going into the spare bedroom that he used as an office and where he kept his equipment, he noticed the shower running in the bathroom across the hall. "What the hell..."

Sam knocked.

"Who's in there?" Sam asked.

"Just me, Dad, be out in a few." It was the voice of Jeb, his 17-year-old son that replied.

"Just great!" Sam said, taking off his boots, and socks.

Sam smiled, as he wiggled his toes in the carpet, he loved to be barefooted, this felt so good. When he was a kid, his mother was always on him about his bare feet. If they went somewhere, Sam never seemed to have a pair of shoes with him. It got so bad that she bought several pairs of flip flops or thongs as they called them back then and left them in the car. His solution was Hamachi sandals. They were so thin, he could fold them up and put them in his back pocket. This was the time when places that served food first started insisting people wear shoes. Sam didn't see a need for shoes, his feet were so calloused back then; he could walk across rocks with no problem, and if he stepped on a bee and it stung him in the foot, he just pulled it out without feeling any pain.

Pulling off his uniform, Sam walked to the bathroom near Lilly's and his bedroom in just his t-shirt and pants. As he got close to the bathroom, he heard the shower in there also. Sam thought, "What the hell, Lilly's home already?"

Sam tried to open the door, but it was locked.

Sam knocked and called Lilly's name. Instead, he heard, "No, it's me," the voice of Midg, his step-daughter called out.

Sam wondered what she was doing home.

Midg was in college at Purdue and was going to stay there over the summer because she had an internship. Sam just shook his head, he seemed to never to know was going on with the kids, but he did know he wouldn't be getting a shower for a while.

Sam sat down on the recliner and kicked back to watch the news until one of the showers became free, but in no time he was asleep. Sam woke up and first noticed his Border Collie, Boo, was asleep on his lap, and Lilly was on the couch watching television.

"What time is it?" he asked.

"You were out, I didn't want to wake you. It's 9:30. We had dinner, I saved you a plate." Boo looked up at him and scratched his ear. Boo probably wished Sam would go back to sleep.

Sam asked Lilly, "Would you mind zapping dinner for me while I take a shower?" He grumbled as he headed to the bathroom.

The hot water felt so good running over his body, he took a washrag, soaked it and put it over his head, and he bent over and let the spray hit his lower back. After just standing there for a few minutes he could feel his muscles loosen, and he felt human again. Sam looked at his hand, still caked in blood, he had thrown the bandana in the trash before going into the house. He was trying to wash it carefully, but soon after the water cleaned off the dried blood, it started bleeding again, and it was throbbing now. Cleaning it thoroughly, looking to make sure all the dirt was out Sam looked at the 3-inch cut, thinking it wasn't that deep, he thought it would be ok.

Sam washed, shaving his face and head, he just wished he could stay in the shower longer, but noticed that the hot water was running out. Sam quickly finished up and got out of the shower. How long had he been in there? It seemed like just minutes.

Sam yelled out to tell Lilly he would be out in a moment, as he was brushing his teeth.

She called back saying, "Good, your dinner is getting cold again, I thought you had drowned!" The cut was still dripping blood so Sam grabbed a bandage pad and wrapped some gauze around his hand.

Going into the kitchen, Sam got his plate and told Lilly he had paperwork that had to get done so he would eat in his office. She grabbed Sam's arm and stopped him, "What did you do to your hand?"

He told her, "It's just a cut."

Lilly was already unwrapping it, and when she saw it she said, "Sam! You need to see a doctor for stitches."

Sam asked why he needed a doctor when he lived with "Nurse Lilly."

"I do filing in a medical office. That's far from being a nurse, and I certainly can't do stitches."

Sam just smiled at her and said, "That's a good thing!"

Lilly still insisted he sit down and let her bandage it properly. After some antiseptic, 4 butterfly bandages, and 10 foot of tape on the bandage pad, then more gauze around the hand, she was done. She told him she would make him an appointment at the doctor's office in the morning. "Oh hell no, I'm not going to the doc for this!" Sam thought to himself. She told him he better check on the bandage before he came to bed, finishing by saying "You better not get blood on my sheets." She gave him another kiss and went back to the kitchen.

Sam was flexing his hand. It was getting stiff as he walked into his office. He sat down, pulled up a supplemental report form on his computer and looked down at his plate. "Damn, I forgot a fork," he thought to himself, "Oh well, finger food." He picked up the pork chop, took a big bite, and fingered the fried potatoes and peas, in between getting his thoughts together and typing. Looking down at his feet, he noticed Boo looking up at him. Sam gave him the pork chop bone, and Boo went over to the corner and enjoyed it.

Lilly brought Sam a cup of coffee, that she knew he would want some, but knew he didn't need it this late at night. Sam slowly sipped the coffee, "Mmmm boy," he said, "That coffee sure hits the spot."

Lilly asked, "How much longer will you be?"

"About an hour or so," He said, "I have the raid report done, but I still have to get the murder report finished."

"Murder?" she said shocked, "I heard about the raid, but a murder too... who?"

Sam told her it was Jason Kelly; he had figured she had heard already. She said "No," Lilly was stunned and sad, she told Sam she was so sorry, she knew Sam liked Jason. "Who found him?" Lilly asked.

"Me," Sam said shaking his head. "Don't tell anyone, we are not releasing the name yet."

Sam sat up suddenly and said "Damn."

Lilly looked at him and said, "What?"

Sam had just remembered and told Lilly, "I was supposed to get a hold of Jason's sister Jenna and let her know what happened." He looked at the time, "It's too late now, I will in the morning."

"Oh Sam, I am so sorry," Lilly said. She started to cry as she gave him a big hug from behind. Sam smiled, her arms felt nice around him. "I know this is hard on you, so I will go to bed, and stay out of your way... unless you want me to stay up." She said, kissing him on the back of his head.

"No, go to bed. It's going to take a while to get my thoughts together, and make sure everything I know is in the report, I'll be to bed later." He looked up and kissed her good night, and said, "Thanks, love you!" She just smiled back and left saying, "More!"

Sam sat there for a minute, thinking about going outside for a cigarette because Lilly didn't like him smoking in the house. Too tired to get up, Sam pulled out a partial pack he had hidden in the back of the desk drawer, and opened the window in front of his desk. Rummaging around in the desk, he found a small tin he used as a hideaway ashtray. Sam got his old Zippo lighter from of his uniform pants. Another thing his dad always told him to carry, however, his father thought of it as a survival tool, not for smoking. Thinking about it, Sam knew his dad would disapprove.

As Sam sat back enjoying the coffee and cigarette, he thought he needed to call dispatch and get the correct times from them so the report would be accurate. Using his cell phone to call the administrative line, Linda "Buzzy" Nelson answered, "Callsworth County Dispatch, Nelson speaking, how can I help you?"

"Hey Buzz, it's Sam, what's going on?" Sam asked.

"It's the calm after the storm Sam. We haven't had a call in hours. What are you doing up?" Buzz said.

"Trying to get the reports on Jason done, and I need some times." Linda pulled up the dispatch log and gave Sam the times of when things had happened. She was saying how awful it was, and she hopes they caught whoever did it quickly. Sam asked who was working the midnight shift, and she told him it was Clifford and Fogerty. Sam told her he would probably call back later to have them pick up the reports. Buzzy started to ask questions, but Sam cut her off telling her, "I got to get busy, Buzzy, or I'll never get to bed." He knew she would talk his arm off if he didn't, and he really needed sleep!

Sam lit up another cigarette, wondering how long that pack had been in that drawer. It was really harsh. Sam had been trying to quit smoking for quite a while, and usually only smoked a few a day, but on days like this, it was back to the habit. He had told Lilly once, "It's hard to quit something you really enjoy, that's why I could never leave you!"

Sam pulled out his notebook and got down to business, trying to recall every detail he could think of. He knew this would be one of the biggest cases of all of their careers and Sam wanted to do it his part right. He was thankful that Murphy was working on the case with Reb Main. Reb was sharp, but Murphy was like a pit bull on steroids, as well as anal retentive, and a stickler for detail. Having Johnny Hazzard helping would also be a benefit; he had a good eye for detail and an education far beyond any of theirs.

It took Sam almost 2 hours and 5 cigarettes to finish the report. He probably would have smoked more, but he had run out. It was a little after 2 am, and Sam called to have one of the midnight shift guys to come get the reports. Buzzy, as usual, started asking all kinds of questions about the investigation, but Sam cut her short again, saying he need to get to bed. He had to work at 7 in the morning, so he asked her to call him at 6 just in case he overslept. Sam printed off 3 copies of the reports; one for himself, one for the department, and the other for the State Attorney's office, who would have been Jason. He wondered who would prosecute the case, now.

Sam walked outside to wait for a patrol car to pull up, got into his cruiser and got a cigarette. As he lit it, Midge's car pulled in the driveway. As she and Jeb got out of the car, Sam said, "Out a little late, aren't you two?" Midg said, "Sam, I'm in college, I'm out late a lot." She gave him a hug and said she missed him.

Sam asked Jeb why he was still up, didn't he have to work the next day. "Dad, tomorrow is Saturday, I always work nights on the weekends. I got off at 11 and met up with Midg and we hung out," replied Jeb.

Weekends didn't mean much to Sam since his days off rotated every week. Midg asked him about his smoking. Sam just shrugged it off. They talked for a bit about what they had been doing all night, and how everyone in town was talking about the drug bust and the murder. They both asked who was dead, it seemed like no one they knew had heard. Sam just told them they would know soon enough. "That's not fair Sam, you know we can keep a secret," Midg said.

Sam just smiled and said, "Life ain't fair!" They both turned and went into the house. They hated to hear that saying, because Sam used it all the time.

Willy Fogerty pulled up, and Sam walked out to meet him, "What's up, Sam?" Willy asked.

"Me, unfortunately… I just wanted to get this paperwork in the office before morning. If I know Murphy, he will be in early to get started." Sam said, handing the reports to Willy.

Willy looked at Sam and said, "You better get some sleep, you look like shit."

"Oh, thanks." Sam sighed as he walked towards the house, shaking his head.

Sam went back into his office, took off his clothes and put on a pair of athletic shorts to get ready for bed. It had been a long day; he didn't know if his body ached from the lack of sleep or all the activity. He did know his bed was going to feel wonderful and he couldn't wait to get there.

Trying to be quiet, Sam started to slip into bed, careful not to wake Lilly. Stopping, he thought, "Oh hell no, I wonder if anyone fed Boo today." Sam got up and looked at Boo's empty bowl, then at Boo, who had been following him around. Sam bent down and petted the dogs head and said: "I got ya, little buddy." Sam opened 2 cans of dog food and put the contents in Boo's bowl. Sam usually mixed 1 can and some dry food, but thought Boo could use a treat.

Going back to bed, Sam got himself comfortable, he laid there for a few minutes thinking about the day, what he could have, or should have done. After a few moments, Sam felt Boo jump up on the bed. He usually slept at Sam's feet, but tonight Boo walked up between Sam and Lilly and curled up next to him. Sam smiled. Boo always seemed to know when Sam had a rough day. In the darkness, petting Boo, Sam could hear Lilly breathing and slipped into a deep sleep.

Chapter 9

"Bop ta la la, bop bop ding ding," Sam's cell phone blasted, jolting him upright in bed. Lilly hated how loud Sam kept the ringer on his cell phone, but while working with the street noise, car radio, police radios, and air conditioner running in the car he kept it loud so not to miss a call.

Sam, his mind in a fog, answered the phone. It was Buzzy's voice, "Wake up sleepy head, it's six o'clock."

"Thanks," Sam told her, not that he wanted to get up.

He started to say goodbye, but she asked him, "Sam, Chief Wallow left a message that Dawn would be off for a few days and that you would be covering day shift by yourself. Is that right Sam?"

"Yeah, I got it, but let the County Deputies know that too, just in case," Sam answered. Suddenly he remembered. "Oh hell, I forgot to take Dawn some food last night. I need to get over there to check on her." He hung up on Buzzy and hopped out of bed.

While getting dressed, Sam called the Purple Lotus, ordered some breakfast sandwiches, but as he was talking to Gail, the owner, he thought... "Dawn doesn't eat meat." He asked Gail, "What does Dawn usually got for breakfast?"

Gail asked, "Is Dawn was ok? I heard she was going to be off for a few days."

"Wow, that news traveled fast." Sam thought. Sam told Gail, "Dawn will be ok, but she's going through a rough time, just wanted to make sure she got a hot breakfast."

Gail said, "Anything for Dawn, just come by I will have something good ready. Do you want anything Sam?"

"Bacon, egg & cheese biscuit, and a large coffee would be great, Gail." He said gratefully.

Sam quickly finished getting dressed, he was on his way out, when Lilly came out of the bedroom asking where he was going so early. Sam explained that he needed to check on Dawn, and he wanted to do that before he signed on duty.

Walking out the door, Sam heard Lilly yell, "Sam, you have been smoking in the house again!" Sam quietly closed the door behind him, pretending not to hear her.

It was 20 after six when Sam got in the hot cruiser again, he really hated hot weather. When he retired, it wouldn't be to the beach, it would be in the Mountains or somewhere it never got above 70 degrees. Sam drove quickly to the Purple Lotus, and as he entered, Gail said it would be just a minute. Looking over at one of the booths, Sam saw Midnight shift officers Tom Clifford and Willy Fogerty sitting having their breakfast with Brandon Teasdale. Sam walked over to talk to them while waiting. Fogerty asked, "Is Dawn was ok?"

Sam nodded his head, saying, "Yeah, she will be, I'm on my way over to check on her."

Tom asked, "Do you want me to hang over to help cover day shift." Sam told them he would be ok on the shift; the Sheriff's Deputies knew he was working solo.

Teasdale chimed in and told Sam, "I'm going to be around the house all day, and if you need any help to just call me."

Sam smiled and said, "Thanks."

Sam saw Gail coming across the room with 2 take out boxes, he reached into his pocket for his wallet, but Gail shook her head and said, "Don't worry about it Sam, just tell Dawn we are thinking of her." Sam thanked her and as he walked out he shoved a $5 bill in the tip jar, waved and just said "Later."

Sam pulled up to Dawn's house, he noticed her sitting on her back porch, curled up on a chair. "Dawn," Sam said as he approached, "Sorry I didn't get by last night."

She looked up and said "Oh...that's ok, Sam" He could tell she had been crying. He always felt awkward in these types of situations, so he just put the boxes down and told her he brought her some breakfast.

She mumbled out, "Thanks." She continued looking down, not saying anymore. They just sat there for a few minutes... Sam saying, trying to break the silence, "Is Greg home?"

"Oh, Sam what am I going to do?" she cried.

Not knowing what else to say Sam just said, "About..."

"Everything... it's all my fault... Jason and I...Greg...I can't find him... with his temper...I think he has done something bad...I'm to blame, Sam," Dawn said sobbing into her hands.

"You don't know that Dawn, we really don't know anything yet, we will find Greg, it will be ok," Sam told her, not really believing it. He was aware that Greg Pearl had a temper, and always thought that Dawn was in an abusive situation, but every time he brought it up, she would change the subject. Was Greg capable of murder? Besides being mean, he was an alcoholic, so no telling, Sam thought.

Sam picked up the box with Dawn's breakfast and handed it to her, telling her, she needed to eat something. "Gail made it special for you, and she said to me to let you know, that you were in her prayers."

Dawn looked in the box, and half smiled, oatmeal with fresh blueberries and toast. She said, "That was so sweet, but I don't think..."

Sam stopped her saying he wasn't going to leave until she ate something. He let her know that she had a lot of friends and they would get her through this. Dawn put some honey from the little packets in the oatmeal, she stirred it for a long time, not eating. Sam had almost finished his sandwich before she took the first bite. She ate a few bites as they talked, mostly at Sam's urging.

Sam looked at the time on his phone, two minutes to 7:00- he reached for his walkie and signed on duty. They talked for a few more minutes. Sam told her he would talk to Murphy and try to get him to get her interview out of the way as soon as possible.

Dawn plead with Sam, "Please talk to Murphy and make him let you sit in on the interview."

Sam said he would do what he could, gave her a hug, and said, "I'll call you later...but you can call me anytime."

Sam put the oatmeal back in Dawn's hands, He had never seen her so vulnerable. As Sam got back into his car, Murphy radioed him to meet him at the station, Sam told him he was en route, and he drove off.

Even though the thermometer in his cruiser said it was 95 degrees outside, as always, Sam had the driver's side window on his car all the way down. His air conditioner was running full blast. Sam liked to be able to hear the sounds of the city, as well as see them. Going down 3rd Street, he waved at Mrs. Val, who was walking her little dog, he wondered how old she was, and how old the dog was It seemed like she had had him forever and that she seemed old when he was a kid.

Arriving at the station, Sam met Murphy who was coming out the door. Murphy had a determined look on his face, which was not uncommon, but today he looked also looked confused, which was unusual. Murphy said, "Hey!" to Sam, then he stopped in thought, looked at Sam and asked, "Did you get in touch with Jason's sister?"

Sam told Murphy, "Not yet, I just plain forgot last night." Murphy said that B.J. was trying to make the notification but could not reach her because he didn't know her married name. Sam said, "Let me take care of it, tell B.J. I have her phone number, I've known her for years."

Sam hated making death notifications, and it was even worse over the phone. He also knew that since he knew her and the family so well, it would be best if it came from him. Murphy asked that Sam try to get it done as soon as possible. Sam said, "I'll go back to the house as soon as I leave here, but I have a couple questions."

Murphy said, "Here comes Buckman, we're headed to the Medical Examiner's Office." "I'll call you when I get back, maybe then I might have some answers."

Sam said, "Stop! Murphy when are you going to interview Dawn? And, can I sit in while it is going on?"

Murphy asked if Dawn was going to get a lawyer. Sam said, "I don't think so, she said, she doesn't need one, but she was blaming herself for it happening."

"Well, I would tell her to get one if I was you, it never hurts," Murphy advised Sam, following with, "I don't care if you are in there. But, if she gets an attorney, he might. Let's see what happens."

Murphy went on to tell Sam that he would be gone most of the day. It was a couple hours over and back, so it probably would not be until evening or the next day before did any interviews, and Buckman was making those decisions.

Sam asked if there was anything else he could do. Murphy said he would e-mail Sam the suspect and witness list and asked Sam to try to see if he could locate them. Not only were there Joe Kerchak, Greg Pearl, and Bobby Ellis on the list. They also wanted to talk to whoever got away from the party at the raid. Murphy asked Sam to find anyone one else that was up that time of the morning that might have seen someone, or something. Randy's Convenience Store would be a good place to start, and whoever was working for the County and State.

When Buckman pulled up, Murphy jumped in the car and as they drove off, Sam told Murphy, "I'll see who I can find."

As he drove back to his house, Sam really wished he hadn't said he would call Jason's sister, Jenna. Having known her since she was a little girl, even though she was a couple years older than Jason, Sam still didn't know her well. Jenna was very shy as a child as well as into her teens, and like her brother, very smart. She studied Veterinarian Science at Purdue University, then moved to California and got her Ph.D. in Marine Biology. While out in the Pacific working, she fell in love with the ship's captain and they got married as soon as they hit land. Sam thought it funny, being a captain at sea, he could marry other people, but not himself.

Sam had not talked to Jenna since Jason's and her mother's funeral. It seems like you only talk to some people at bad times, Sam thought. Getting back to the house, Sam looked around for the old address book, where the number should be. They didn't use the book very often anymore since, like everyone, they kept the phone numbers they needed in their phones. Looking around in his office and their bedroom, it wasn't there. Sam thought of the little table in the living room where their house phone use to be. There Sam found the leather covered book in the drawer, opened it up and looked through the pages. "Wow," he thought, "So many people in here that are dead or I have not seen in years, where does the time go?"

Sitting down at the kitchen table, he found her number, still under Jenna Kelly. Sam collected his thoughts, how would he say this? How would she react? Sam could think of a million other things he would like to be doing at that moment! He hoped her husband answered... hmmm... What was his name?

Sam looked but his name was not in the book, and he could not even think of Jenna's married name. Sam slowly called the number, almost wishing it was not connected anymore! On the third ring Sam heard a female voice say hello. He hesitated, and she repeated herself, "Hello.... Is anyone there?" She sounded like she was asleep, Sam forgot to figure the time difference. He thought, "It's 8:20 am here, it must be 6:20 am there, Damn!"

"Hey Jenna, this is Sam Nickles." He noticed a shake in his voice and tried to clear his throat.

"Sam!" she said excitedly, "How are you?"

"Uh, I'm ok," Trying to think what to say, Sam asked. "Is your husband home?" "Yes, do you need to talk to him?" she asked.

"Well... uh... no." He thought this should come straight from him? "What's wrong, Sam, is Jason ok?" she inquired, now sounding nervous.

"Jenna, I'm so sorry, but Jason's dead," Sam said it quickly, to just get it out.

"Dead?"

Sam could hear a break in her voice, and in the background, her husband said, "Jen, what's wrong?"

"How Sam…. what happened…when?" Jenna asked.

Sam knew she was crying, now. Sam tried explained what had happened but had to stop as she was relaying the information to her husband. Jenna called her husband Cappy, but never by his name. She was saying that she could not figure out why anyone would hurt Jason, he was always so kind. Sam assured her that they would find out who did it and they already had some leads.

After talking for about 10 minutes, during that time Sam told her that she should call Peeks Funeral Home for the arrangements. He also told her that Murphy Dam or John Buckman would probably be calling for any information that she might have.

"Well, I know…" Jenna started to say something, but then stopped, she then said: "We might be hard to reach, we'll be on the next flight to get there." She ended by saying, "I'll talk to you as soon as I arrive." She hung up. He was glad that was over, but what did she want to say, what did she know? This was getting more confusing all the time. Sam sat down on the couch and closed his eyes, to think.

Chapter 10

"City four, County nine" (Sam's and Chief Deputy Mike Oldam's call signs) The voice over the radio, shook Sam out of his slumber. Oldam was calling Sam, and Sam answered back, "Go ahead," while shaking his head to get the cobwebs out. Oldam asked Sam to meet him at Jason's house. Sam got up, stretched, and started for the door trying to wake up. He couldn't believe he fell asleep that easily. He could never take a nap in the middle of the day a few years ago, now a twenty-minute nap was like a beautiful treasure.

On the way to Jason's, Sam was not even sure if anyone had been to the house yet, and he wondered what Mike wanted. As Sam was driving to Jason's, playing on the radio was "Lookin Out the Back Door." This song always made him smile, and today, he needed something to smile about.

It was about 9:30 am as Sam pulled up on the road in front of Jason's driveway. There was yellow *Police - Do Not Cross* tape.

"Well, someone has been here." Sam thought. Looking across the field, Sam saw Oldam back in the field, at the back fence that went around Jason's place. Oldam was walking towards Sam, waving. Sam started towards him, but Mike told him just to wait there.

"Sam, Buckman asked me to see if I could pick up the trail of Jason's horse after it went onto Deerhead Lane," Oldam explained. He found what he thought was the trail going back into the woods. It goes about a hundred yards through the field, then I followed it through the woods to a place where Jason could have seen the back of Tommy Little's property. "Sam, it looked he stopped there for a while," Oldam said.

"That's strange, where else did it go?" Sam asked. "Just straight south to the back of Poleman's place and along the fence line to the back of his place," Oldam explained.

"Ok, we knew it would probably go there, so what is the problem?" Sam asked.

"There is a cell phone just outside of Jason's fence, just back there." Oldam replied,

"Do you have a camera, evidence bags or anything?" Sam inquired.

"Well, back in my car, way over on Deerhead Lane."

Sam went to the trunk of his cruiser and got some evidence bags, and marking flags. "Do you have a camera on your cell?" Sam Asked, "Yeah, but it doesn't work." Oldam said, shrugging.

Mike Oldam and Sam walked back to where Mike had found the cell phone; Sam photographed the area and the phone. They marked the spot where it was lying, and moved it into an evidence bag, marking the bag.

Oldam asked, "Should I put your name as the person taking it into evidence?"

Sam said, "It will be better in your name since it's a Sheriff's Department case."

Sam thought to himself, he would have liked to have seen what was on that phone, but it was too late now. It was already sealed with evidence tape.

Mike showed Sam where he thought that Jason had jumped the fence on the horse, probably when he lost the phone. They discussed whether they should go on inside the property. Sam thought not, because they did not know what the investigators had done. "Is that all you found out here?" Sam asked.

"Yeah, there was no place else where it looked like Jason had stopped and nothing else along the path," Mike answered.

"Ok, well it's hot, and there is still a lot to do, let's wrap this up," Mike asked Sam for a ride back to his car.

"No problem, hop in," Sam said.

Discussing the case on the trip back to Dearhead Lane, Oldam said, "I think that asshole Joe did it. He was in the right place and at the right time. I'd sure like to get my hands on him." Mike punched Sam's dashboard. Sam gave him a look! "Oops, sorry, Sam. It's just- I'm so mad!"

Sam drove on, keeping his thoughts of Joe to himself. At Mike's car, they talked for a minute, and Mike got the evidence together, put it in his car, and came back and thanked Sam for his help.

"Not a problem. Working together, we will figure this out." Sam said, then continued, "Make sure you let Buckman know what you found, and I'll tell Murphy."

Sam advised dispatch that he was done at Jason's, and they cleared him at 10:21. "Good," Sam thought. He wanted to get to Randy's before they got busy at lunchtime. There were only a couple of cars in the lot as Sam arrived, and he hoped it was the right time to talk to Randy. At times, Randy could be a little scatterbrained.

Randy was working the register when Sam walked in. Sam asked Randy if they could talk when he got a minute. Randy nodded yes, while checking out a customer. Sam went over and got a cup of coffee while he waited. Randy's coffee was so hot it would take the skin off of the roof of your mouth, so Sam put in some ice from the soda machine along with powdered creamer and artificial sweetener. Sam thought, at least the coffee is real.

Randy walked up as Sam was putting a lid on his coffee and sticking a straw through the lid. "You drink your coffee through a straw?" Randy said, looking at Sam strangely.

"Yeah, it keeps it from sloshing out of the cup in the car," Sam said and asked. "Do you have your security tapes from last night?"

Randy said the video should be there and he could load them to a disk as soon as Angie came on shift. No sooner than he got that out of his mouth, the bell on the door rang, and Angie came in with a big smile that always seemed to be on her face. Randy asked her if she would take the register while he talked to Sam, Angie saluted Randy with a smile and went to work.

Sam and Randy went into the backroom of the store where the surveillance recorder was. While Randy was pulling the videos up, Sam asked who was working Thursday night and Friday morning. Randy said he worked late that night, till 11:00 pm, and then his nephew, Buddy, came in and worked until 7:00 am. Randy said that then he came back in for the morning shift.

"I've been shorthanded lately; hard to find good, reliable help," Randy complained.

"I hear that a lot." Sam replied, "Everyone says it's easy to find people who want a job, but they don't want to actually work. You watch out Randy, those kinds of hours will make an old man out of you!"

"I know, I meet my self-coming and going, not enough sleep," Randy

said.

Running the video in rewind, Randy found the time the night before.

"What day do you want me to record for you, Sam?" Randy asked, along with, "And at what times."

Sam figured that between 6:00 pm on Thursday and 10:00 am on Friday should do it. That would have everyone coming and going for several hours before and a few hours after he found the body. "What's this all about Sam, I heard there was a murder?" Randy asked.

Sam told Randy, "You heard right, but that's all I can say right now," Continuing he asked Randy, "Please keep it quiet about getting the surveillance footage too."

"No problem Sam, you guys are always looking out for me. I got your back this time," Randy said, handing Sam the disk.

"Anything unusual that night?" Sam asked Randy.

"No just the usual suspects," Randy replied laughing, "No, really it was quiet." Looking at Sam, thinking this was not a joking matter.

Sam asked when he could talk to Buddy, Randy said, "He's probably sleeping right now, but he will be working the midnight shift again tonight."

Sam stopped to buy a Snickers bar, and as he was paying Angie for it, Sherrie Hall walked in. "Caught you again, Sam," Sherrie broke in.

"Just leaving again, sorry Sherrie," Sam said regretfully. Sam would really like to stop and talk to her, but this was not a convenient time.

"Oh… Ok, But I do really need to speak with you, when do you think we can catch up?" Sherrie asked.

Not thinking really well, Sam said. "I will be off later, how about 7 tonight."

"Drinks at the Fuwalda?" She asked.

Sam quickly replied. "Let's make it coffee at Rose's Diner."

"Ok, it a date!" Sherrie said giving Sam a hug. "Oh boy," Sam, thought, "What am I getting myself into?" Sam turned around as he walked out the door and looked at Sherrie, thinking...

After Sam had left Randy's, he went out to the jail to see if there was any information he needed to catch up on. Sherrie Hall was drifting in and out of his mind, why did she come back right now? She shows up, and his world gets all crazy, seems she has always had that effect on him.

Sam tried to put her out of his mind. As he walked into the sheriff's office he ran into Clifford Duggs with Henry Watson, the man that owned the local Chevy dealership. "Hey Cliff, what's going on?"

"Getten bailed out, Tam, to wook!" Cliff said.

"That damn Joe Kerchak was supposed to come by to wash cars. I haven't seen hide nor hair of him. Cliff does a better job anyway," Henry broke in.

"Yeah, and works cheaper," Sam thought.

"When did you last talk to Joe, Henry?" Sam asked. Henry explained that Joe came by his lot on Thursday morning looking for work and he told him to come in on Friday morning to wash cars and clean up the lot. "I guess that sounded like too much work for him," Henry said.

"I wook good Tam if ya need tum help," Cliff offered.

"Uh, maybe I'll find you something for you to do sometime, Cliff," Sam said, patting Cliff on the back.

Henry and Cliff walked out, Sam turned and laughed watching Cliff's long bouncy stride. His skinny body, huge feet, and hands, he always reminded Sam of some 1950's cartoon character. Everything about Cliff seemed just not right. His face was all kinds of crooked. Clifford was once riding his bicycle late at night, drunk as usual, and came around a corner and ran into the back of a parked semi-trailer in the dark. The bike went under the trailer, but Cliff's face took the full impact of the back of the trailer. He broke several bones in his face, cutting it up terribly. Sam wasn't the first officer on the scene that night, but when then-Officer Wallow found Cliff, he thought he was dead. When Sam got there, he was surprised that the ambulance crew was working on him, it looked like there was nothing left of his face. His jaw was hanging loose and eyes were swelled shut and bleeding. He was a mess, but then he usually was.

Cliff spent a couple of months in the hospital. Sam would visit him from time to time, taking him colored pencils and paper, after he could see. When he could eat again, Sam would bring Cliff his favorites: fried pork skins, Twinkies, and Big Red Soda. Sam knew Cliff didn't have any family, except for a sister, not his Mother/Sister, but another sister. She lived in some kind of nursing home because she was blind and confined to a wheelchair. Sam had met her once at Cliff's mother's funeral. Despite her disabilities, Sam found her to be intelligent, witty, and very sweet. Sam would write letters for Cliff to send to her, but also write, just to let her know he was ok. The hospital staff would read the letters and write Sam so he could read them to Cliff. Even though all the trouble Cliff had caused Sam over the years, Sam liked him. Cliff had a lot of problems, so Sam always tried to watch out for him.

Sam turned to go into the jail, but just as he got to the metal detector his phone rang. He stopped, it was one of his snitches who told Sam that he just saw Joe Kerchak going into the back door of Dawson's Market. Joe's Mother worked at the deli there, and Joe was probably there to hit her up for some money. Sam knew Joe would not stay for too long, Dawson wouldn't allow it. So, he hurried to his car and started across town.

While en route Sam checked the location of the County Deputies that were on duty. Just his luck, both were several miles outside the city working an accident. With regret, Sam quickly called Teasdale. Sam thought he better have some help. He knew Joe would run, he always ran. If caught Joe was a fighter. Depending on what kind of drugs or alcohol he was on, he would even fight Sam, and Joe could be a handful.

Teasdale answered on the first ring, almost like he was waiting for Sam's call. Sam told him to park on the East side of Dawson's market and watch the front door. Teasdale said, "Yes Sir, on my way!" and hung up before Sam could say anything else.

Sam got to the rear of the store and didn't see any movement. He advised Dispatch where he was and why, and as he was got out of his car. Teasdale radioed Sam that he was about 30 seconds out.

Walking up to the rear door, Sam slowly opened it to peek in. As luck would have it, Joe was just inside looking right at the door! "Oh, hell no," Sam thought as he saw Joe turn, then start to run. Sam pulled the door open, ran in, bumping into Joe's mother as he sprinted after Joe. Joe jumped over the deli counter and took off. As Sam went through the opening next to the meat cooler, he heard Joe's mother yell, "Sam, don't hurt my baby."

Sam thought, "6'4" baby gorilla!"

Joe started up Aisle C, and Sam cut up Aisle B. As Sam ran he could hear cans and boxes hitting the floor as Joe was raking them off of the shelf in hope to slow Sam down. Sam had been in this rodeo before as a rookie, he had chased a suspect through Dawson's and ended up on the floor after slipping on cans and broken glass of spaghetti sauce. All he could do was watch the suspect run away.

118

That wasn't going to happen this time, as Sam got to the end of the aisle, he saw Joe push his way through one of the checkout lanes knocking a woman out of his way, Joe was heading for the door, and Sam smiled, Joe was heading for the *IN* door.

It all happened so fast, but it happened just as Sam knew it would when he saw Joe's intended escape route. The doors were the electronic type that opens when you step on the pad, but not the wrong way, and the door would not push out. As Sam cut through the open checkout lane, he was only a few of feet behind Joe. Sam could see Teasdale walking up to the IN door, and was right in front of it as Joe hit it running full speed. Joe hoped to push the door open and knock Teasdale out of the way, but instead he bounced off of door like he hit a glass trampoline. The look on Teasdale's face was classic. Brandon thought Joe was going to run over him like a freight train and wasn't ready for the impact. His eyes were at first as big as chicken eggs, he squinted getting ready for the full body hit, then a little peek when the collision didn't come.

As Joe staggered from the impact, Sam was there, spinning Joe around and sweeping his feet out from under him. Sam then dropped all of his weight on the center of Joe's back, knocking the air out of Joe's lungs. Sam learned from wrestling, ya can't fight if ya can't breathe and he used that to his advantage. It didn't take but a couple of seconds for Sam to get the cuffs on Joe, again using two sets of cuffs because of Joe's size. Sam was thinking, "Damn, Joe has gotten bigger." He could only get two clicks on the handcuffs around Joe's massive wrists.

When Sam looked up, Teasdale was standing over him with his Tazer pointing at him and Joe. Sam thought, "He's off duty, does he carry that thing with him all the time?" Sam said in a quiet but demanding voice. "Put that damn thing away before you taze me, and I have to shoot you!" All of the other people in the store were just standing with their mouths agape, not believing what they saw. Sam waved at them, with a smile said, "It's all ok folks, just another day in my world." He continued, "Please hang around, so we can get your information."

Teasdale kneeled next to Sam as they searched Joe, and said: "Damn, I thought he was going to nail me for sure Sam, he looked like a bull coming straight at me."

Sam told Teasdale, "Watch out for knives, he will have several." Joe was getting his breath back and started complaining that he didn't do anything. Sam said, "Joe we have two warrants out for your arrest, so you have the right to remain silent, use it!"

They found three knives on Joe, one being Joe's favorite foot-long Bowie Knife that appeared to have blood on it, a stiletto and a box cutter. They also found a pack of Black Jack gum, with a marijuana joint hidden inside of it, along with a buck and a quarter in change.

As they were getting Joe to his feet, Joe's mother was complaining about how they were treating her angel. Dawson came to the front of the store and told her. "You better quit worrying about Joe, and more about your job. There is a big mess to be cleaned up that your angel, Joe, caused." She quietly slipped off to the back of the store.

Sam asked Teasdale if he would take the report from Dawson for the damage so he could take Joe to the jail. "I need to talk to him after I book him,"

Teasdale saluted and said, "Aye Aye, Skipper! That was fun!"

Sam just chuckled, thinking. "That Teasdale is a goofball, but ya gotta like him."

Sam walked Joe out the back of the store where his car was. Sam squeezed Joe into the back seat, with him complaining about the cuffs being too tight like he always did. Sam told Joe, "Quit whining, you know we will be at the jail in a few minutes, and you know I am not taking the cuffs off until we get there." Sam slowly walked around the car, got in the driver seat feeling pain in his back. As he was starting up the cruiser, sweat rolled down his face. Sam took a minute to catch his breath.

Joe piped up from the backseat, "What's the matter Sam, ya getting old?

Sam answered. "Yeah, as a matter of fact, I am, but this old man just busted your ass, didn't he?!" Joe mumbled something and remained quiet for the rest of the trip to the jail.

Chapter 11

Sam started the booking process on Joe Kerchak., As usual, he was handcuffed to the bench, but two of the jailers hung around due to past dealings with him. Joe was read his rights, while the jail personnel was present to be witnesses along with the video tape. One of the jailers, Bryan O'Riley, brought Sam Joe's jail packet. The folder was about 3 inches thick. Sam looked at Joe, held up the records and said, "Really Joe, when are you going to quit this crap?!"

"What crap? You don't have anything on me. This is bullshit, I ain't done nothing!" Joe yelled.

"Joe, we have two warrants on you, assault with bodily injury at a fight at the Fuwalda three nights ago." Sam started. Joe started complaining, saying, "Hey that other guy started it...."

Sam held up his hand and stopped him. Sam continued, "Then you ran from officers at the drug raid on Tommy Little's house two nights ago, that's warrant number two."

Again Joe started in, but not very convincingly, saying, "They can't prove I was there, those officers can't say it was me, in the dark and that far ways."

Again Sam held his hand up and stopped him again, Sam mentioned, "I saw you by the park when you ran from me, but I'm not even going to mess with that, you got enough problems." Sam looked at Joe shaking his head, and said, "Then you ran from me again today, explain that Joe."

Joe just looked at the ground, shuffled his feet, and said: "Damn Sam, seems like every time we meet up, I get in trouble."

"We? Joe, you always are where trouble is happening." Sam looked at Joe curiously. "So, what happened after you ran from the party?"

"Ok, I ran and hid, you guys were everywhere, I didn't know what was going on, I hadn't even started partying yet, but knew I'd get blamed for something" Joe confessed.

Sam asked, "Where did you hide?"

Joe paused, thinking. Then, he simply said, "I can't tell ya."

"Come on, Joe, we got the knives that you had on you at Dawson's, one of them is going to have Jason's blood on it, why don't you just admit you killed him," said Sam.

Joe came up off of the bench, pulling at the cuffs, screaming "Jason who, I haven't killed anyone, I beat up Larry at the bar, but I didn't cut the pussy!"

Sam told Joe to sit down and chill out. Joe could tell by the look on Sam's face, that he wasn't in any mood to mess around. Sam continued "Jason Kelly, you know the States Attorney that you threatened, and that we can put you in the area, and that his throat was slit with a large knife."

Joe got real nervous, saying, "Really, Sam you gotta believe me, I'll tell you about all the other stuff, but I didn't kill no one."

"Then tell me where were you, and who you were with?" Sam asked.

"If I tell you that Sam, I'll get into more trouble, I'm screwed."

"Yeah well Joe, but it doesn't get much worse than murder, you better weigh your options," Sam told him. Joe just sat for a long time, thinking, while Sam filled out the booking paperwork.

Sam looked up after finishing his paperwork and noticed something he had never seen, Joe was visibly nervous, his eyes were darting around, hand shaking, feet shuffling. Joe was holding something back or knew something dangerous. No matter what crime they had on Joe in the past, he always kept that tough persona on the outside, usually cocky and carefree.

"Ok Joe, I'm leaving, if you have any more to tell me, do it now. I don't have the time or the patience to sit around here to hear your bullshit," Sam commented.

Joe, shaking his head, said, "Ok, Ok, I'm screwed either way. I was at Miss Val's all night that night."

"Miss Val's?" Sam replied, giving Joe a questioning look. "Come on, you can do better that that."

"Really, Sam, go ask her, that's all I am saying, I think I've said too much already." Joe said. Then, after thinking, he added, "Hey, I want a lawyer."

Sam said, "Interview Over."

Sam walked out talking to himself, "Miss Val's? What kind of bullshit is that? Even for Joe, that was a strange thing to say. But, at least it will be easy to check out."

Sam walked up to the jail's command room to talk to the jailers. He asked them to keep Joe isolated for a little while, at least until Murphy or Buckman had a chance to decide what to do with him.

Sam looked at the monitors in the control room. Watching the inmates going back and forth, playing cards, some watching television, he recognized several faces. Looking over at the cell log board, Sam thought about how many of the names belonged to people he had arrested over and over throughout the years. Some of the names were the same last names as in the past, just with different first names. Sam knew he had arrested three generations of the same families. That's pretty sad, he thought- bad habits passed down through generations.

Ryan McNinny, the jailer working the control room, asked Sam if he could keep an eye on things while he went to the can. Sam just nodded yes in thought. "There're donuts over there Sam, we know you boys in blue can't resist a fresh donut," McNinny said as he was walking out.

Looking at McNinny as he walked out, Sam was thinking, "It's easy to resist donuts, but it's getting tough resisting the urge to slap the crap out of you!"

Sam took the whole bag of donuts and hid them in the lower drawer under the control panel. When McNinny came back in Sam said, "Those were good!" and walked out. He could hear McNinny yelling something about eating them all. As Sam walked through the outer office, he laughed and told Deputy Chief Oldam to tell McNinny to look in the bottom drawer... in about an hour. Oldam hearing McNinny yell and Sam laughing, understood and just smiled back and winked at Sam.

Sam walked out and squinted his eyes because of the sun, saying, "Damn... Oh well, at least there is a little bit of a breeze." Sam could smell the Wabash River. Sam loved the river, but not the smell. It was a cross between fish and dead vegetation. As he walked to his car, Joe's statement bothered him. He thought to himself, why would he say that... it was odd... and easy to check out, it was for sure Miss Val would not lie for him.

Climbing back in his car, Sam got hot air from the air conditioner, and he quickly rolled the windows down and backed out to get some air moving until the cold air kicked in. Sam had a lot to do but wanted to go talk to Miss Val first- this really had him intrigued. He wanted to disprove Joe's alibi, so that if they got to question him again, they would be able to come down hard on him. Something was up with Joe.

As Sam turned onto 2nd Street on the way to Miss Val's, he was driving in front of her deceased sister's house, that of Miss Liz. What a pair they were. Sam remembered, they were both classy ladies, but neither ever married. Their father had left them a lot of money, but they both lived very simple lives. They never wanted for anything, but were always there to help people in need. Well, Miss Liz did until her mind started to go.

Sam's train of thought got interrupted when he saw Bobby Ellis, walking in front of Miss Liz's old house. Sam pulled over to the curb and put the window down and yelled for Bobby to stop, saying he needed to talk to him. As usual, Bobby looked nervous, but stopped and waited for Sam. "What did I do Sam?" Bobby asked.

"I don't know; you tell me, Bobby?" Sam said with a smile. This just made Bobby more nervous and he was almost dancing, shuffling on his feet. "No, Bobby, I just need a little information." Sam retorted.

"Whew, Sam d-don't d-do that to me," Bobby said with a stutter, "you guys make me nervous."

"Why?" Sam asked. Bobby just stood there looking at anywhere but at Sam. Sam said, "Listen, Bobby, I just need to know if you were passing your papers on Friday morning?"

"Yeah, I deliver them every day, why?" Bobby replied.

Sam hadn't really thought about what to ask Bobby. He was a possible suspect, and at least a witness. He didn't want to give him too much information, just in case he was involved. Sam asked what time Bobby started and finished up. Bobby told him that he picked up the papers in front of the Purple Lotus at 3:00 am as usual. Bobby said, "I usually take the papers home to roll them, but my air conditioner in my trailer was not working, so I went to the city park and rolled them in my car where I could stay cool."

"Did you see anyone?" asked Sam.

"No, not at that time, in the park," Ellis replied.

Bobby said, "I started passing the papers about 4:00 am, I remember because I had been listening to Coast to Coast AM on the radio and it had just got over, so I turned over to hear some music. I got done about 6:30 the sun was coming up. Is that it, Sam?" Bobby asked, still shaking.

"Did you see or talk to anyone?" Sam asked.

Bobby explained that there were not many people out at 4:00 am, he stopped in at Randy's and got some coffee and jerky. "Buddy was working, but we don't say much to each other, a feud over a girl, years ago."

Bobby shrugged. "Oh yeah, Greg Pearl, he was going in as I was leaving. He seemed like he was in a hurry. I never thought that slug ever did anything fast, and I have never seen him out that early."

Sam asked, "What time was that?"

Bobby said, "It was just a little after four o'clock, I had just started passing the papers." Bobby told Sam that Greg almost ran into him and that he had said hi, but Greg just kind of growled like usual.

"Ok, anyone else in the early hours?" Sam asked.

Bobby though and said, "I saw Jason Kelly, but I didn't talk to him."

"Where and when did you see Jason?" Sam asked, shocked.

"It was just a few minutes after I left Randy's. I only have a few houses on Cotton Mill Road so I was going to knock them out first since I was on that side of town." Bobby went on to explain that he saw a light in Jason Kelly's barn, and saw Jason ride his horse out of the barn and go north, jumping the fence. "After that, I don't know where he went, it was too dark." Bobby finished.

Sam asked if Bobby knew where Greg went to, but Bobby said, "I didn't even see him leave Randy's." The rest of the people Bobby saw that morning were later that morning, store owners, workers going to work and such. Sam got some contact information from Bobby and told him that Murphy may want to talk to him.

"Oh great, that guy really makes me nervous," Bobby said.

"Do you have a guilty conscience, Bobby?" Sam joked.

"No," Bobby said his voice shaking again.

Sam stood for a moment, jotting down some notes. Bobby started walking away but turned back and asked, "Hey Sam, I saw a lot of cops out that night, what was going on?"

"A whole lot more than should have been," Sam replied, looking back at his notes.

Bobby stood there for a minute and then said, "Sam, you know I did see something else strange that morning." Sam looked at Bobby, and waited. "I noticed Aaron Peeks sitting in his car at the city park about five o'clock am."

"Where at the park?" Sam wanted to know.

Bobby stood and thought for a while, then explained, "He was by the main entrance. He was in that creepy old black Cadillac funeral-looking thing he drives."

That got Sam's attention. He asked if he saw Aaron leave or go anywhere else, but Bobby said he didn't see him the rest of the morning. Sam asked if Bobby remembered anything else, but Bobby thought that was everything. Sam gave him a card with is cell phone number and told him if he thought of anything, call him, anytime!

Sam stood there and realized that he was soaked in sweat. He took his notes and went back to his car. He was glad that he had left it running. Looking over his notes, Sam thought how every time he talks to someone, it adds to the list of other people they need to talk to or check out. Sitting back in the seat enjoying the air, Sam looked over at Miss Liz's and started to laugh. He would always remember that house as being the scene for one of the funniest nights he ever worked, but also was sad, now that Miss Liz was gone.

It was about three years in the past, late fall, close to Halloween. People who knew Miss Liz could tell that she was just not quite as sharp as she had always been. She had to have been in her mid eighties. No one really knew how old the sisters were, or even who was oldest, and they were not saying. Sam though Miss Val to be about ninety, but was not sure, he tried running her driver's license once, but nothing came up on file. She had a car and drove, but …. Sam decided not to even go there.

The kids in town had been extra busy during that Halloween season. Streams of toilet paper seemed to hang from trees in every block sometime during the week. TPing had been a tradition in town as far back before Sam was a kid. He loved to TP the teacher's houses.

With all this extra activity, Miss Liz was calling in complaints of people in her yard. Officers would go there at least once a night, sometimes more, but never found anyone. Suddenly, the calls got stranger. Miss Liz said someone was in her house. Officers rushed over but found nothing again. It was on about the fifth call, where she was saying people were in her house, she showed the officers how the "people" were getting in. Miss Liz told them that they were little people, about two feet tall, who were coming in from the furnace grates, and they were cutting her hair as she slept. She had been losing her hair; maybe that was how her mind justified it.

For about three weeks, officers, mostly mid-night shift, would get a call to her house every night. All the officers liked her, and she was always very nice, so they would check they house and tell her no one was there. It was getting worse, they were sometimes getting two calls a night, and she told them that they were too noisy arriving there and were scaring the little people off.

Officers went and talked to the County Health Nurse. She did what she could do, but Miss Liz was not a danger to herself. Other people went to speak to Miss Val, her sister. Miss Val was torn. She knew something needed to be done, but could not bring herself to put Liz in a nursing home. Miss Liz refused to move in and live with Val for some unknown reason.

Sam and Dawn were at Randy's getting some drinks one night when Murphy happened to walk in. While talking, a call came in to go to Miss Liz's. Sam and Dawn groaned, knowing it was another bogus call. Before they left, Murphy said he had an idea. They asked what it was, but he just told them to follow his lead when they got there.

Everyone arrived and flooded the house with spotlights. Sam and Dawn went to the front door, Murphy to the rear, just in case. After Miss Liz had answered the door, they went in, and Sam let Murphy in the back door.

They checked the residence and everything was secure.

Dawn sat down with Miss Liz, who was shaking, saying, "Didn't you see him? He just ran out."

"So sorry, we missed him again Miss Liz, but I have a plan if you will let us do it." Murphy asked. Miss Liz said she would let them do whatever they needed to stop this living hell!

The next night, Dawn and Sam went to Miss Liz's house at about dark. Murphy sat in his patrol car down the street watching the outside. Dawn told Miss Liz that they were going to hide living room, so she should go about here nightly routine. Miss Liz brought them in coffee and cookies, then started spreading some afghans and pillows on the floor. Dawn, who was sitting on the couch, asked what she was doing. And Miss Liz looked at her and said with and matter of fact attitude, "Well you can't sit in the chairs, they could see you from the windows."

So Sam and Dawn crawled down on the floor, laughing. Laying on the afghans, they just looked at each other, trying to be quiet. Miss Liz asked if they needed anything else, and they told her they would handle everything for then on. Miss Liz told them she was going to go to bed and read before going to sleep. Everything was quiet, then Miss Liz yelled out "If ya need anything just holler!" This made both Sam and Dawn jump, then laugh.

Dawn and Murphy were talking quietly, munching on cookies, and kidding each other. Dawn said, "Great date, Sam, what a way to spend a night off."

"Hey, I know how to show a girl a good time," Sam replied, bumping her shoulder with his.

They did a radio check with Murphy, suddenly they heard this deep rumble. They both cocked their heads to the listen, they heard it again. Sitting up and listening, they noticed the rhythmic pattern of Miss Liz snoring loud enough to wake the dead. This tickled both of them, this prim & proper little lady snoring like a buzz saw. They were giggling so hard that they had their faces down into the pillows to try to muffle the sound. Every time they would look up hear the noise and look at each other they would crack up again.

It took Dawn and Sam about ten minutes to regain their composure, and it was just in time. Miss Liz bolted out of bed, and screamed, "There he is, get him!" Dawn and Sam jumped to their feet, ran around the house, yelling "We'll get him!" Sam called Murphy on the radio and said "Now!" They were shining their flashlights around when Miss Liz said, "He's going to get outside." Dawn and Sam ran towards the door.

Murphy was almost dozing off down the block, waiting to hear something. Suddenly Murphy heard "Now," on the radio, he shook himself awake and took off towards Miss Liz's house. Murphy hit all of his lights and sirens, sped up the half block, screeching his tires as he stopped the car. Jumping out of his cruiser, he ran into the yard.

Dawn and Sam came out the front door with Miss Liz right behind them. They all stopped dead in their tracks on the front porch. What a sight it was, red and blue lights flashing, spotlight on, wig wags making the scene strobe from light to dark, with the sound of the siren blaring. In the middle of all this was Murphy flinging around a half size person like a rag doll. Dawn and Sam could not believe what they were seeing. Murphy really caught a miniature hair-cutting criminal. Miss Liz was yelling, "He got him, he got him! Bless you, Officer Murphy!" Murphy got the bad guy under control, handcuffed the tiny suspect and tossed him in the back of his patrol car, got in and drove away.

Dawn and Sam stood for a moment looking at each other in amazement until the silence was broken by Miss Liz thanking them. Miss Liz asked them to have Officer Murphy to come by tomorrow, that she was going to bake him an apple pie. With that, Miss Liz said, "Goodnight." She turned went inside and locked the door.

Sam looked at Dawn and said, "What the hell was that?" They walked down the block towards Sam's truck and radioed Murphy, asking where he was.

"I'm at the city park," he replied and they could tell he was laughing.

They drove to the park and pulled up beside Murphy's patrol car, and Sam asked again, "What the hell was that?"

Murphy could hardly contain himself laughing, he reached into the back seat and pulled out a Charlie McCarty ventriloquist dummy.

"Where did you get that thing?" Sam asked.

Murphy said, "I've had it since I was a kid. It's been in my basement for years, thought it would add some realism to the act."

"It would have been nice if you had told us," Dawn chimed in.

"Oh no, the look on your faces was priceless, and hey, it worked," Murphy said with a smile.

They all got a good laugh, and since this was an off-duty detail, they decided to go to the Fuwalda and have a couple of beers to celebrate a job well done. They even took Charlie in and bought him one. They would tell everyone that he was the new officer, to deal with small crimes.

Sam looked at Miss Liz's old house one last time before driving off. They never got another call from her place until about 5 months later. That was when her sister, Miss Val had found Miss Liz in her bed, dead, from a massive heart attack. Miss Val told them at the funeral how thankful she was for the peace of mind they had given Miss Liz in her last few months. Sam drove off down the tree lined street smiling.

As Sam pulled up to Miss Val's house, he could see her out working in the garden. When he got out of his car, she looked up from the roses she was cutting. He was walking towards her when she greeted him saying, "Well if it isn't Yosemite Sam!"

Sam chuckled, no one had called him that since junior high. Those crazy school day nicknames, Sam got his because of his red hair and because he mumbled and sometimes was hard to understand. Now, since he was bald, the name didn't seem to fit. Even though he still mumbled a lot. Sam asked, "How are you, Miss Val? It's terribly hot for you to be out this time of day."

"Oh Sammy, I've been working out in the heat since I was a kid, didn't bother me then, doesn't bother me now." Miss Val told him.

Sam came to the point of the visit quickly and said. "Miss Val, I need to ask you some questions about some things that happened last night." Sam could immediately see a change in Miss Val's demeanor, he could tell she was nervous and would not look at him directly. "Hmmm," Sam thought, "She does know something." He asked, "Can we sit on the porch?"

"Gracious, no. Let's go inside, I'll get you a piece of pie and some tea." Miss Val answered.

They went into Miss Val's house, which was like stepping back into the past. The Victorian was full of antiques. Everything was prim and proper, neat as a pin. She sat Sam down at the big oak dining table and went off into the kitchen. Sam noticed there was no air conditioning, but the house was surprisingly comfortable for a day as hot as this one was. He looked around and noticed there was a large ceiling fan above him, but also a big window fan pulling the air through the house.

Miss Val came back into the dining room with a huge slice of apple pie and a large glass of ice tea. Sam could not resist the pie; he remembered her pies that she made for the school when he was a kid. Even when he was wrestling and watching his weight, one of the few treats Sam would allow himself was Miss Val's apple pie in the cafeteria.

Sam took the first bite and just let it sit on his tongue." Mmmmm."

Sam thought to himself, "I could eat this every day." He took a couple more bites and a drink of tea, then said to Miss Val, "I guess you heard about the murder?"

"Yes, Sam that's awful, but I haven't heard who it was." She asked.

"Well, we haven't released the name, but we have a suspect," Sam said.

"That's good, I hate to think they are still out there," Miss Val said.

Sam looked at Miss Val and said, "It's Joe Kerchak, and he claims he was with you at that time?"

She looked away, was fidgeting with her hands and the doilies on the table. Her voice shaking, she said, "Sam, I don't want to get him in trouble, he is really a good boy deep down, he just never had any upbringing."

"Miss Val, being a suspect in a murder is about as much trouble as he can get in…" Sam paused thinking she would say something but she didn't so he said, "If you know anything about Friday morning, you need to tell me!"

"Ok, Sam… but I don't want to make things worse for him," Miss Val

said.

"You can't," Sam reassured her.

She started, "Ok, ok… I was asleep the other night, and about a quarter after three I heard a noise downstairs."

"You sleep upstairs?" Sam asked.

"Yes," she answered.

"Are you sure about the time?" Sam asked.

"Positive, I have one of those clocks that project the time on the ceiling real big, and it said 3:12."

"Ok, then what happened?" Sam asked.

Val continued, "I listened for a minute, I could hear the kitchen door open and close, it squeaks, ya know."

Sam just nodded.

"So, I grabbed my shotgun," Val said.

"Your shotgun!" Sam was shocked.

"Yeah, Papa taught us to shoot guns when we were young girls, we went hunting with him all the time. It put food on the table," Val told Sam.

"Ok, ok then what happened?" Sam asked, still surprised.

"I went down the back stairs that go into the kitchen, I could see someone moving around, so I shucked a shell in, turned on the light, and yelled STOP!" She paused and smiled, then said, "I think I scared the poop out of him." She said.

"And it was Joe?" Sam asked. He was thinking, at that time it wasn't too long after the drug raid.

Miss Val nodded yes, and said, "He started apologizing, saying he was sorry. Joe didn't think I would be home, and he needed a place to hide."

"Why would Joe think you wouldn't be home Ma'am?" Sam asked.

Miss Val explained, "I saw him a couple days before and asked him if he would mow my yard on Saturday. I was going out of town to visit my cousin and her new baby in Springfield. The plan was to leave on Thursday and come home on Monday... but the baby got sick, and Ruth didn't think I should come."

Sam said," Miss Val... you shouldn't tell people like Joe you are leaving town." Sam felt like he was scolding her and didn't want to sound mean, so he said, "But you can come to the station and fill out a vacation watch card when you leave so we can watch your house."

"Oh I've known Joe since he was a little boy, he used to play around here all the time. I always gave him cookies and milk to do little things for me. When he got older, he would come by to earn a little spending money." Miss Val said.

Sam, thought, "Yeah, to buy drugs," but said, "Ok, but did you run him off that night?"

Miss Val explained that she had told him to lie down on the floor like they do on COPS on TV and he did. She told him that she was going to call the police, but he begged her not to. Joe even said he would mow her yard for free.

"I asked him what he was hiding from and he told me about being at a party, the police raided it and he ran." Miss Val said, then continued. "I asked him when he was going to grow up and act right."

Miss Val said that they had delved into a long conversation about his past, his problems with drugs and alcohol. She talked about how they ate some pecan pie and drank some milk. Joe had told her that he was trying, but every time he got a job, someone would make him mad, then he would get into a fight, and now no one in town would hire him.

Miss Val and Joe swapped stories from when he was young, talked about his father spending his life in prison, as well as his older brother. Joe told her that he had always known what his mother did to support him, but he never let her know that he knew. Miss Val said they cried together, prayed together and laughed together too.

"He is really just a misunderstood little boy that has never grown up," she concluded.

"Well… he's a big boy now and needs to man up, be responsible for his actions. What time did he leave?" Sam asked.

Miss Val thought a minute, and said, "I believe it was around noon. He fell asleep in the chair in the living room about 6 am, and I just let him sleep." She paused for a moment and continued, "I was baking the apple pie you are eating, and the aroma woke him. I made him a fried bologna sandwich and a piece of pie. He ate, and we talked some more. Before leaving, he thanked me for everything, and asked if I still wanted him to mow." She thought again and said, "Yea around noon or 12:30 was when he left, but he still hasn't come back to mow."

"Ok," Sam said shaking his head, "So... I guess you don't want to press charges for him breaking into your house?"

"Oh heavens no, will this help him?" she asked.

"I'm not sure yet ma'am, because I'm not positive what time the murder happened, but it sure won't hurt him. But right now, Joe is in jail on some other charges, so you should find someone else to mow your lawn." Sam said as he got up from the table, the taste of the pie lingering in his mouth, begging for another piece.

"Well, I really needed to get going, I still have a lot to do," Sam told Miss Val.

On his way out, Sam looked in the corner of the room. He eyed the shotgun. It looked older, but in good shape. Sam asked if he could look at it. Miss Val picked it up, checked the chamber and safety and said, "All safe, here ya go." She was obviously taught gun safety, and Sam took it and looked over the weapon.

"When did you get this?" Sam asked.

"Daddy gave identical ones to Elizabeth and me around 1950 or so, I can't really remember exactly. I have hers upstairs, I took it when she started… when she got sick," Miss Val said.

The gun was in excellent shape, and Sam thought it was probably one of the first 870 Remington's produced and worth a lot of money. Sam shucked a shell out and looked at it: 00 buck. That would do the job on anyone breaking in, but the shell looked almost as old as the gun.

"Miss Val, this is a very nice shotgun, but I think you need to get some new shells, these may or may not work… I have some at home that I could drop by," Sam told her. Miss Val told him not to bother, this incident made her think that the shotgun may be getting too big for her, at her age. She said she always wanted a 9mm pistol and thought this would be a good time to get one. "I'll get some new shotgun shells too, Sam, just in case," Miss Val said with a wink. Sam just grinned, shaking his head thinking, "This lady is something else!"

"Thank you, Miss Val, for letting me know what happened, and special thanks for the piece of pie. It was as wonderful as ever," Sam said to her as he started for the door.

Miss Val said, "Wait!" She walked back into the kitchen, and came out with a whole apple pie, giving it to Sam, saying, "Now, you share some of that with your lovely wife now."

Sam smiled saying he would, he walked out to the car smelling the pie with his mouth watering.

Chapter 12

Inside his car was frigid. Sam hadn't expected to be at Miss Val's that long and had left the car running. The cold air felt good, so Sam sat back and enjoyed it. Sam looked at the clock on the radio as he turned it on: 2:35 pm, less than a half hour to go in the shift. On the car radio, "Give Me Three Steps," by Lynyrd Skynyrd was playing as dispatch called Sam, "Dispatch to City four."

Sam answered, with a sigh, "City four."

The voice on the radio said, "Go to The Fuwalda, Terrance is there causing a problem."

Sam acknowledged he was clear on the call. "Damn," he said to himself, as he put the car in gear and headed that way.

Sam, as all the officers and anyone in emergency services in the area knew, Terrance Poe, was just a nasty drunk. He always had, for some reason, always insisted on being called Terrance, never Terry. Dispatch knew if they just said Terrance, Sam would know who they were talking about. Sam always hated dealing with Terrance. Not only was he always intoxicated, but it seemed he never took a bath, and he stunk. Terrance lived in a dirty little shack, and Sam never knew him to work. He got a government check and sponged off his relatives to support his habit.

Terrance did hold one distinction that he was proud of. On his birthday, a few years back, Sam had found Terrance passed out on the courthouse lawn. After a good hard sternum rub, Sam had gotten him awake and on his feet. It was only one o'clock in the afternoon, so Sam knew the best course was to go ahead and arrest him. If Sam had taken him home, they would be dealing with him later in the night. Sam loaded Terrance in the patrol car and drove him to the jail, all the way Terrance singing Happy Birthday to himself. Sam almost had to carry Terrance into the booking hall at the lock up, which wasn't hard, since he was only 5'5" and didn't weigh much more than 100 pounds. But, his stench made Sam gag.

Sam was met in the booking room of the jail by Jailer Ryan McNinny. McNinny said, "Damn, I thought it was going to be a nice quiet day. Did you have to bring him in?"

"Uh…Yeah," Sam said, "He was passed out at the courthouse, and he is really hammered."

"What did the asshole test, Sam?" asked Ryan.

"I don't know; he was so out of it, I didn't see any reason to test him…

look at him." Sam pointed to Terrance, already asleep on the booking room bench.

"Well I have to know for the intake card, so we will know when to send him to court, or for when he gets bailed out," Ryan said, as he grabbed the Alco-sensor and tried to wake Terrance.

Sam was going through the file cabinets to get Terrance's file, so he didn't have to ask him for his information. Sam thought he could probably fill out the booking card from memory. Opening the drawer marked O -Q, it wasn't hard to find Terrance's file. Actually, there were 4 of them. He had been arrested so many times over the years, that one file would not hold it all. Standard procedure was: arrest him, he would plead guilty, the judge would give him six months, he would serve about three months with good time. While in jail, he would get cleaned up, fed well and the county doctor would look at him. After he got out it would only be a few weeks, and he would be back in again. The record shortest turn-around was 4 and a half hours from release to booking. They tried rehab, Antabuse, trying to get the bars and liquor stores to stop serving him, but nothing so far had worked.

"Point fifty-two percent," McNinny exclaimed.

"What? That can't be right, no way, he would be dead.," said Sam.

"If I can get this Alco-sensor to clear, I'll check it again…but if it's the same…, you know what that means, Sam."

Sam knew what that meant alright, it was going to ruin his day, is what it meant. Anything over .25% and the jail would not accept a prisoner due to the fact they could die. Sam would have to take him to the hospital where he would remain until his blood alcohol level dropped to a safe level. It was almost a half hour drive there and no telling how long he would be there with that high of a level.

"It came up point fifty-two percent again, Sam. Sorry," said McNinny.

"Damn… Well, help me load him up," said Sam.

So they loaded Terrance back into the patrol car. Sam advised dispatch of where he was going. He called the Chief to let him know he would be out of town, then called his partner Dawn to tell her. Dawn said she would be ok, it was only about an hour and a half until evening shift signed on. Dawn said, "You got the bad detail, is he smellin'?"

"All the windows are down if that tells you anything," Sam answered.

Almost the whole trip there, Terrance sang, gibbered about something, or asked to go home. He would fall asleep occasionally, but if the car hit a bump, he would wake up.

Luckily, the ER was not busy when they got there. Sam walked Terrance in, and a nurse almost immediately took them back to an examination room. Once in the room, the nurse asked Terrance his name.

He replied by singing, "My name is Poncho, I live on a rancho, I eat…"

Sam knew the rest of the obscene song, so he grabbed Terrance and put his hand over Terrance's mouth.

Mad, Sam got up in Terrance's face and told him, with a growl, "We are going to be nice and polite, aren't we!" Terrance just shook his head, yes, knowing Sam was not messing around.

"What seems to be Mr. Poe's problem today, besides having a little too much to drink?" the Nurse asked, sarcastically.

"A little too much, he tested .52% on our PBT. The jail would not take him," Sam said.

"Well… that can't be right, we'll draw blood and get a correct test, and maybe get you out faster. I bet you, and everyone here would like that," the nurse said, holding her nose.

A tech came in and drew blood. Sam waited… and waited.

Finally, a doctor came into the examination room, "Mr. Fisher, you should be dead." The doctor stood looking at the report shaking his head.

Terrance said, "Beer is my buddy, whiskey is my friend, we'll be together to the bitter end."

Sam said, "Stop." Terrance did, biting his lower lip.

"Well if you don't quit drinking, the bitter end won't be too far away." The doctor told Terrance. He then asked Sam, "What was he drinking to get into this shape? You said he tested .52% at the jail."

"Yeah point fifty-two percent. But, I don't have the slightest idea what he drank, with him, it could have been anything," Sam replied.

"He tested the same here also, so he was still probably still on his way up when you tested him, so at one point when you were transporting him he might have gone point fifty-three percent or even point fifty-four percent... Unbelievable!" the doctor remarked.

Terrance giggled, looked at Sam, and tried to whisper, "I got me some good Tennessee Moon...Smoooooth!"

"That explains some of it... some of that stuff is almost pure alcohol, a hundred and ninety proof... WOW!" exclaimed Sam.

"Terrance, you now hold the record of having the highest blood/alcohol level ever recorded in a living person in this hospital. How you are still talking to us...I have no idea." the doctor said.

Sam told the doctor that it was the highest he had ever seen also, then asked, "What will you do with him?"

The doctor explained to Sam some medical and physiological reasons for why Terrance's body was handling the alcohol, mostly stuff Sam didn't understand. The question Sam most wanted to be answered was when they could leave. The doctor said he would check back in about an hour.

"If he's doing ok- his blood alcohol levels would still be high, but it would probably be ok to release him," the doctor said, but warned Sam, "With a BAC that high, Terry's detoxification is going to be rough, so you will want to keep an eye on him."

Sam said, "I'll pass that on to the jail staff."

Terrance sat up and looked at the doctor and said, "It's Terrance, if you please." Then, he lay back down.

The doctor and Sam looked at each other and just shook their heads.

When the doctor did come back, after about an hour and forty-five minutes, Terrance was napping but woke up when the doctor shook him. The doctor didn't see any reason to keep Terrance any longer. There was nothing they could do for him. He told the nurse to get the discharge papers ready, and after another half hour of waiting, Sam and Terrance were on their way back to the jail, Terrance singing all the way.

From then on, every time Sam saw Terrance, Terrance would remind Sam of his record.

Today, pulling up in front of the Fuwalda, Sam was not happy about having to deal with Terrance this late in the shift. Out of habit, Sam had kept his right eye shut during the drive. Sam knew the inside of the bar would be dark, and at least one eye would be used to the dark conditions. He opened both eyes as he walked in and noticed Black Michael behind the bar.

Sam had known Michael Finnegan since they were kids, they were in the same grade at school, he remembered Michael as being a short, stocky kid, who said his father was Irish and mother was Cherokee. The Native American blood explained his black hair, although it was not straight, it was full of curls. A lot of kids got nicknames in those days, some were given them by teachers, as was Michael's. In 3rd grade, Michael and Sam both got their nicknames. There were 2 Sams in his class and Sam became known as Yosemite Sam because of his red hair, but his name didn't stick. Sam never did like the nickname anyway. There were 5 Michaels in that class. For the teacher to keep them straight, it was Black Michael, Blond Michael, Brown Michael, due to their hair color and there was Mike, and Mikey who also had brown hair!

Michael, unlike Sam, had embraced his nickname. He thought it made him sound tough, which was good for a bar owner. Michael was destined to take over his father's bar. He grew up living above it and started working in the kitchen and behind the bar, way before he was of age to do so, legally. Another reason Black Michael liked the name was that it was a character in one of his favorite books. Sam knew this because he had given Michael a copy of that book. It was the first of a series of books that Sam liked best. They often would sit and discuss the different books for hours.

Michael had even changed the name of the bar after his father died. He wanted it to go along with his nickname. On the window at the front of the bar, under the name "Fuwalda" in the fancy script was the words "Owner: Black Michael Finnegan." When asked about the meaning of the name of the bar, Black Michael would say, "If I tell ye, I'd have to kill ye," in his best pirate voice. But Sam knew, and it was always a private joke between them.

On that day at the Fuwalda, Sam looked down the bar and asked, "What's going on Michael?" Michael pointed to Terrance, who was slumped over at the far end of the bar.

"He came in here about a half hour ago, I usually don't serve him, but he didn't really seem drunk and just ordered a beer," said Michael.

"Ok," said Sam. "Let's see if we can get him up?"

Sam shook Terrance, and he looked up with a start. "Sam, how ya doin?"

"Tying one on again, Terrance, is it your birthday again?" Sam asked.

"No… well yeah, it is my birthday as a matter a fact… but I'm not drunk… just tired, didn't sleep last night."

Sam thought, and remembered the date of birth that he had written down so many time and yep, it was Terrance's birthday.

"Why didn't you sleep, Terrance?" asked Sam.

"Well, a buddy of mine was having some problems, and I was on the phone talking to him all night," Terrance replied.

"And who was this buddy?"

"Greg," Terrance said.

"Greg Pearl?" Sam questioned.

"Yeah, he was driving all night, that bitch of a wife…"

"Stop!" Sam said, cutting him off mid-sentence, knowing something bad about Dawn was coming next. "Come with me," Sam said, taking Terrance by the arm, walking him out to the patrol car. "I got this Michael, thanks, see ya later."

"One on the house, anytime, Sam," Black Michael said.

Sam put Terrance in the back of the patrol car and drove off.

"Are you taking me to jail again Sam? Really I'm not drunk, I've just had a few beers," Terrance whined.

"No, I'm taking you home, and you are going to stay there," Sam told him. "What's up with Greg Pearl?" Sam asked like he didn't know anything.

Terrance explained that Greg had come to his house a couple days ago, and asked if he could crash there. "He almost drank me out of the house and home. I've seen Greg drink but not like that," Terrance explained. "He told me that he had been gambling and lost a lot of their savings. He was mad and was drinking because he found some texts on his wife's phone, and he thinks she is having an affair. I didn't know what he was going to do, so we drank until he passed out."

Terrance went on to tell Sam, "That afternoon Greg had got up and went to the ATM. He got some more money and gave me some for helping him, and asked if he could stay another night. Greg then told me he was going to go back to Missouri, he said he was from there."

Terrance explained he tried to talk Greg out of it, but he said Greg had his mind set. Terrence said, "I was worried about Greg, so I stayed up with him all night. Greg tried to sleep but would get up and pace the floor. He left real early this morning, and I have been on the phone with him most of the day to keep him awake as he drove."

"Where was he going in Missouri?" Sam asked.

"Cambellsville, Camptown, something like that, I don't remember," replied Terrance.

"OK, think, Terrance, when did Greg show up at your house, and when did he leave?" Sam asked.

"Hmmm... let's see, he came over about dinner time on Thursday, yeah that's right, *Wheel of Fortune* was on, and he left about 4 am today," said Terrance.

"And you were always with him during those times?"

"Yeah, the only time we left was when we went to the ATM and liquor store. Greg took a bottle of Jim Beam with him. I told him not to drink and drive, even I don't do that, Sam, I don't even own a car," Terrance proudly said.

'Yeah, yeah I know, Terrance, I know." Sam said, "Are you sure he didn't leave at any time?"

"Positive, Sam, I stayed up with him, that's why I'm so tired. I thought he might try to do something stupid, I was worried about him. I didn't want him to leave, I don't know what he is going to do, but Greg said he had kin where he was going." Terrance had gone on to explain.

Pulling up in front of Terrance's shack, Sam told him to let him know if he remembered where Greg went or if he hears from him. Sam got Terrance's phone number, even though it probably was on his booking card at the jail. As Terrance got out of the car, Sam told him, "Don't get silly celebrating your birthday, I don't want a replay of a few years ago!"

"I'll try to be good, Sam, but I'm still the champ!" Terrance said with a laugh.

Sam drove off, thinking, "This case is getting stranger by the minute."

The evening shift had already signed on. It was 7:20 pm and Sam was way past ready to go home. Sam called dispatch and announced, "Ten twenty-four, ten eight,"(assignment completed, back in service). He also asked, "Signal twenty-seven?" This was to ask if there were any messages for him.

Dispatch replied, "Signal twenty-eight" (no messages). So, Sam went off duty.

Sam drove the last few blocks home thinking over the events of the day. He pulled into the drive and sat in the patrol car, enjoying the quiet and finishing up his daily log. Sam pulled the small notebook out of his shirt pocket, looked over the notes he took at Miss Val's and wrote several notes about the times that Greg Pearl was with Terrance Fisher. Sam didn't know where this case was going, but it was getting more interesting as it went along. Perhaps a lot of questions would be cleared up at the meeting that was called for 7:00 am the next morning. The coroner, investigators and everyone else involved would be there, Sam hope they had some answers. The investigators would be talking to Dawn sometime that morning. Sam thought he should call her to check on her, with the day being so busy he had not even had time to talk to her.

Sam called Dawn while still in his cruiser. When she answered, Dawn asked if she could call him back. Dawn said that Jenna just arrived at the Saint Louis's Lambert Airport with her husband and she was on the other line with her. Sam said, "Sure, whenever you get a chance, I'll be home all night."

Sam had noticed there were no cars in the driveway at his house, but he hollered, "I'm home!" as he walked in the doorway. As usual, Boo was waiting for him at the door, jumping and wagging his tail, dancing around. Sam knew he had been there by himself all day, so he walked to the back sliding doors and let Boo out, who immediately went to the first tree he came to and did his business. While watching Boo out in the back yard, barking at the birds, Sam took off his gun belt, shirt, boots, and socks. He grabbed a coke out of the fridge and walked out the back door, stepping off of the patio, Sam smiled as he felt the cool grass on his feet, and wiggled his toes as he felt a gentle breeze on his face.

Calling Boo back in, Sam checked a roast in a crock pot with some potatoes, carrots, onions, and celery. It was good and done, the aroma was making Sam's' mouth water. Sam wondered where everyone was but wasn't worried, they would probably be home soon. He then gathered up some towels from the bathroom hamper and put them in the washer. Sam changed into a pair of jeans and a t-shirt, washed the breakfast dishes, then plopped down in his favorite chair and turned on the TV. It wasn't long he was sleeping with Boo at his feet.

When Lilly got home, they ate and talked about the day. He helped her clean up the dinner dishes, and then took a long-needed soak in the bath tub. In the tub of hot water, Sam relaxed and drifted off to sleep again. That was, until his cell phone rang and woke him. Sam answered, as usual, "Sam Nickle's McCracken Police, can I help you?" It was Buddy, the midnight shift worker at Randy's Convenience Store. "Hey Sam, Buddy said, "Randy said you wanted to talk to me."

Err... yeah, Buddy do you remember who came into the store on Friday morning while you were working?" Sam said, trying to get the cobwebs out of his brain after his little nap.

"Uh, well... there were several early, but it was pretty dead after about 3 o'clock." Buddy replied.

"Ok then... just those after 3:00 am?" Sam asked for.

"There was Aaron, about 4 o'clock, I think... yeah, it was a few minutes after 4 because he had bought a Monster, and I told him it would keep him awake. He said he liked being awake at that time of the night. Then there was that asshole, Greg that came in, he seemed kinda drunk and ruder than usual."

Sam stopped him and asked," You mean Greg Pearl?"

"Yep, the one and only Greg Pearl, the biggest jerk in town, married to Dawn the lady cop."

"Did he stay long?" Sam asked.

"Nope, he just got a forty-four-ounce coke and some chips. I remember because he paid for it with a hundred-dollar bill from a big wad he had. Hell, it took almost all my cash, I had to give him change. Then, he left." Buddy stopped, but then said, "You know... he was acting real nervous. Aaron even said something about it, and that he was going to see where Greg was going that time of the morning."

"So Greg and Aaron left about the same time?" Sam asked Buddy.

"Yeah, that was about four twenty, four thirty, something like that," Buddy replied.

Buddy said that the next couple hours were slow, until about 6:00 am and the morning crowd started to come in. He gave Sam the names of several people. Sam was trying to remember everything and noticed that his bath water was getting cold. Buddy told him that Randy had come in about 6:30 and started working the register, so he could finish stocking the coolers. He remembered that as he was coming back out front, Dawn walked in and asked Buddy if he was keeping her green tea stocked up.

Sam butted in and asked, "What time was that, and how long did she stay?"

"It must have been right around seven o'clock, when she came in, give or take a few minutes because I clocked out at seven twelve am, but hung around for a bit."

"What time did she leave?" Sam asked.

"You know, I don't know, she was giving direction and talking to some people I didn't know. She explained the best way to get to Shawnee Forrest and what was there. They were tourists I guess. Anyway, I left about seven thirty am, and she was still there."

Sam was getting cold and told Buddy, "Thanks, you have been a lot of help. I'll get back with you if I need anything else."

Buddy said, "Anytime Sam, talk to ya later."

Sam got out of the tub, dried off, put on a pair of shorts and a t-shirt, got a Coke from the refrigerator, then sat down and talked to Lilly while she watched TV. Usually at 10:00 pm, Sam watched the news, but he was tired. He just let Boo out for the last time of the night, kissed Lilly good night and went to bed.

Chapter 13

Sam woke early. It was going to be a busy day for a Sunday. The investigators had called this meeting on Sunday morning thinking they could work without many interruptions. The meeting was at 7:00 am in the training room at the jail. Since this was going to be a joint investigation, there would be several people there. As Sam got dressed, he went over the things he wanted to do before signing on duty and going to the meeting. Most of all he would go by Dawn's house, to see if she was awake, and make sure she was doing ok. Sam had been worried about her Every time he saw her, she was crying.

It was only 6:00 am, so Sam had plenty of time. The first stop was Randy's for some coffee and something to eat. Sam walked outside, stopped and let a brisk breeze blow into his face. It wasn't nearly as hot, but it was still early. It had the makings of a beautiful day so far. Sam drove straight to Randy's but doing his routine visual checks of the homes and business while en route. After working in a town as long as Sam had, you get used to people's and businesses' habits. You notice things that look out of place. Luckily, on this morning everything seemed quiet, peaceful, even.

Sam got a large cup of coffee and doctored it up with some creamer and sweetner, plus a few pieces of ice to take the edge off. Sam grabbed a lid and straw, went over to the counter where the donuts were.

Looking in the case, Sam asked Angie, "Where are all the donuts?"

"Needing cop food, Sam?" she said, giggling. Sam half smiled. "The Presbyterians beat you to them, they were having a big social today, and they didn't make enough goodies. Sorry, Sam. The Twinkies are fresh…well as fresh as Twinkies can be," Angie said, laughing.

Sam opted for some granola bars and picked up a few for Dawn along with a bottle of green tea. Angie asked if there was any news on the murder.

Sam just shook his head no, said, "Thank you," as she handed him his change, and he left. He wasn't in the mood for chatter, especially about this case.

As Sam pulled up to Dawn's house he noticed two figures sitting in the screened in porch. He could see one waving at him. He parked the crusier and walked towards the porch. At first he didn't recognize the second woman, but as he got closer she smiled, and he knew it was Jenna. Sam walked through the door Jenna met him with a big hug saying, "My brother from another mother." She pulled away and looked him in the eyes, and

Sam could see her eyes welling up and could feel the tears in his eyes also. Sam didn't think he had made much of an impression on her when she lived there, but apparently, he had.

Sam handed Dawn the tea and granola bars, apologizing for not bring Jenna something, not knowing she was going to be there. "You made good time," said Sam. "Yes, Cappy got us on a non-stop flight, by the time we got packed and drove to the airport we barely made the flight."

"How are you two doing…and where is your husband, Jenna?" Sam asked.

They both looked at each other and reached out and held hands. "We're coping," Dawn said.

Jenna told Sam, "Cappy's still sleeping, I'm sure you will meet him later."

Sam watched Jenna as she talked, it had been years since he had seen her. There were a lot of changes from the shy, pale, quiet girl he knew growing up, to this outgoing, tanned, windblown blond woman. The few wrinkles on her face gave her character, you could tell she had spent a lot of time on the sea, and she was fit and healthy-looking.

"Sam, I am so glad you came by, I have so many questions. Dawn has told me what she knows, but it seems she is out of the loop on this one," Jenna said.

Sam told her, "Well… the is only so much I can say, Jenna, but I'll tell you what I can."

They chatted for a while, Sam avoiding questions that directly involved the case or the evidence. Sam told them he might be able to tell them more after this morning's meeting.

Sam looked at his phone and told them that he needed to be going, saying his goodbyes and gave them both a hug. The meeting was in about fifteen minutes. Dawn said that she would see him at noon. That was when she was scheduled to talk to Murphy and the other investigators.

"You're still planning on sitting in aren't you, Sam?" Dawn asked.

"As far as I know, I will be there for you," Sam said and gave her a smile.

Chapter 14

As Sam pulled into the sheriff's office's parking lot, he was surprised to see so many marked police cruisers. There were also several unmarked Crown Vics that were probably detectives' cars. As he drove through he noticed the plates on one car. It was from the States Attorney's office in Springfield. This is going to be a full-scale investigation and a lot of people involved.

Sam found a parking spot behind the jail and while he was parking, he noticed Murphy standing by the door waiting to be buzzed in. He yelled for Murphy to hold up.

"How's it going, Murph?" Sam shouted as he walked up.

"Crazy," replied Murphy. "Just bat shit crazy, my phone won't stop ringing!"

"Let's go over here, I want to talk to you before we go in," Sam said, motioning Murphy around the side of the building. "What do you think about Dawn?"

"I don't think she could have done it. Even if they were having a lovers' spat, I just can't see her doing something like that. However, her timing... uh... leaving the raid and time no one saw her, makes it look bad." Murphy answered reluctantly.

"I know... maybe something will come up in the interviews." Sam sadly said.

Murphy put his hand on Sam's shoulder, looked at him and said, "Look, I know you two are tight. She may not be my favorite, but she is a good cop and a decent individual. I'm going to do everything I can do to get the real killer, and my instincts say it's not her, it just doesn't make sense."

Sam smiled at Murphy and nodded his head.

Murphy slapped Sam on the back and said, "Cheer up! Let's go find a killer."

They walked over, rang the bell, waited to hear the buzzer so they could open the door and go in.

The training room was packed, not just investigators, but street officers wanting to get caught up in the investigation. Sam was glad to see them there, the more ears on the street knowing what to listen for the better. Sam also knew each officer has their own set of snitches, those are the people that know what other criminals are doing, as the everyday citizen has no clue what goes on in the criminal world.

Sheriff's Detective Buckman announced for everyone to take their seats and waved for Murphy and Sam to come up front. There were a lot of faces in the front 2 rows that Sam didn't know. They were all in off-duty clothes, so it was hard to tell who they were with. The was one guy who was standing near Buckman, with his haircut, overly pressed clothes, and just the way he stood, Sam would bet that he was FBI.

Buckman started talking after everyone got quiet, "Ok, everyone knows why we are here. It's always hard to lose one of your own, and I know we all felt that way about Jason. I'm just going to let everyone tell who they are and what agency they are with, I know we have some younger officers that haven't met everyone. Remember when you are all out there and get information, it all goes through this office, Deputy Kent Phillips or Myself."

As they went through the introductions, Sam was right about the guy from the FBI. He was there to be able to process any evidence through their lab, if need be, or to pull from any of their resources. The States Attorney's office had sent a female investigator, Adele Melrose, who looked to be about Sam's age. The Illinois State Police sent 2 detectives who both looked to be in their mid-30's, and the States Forensic Pathologist who did the autopsy was there.

The Pathologist was a funny-looking little man, very short, with bushy white hair and eyebrows. If his feet were bigger, Sam would have thought he was a Hobbit. The introductions went on for several minutes, and everyone gave their name and department, even the street officers. While this was going on, Karla DeCarla was passing out stickers for name tags and pieces of thick paper to be used for everyone's name at their seats. She was there to keep a record of everything said or discussed. Karla was thorough at her job and left nothing to chance. She had set up a video camera, had a digital audio recorder and was taking notes. This was just the way she was, you could ask for anything at the Sheriff's Office, and she knew the information or where to get in, that probably why she has been there through three Sheriffs.

Buckman started out giving a timeline of the events before and after finding the body. It looked like he had taken most of it from the report that Sam had turned in. After he had finished, Buckman asked Sam if that looked correct as it was written on the whiteboard. Sam looked at his notes and a copy of the report and said everything looked accurate.

Buckman then went through a brief biography of Jason Kelly for those who did not know him and what he had done throughout his life. Many of the people only knew Jason since he came back to McCracken's Bluff and didn't know that he worked as a Deputy State's Attorneys in Lake County. The States Attorney's Office and the FBI were concerned that his murder was linked to one of the cases he worked up there, several of those cases were gang or organized crime cases.

The FBI Agent, Glenn Henley, spoke next he said, "The FBI and its resources are available for anything you need. We will work with you and the States Attorney's office, and if you need us to conduct interviews outside your jurisdiction or access to our forensics lab for anything, just ask." It was short and to the point. "Typical," FBI Sam thought.

The States Pathologist, Dr. Joseph Knowles, spoke next. He didn't stand at the podium, probably because he could barely see over it. Dr. Knowles spoke in a very deep gruff voice that Sam giggled at because it didn't match his stature at all. Dr. Knowles started out saying that the drug and alcohol screen came back negative, to no one's surprise who knew Jason.

Next came pictures of the body and Dr. Knowles explained that the only injuries were an 81.28 millimeter or 3.2 inch cut on his neck and some bruising on the front and top of his head, most likely from the fall from the horse. He switched the slide to a close up of the cut on the neck. As he continued to say that the cut was not a slice as with the sharp edge of a knife, Warren Teasdale's hand shot up, waving furiously. The doctor looked up and said, "Yes Officer, do you have a question?" Teasdale said, in an excited voice, "Do you think the horse could have done it?"

You could hear a groan throughout the room, and the look on Dr. Knowles was priceless, saying, "No it was not a bite mark from a horse, the horse did not do it."

Teasdale sat down sheepishly, and others snickered around him. The Doctor trying to quiet the room said, "It's ok, we have to look at all possibilities at this point." Teasdale sat up, smiling.

Continuing after everyone got quiet, Dr. Knowles went on to say, "The cut was a gashing cut. It could have been with a knife with a sharp point cutting sideways so that the blade ripped instead of slicing." He demonstrated using a big knife, flinging the blade sideways. "However, he continued, the person holding the knife would have to have been at near the same height as the victim." He then demonstrated that the blade would have to have been level, not at an upward thrust. "With the ripping in the incision, this could have been made with any metal object made of steel or copper as in a piece of piping. We found small metal fragments in the wound." He paused looking over at Officer Johnny Hazzard. "Or I should say, Officer Hazzard found them in the blood on the sterile pads the paramedics used to wipe Jason's neck. These are minuscule and are being sent to the FBI lab for identification of the metals." Dr. Knowles changed the slide showing the metal fragments. He continued. "The makeup of metals will give us a better idea of what they came from."

Dr. Knowles went on to say with the size of the cut and the fact that it almost severed the carotid artery, Jason would have bled out in minutes, causing him to fall from the horse. The doctor stated, "The Carotid artery was almost cut half way through. Either it was a very planned out and executed attack because the placement was perfect, or someone got awfully lucky. If someone had been there when it happened, he still probably could not have been saved."

He estimated the time of death between 5:00 am and 8:00 am, "I'm thinking closer to 8:00 am, a little before the time when Officer Nickles got the call." He looked at his notes then Dr. Knowles said, "It was hard to pinpoint because it was so hot where he was laying, and there wasn't much body cooling."

The doctor had shown several pictures of the body and Sam was glad that was over. He was not squeamish, but the sight of his friend really depressed him. Dr. Knowles explained that was about all he had to report, and he asked if there are any questions. Murphy Damn chimed in and asked, "Did you say that there are definitely two types of metal in the cut?"

Dr. Knowles said, "Yes, one was magnetic the other was not, I am not sure what kind of metals they were. One also was silver-tone which makes me think some iron alloy. The non-magnetic was a yellow hue as in brass or copper. They are tiny slivers. We will know more when the lab looks at them."

You could tell Murphy was thinking. He asked, "Don't you find it odd that there are two types of metal? Is that unusual from what you typically find?"

"Yes." The doctor replied, "I don't recall ever seeing that in a single wound like this. Again, a lot about this wound is odd, the shape of the cut, that the victim was high up on horseback, it looks to be so targeted. We need to think of the suspect using what we would not think of as an everyday weapon or the regular use of a weapon."

"So… it appears we are not looking for… or at… hmm, this thing just doesn't make any sense," said Murphy.

"No," the doctor said, looking directly at Murphy. "But, often when things are most unusual, it makes it easier to prove, because there is only one path." With that, the doctor looked around the room, but no one else spoke up. He put up his last slide which had his name, phone number, and e-mail address and told everyone to feel free to contact him if they had information or a question. Looking around and with no one saying anything, the doctor sat down at the table in the front.

Detective Buckman introduced Lieutenant Dick Reed from the Illinois State Police. Reed just advised that the State Police Post from his district would be available to help in any way needed. Reed said he would keep his people updated on the investigation so they would know what we may be looking for, or who we were looking at. Reed was an outstanding trooper, both in the way he did his job and his appearance. He always had a perfect uniform, was always in shape, and when he told you something you knew he meant it. Reed had always been liked by all of the officers in the area, and you never heard a bad word about him.

Lt. Reed also pointed out the detective from his post, Sargent William Chapman who would be assisting Murphy Dam and John Buckman in the investigation. Reed finished up, saying, "We understand this is your case, but we also worked with and admired Jason Kelly and want to find out who did this just as bad as you do. We will assist you any way we can. Questions?"

Again there were no questions. Teasdale started to raise his hand, but looked around and stopped. About an hour had gone by, and Buckman told everyone to take 10 and pointed out the donuts, coffee and other drinks that had been set up outside in the hallway.

Sam grabbed a chocolate covered long john and a cup of coffee and went outside for a quick smoke. While he was lighting up, Brandon Teasdale walked out and came up to Sam and said, "Sam, you saw the body, don't you think the horse could have bucked him off and bit him in the neck?"

"No, I don't," Sam replied, shaking his head.

"Well then who do you think did it Sam, Joe Kerchak, huh… do you think he did it?" Teasdale asked.

Sam just looked at Teasdale and said, "No, he didn't do it either." Sam turned to walk in, putting his half-smoked cigarette in the butt can.

Teasdale followed, repeatedly asking, "How do you know that Sam? Really, Sam, how do you know?"

Sam just kept walking, saying, "You'll find out."

Sam returned to the training room and took his seat, he then realized that he had left his coffee outside. He started to get another cup, but Buckman asked everyone to take their seats.

When everyone had quieted down, Detective Buckman turned around a large rolling white board with names and some pictures of people of interest in the murder. Looking around the room, Sam could sense some uneasiness in the room, just as he felt when he saw Dawn's name on the board. Many officers could not understand why Dawn Pearl's name was there, but it was B.J. Peeks, the coroner, who spoke up first seeing his son, Aaron's name up there. "What the hell...!" B.J. said pointing to the board.

Buckman held up his hand saying, "Hold up... these are just people we need to talk to because they were seen out at the time of the murder and many know something, or others have ties to the victim and some with a grudge... so let's take it slow and go through the list.

Sam, and everyone else scanned the list, some writing it down and others just making notes of what they knew. Sam went down, reading each name.

Local People:

Joe Kerchak

Dawn Pearl

Bobby Ellis

Aaron Peeks

Greg Pearl

Poss Bundy

Jim Bass

Otis Bass

Shorty Walker

Chicago People:

Emanuel Bent

Rico Montoya

Jamal Jabir

Tommy Martin

Detective Buckman explained that the local officers need to focus on the locals and that the State Attorney's office would work on the ones from Chicago. These were people who Jason had put in prison and are out and made threats in the past.

"So," Buckman continued., "Any additions or people we can strike off right now?"

With Joe Kerchak at the top of the list, Sam thought he might as well tell his story of Joe's alibi. Sam stood up and said, "You can take Joe

Kerchak of the list, he couldn't have done it." Sam could see the look of surprise on several faces in the room, and even a few groans of disappointment.

Sam told the story of Joe, Miss Val, and the shotgun, there were several laughs and a few comments, but in the end, Buckman took Kerchak's name off of the list.

After everyone had settled down, Sam continued, "Greg Pearl is another story, he and Dawn got into an argument the day before Jason's murder." Sam stopped for a moment thinking how to put the next words together.

He knew it was going to get out anyway so he thought that he might as well put it in the best light he could, so then continued, "Dawn had been seeing Jason and Greg found out about it."

Searching for words, Sam said, "Greg... had been physically and emotionally abusing Dawn and she was trying to get away from him…she went to Jason for help and well… things happened." The room was quiet. Sam knew there was not much love for Greg Pearl in the law enforcement community. Most thought he was shady and generally an ass.

"Anyway," Sam went on, "Greg left home that morning and didn't come back to the house that night. Greg was holed up at Terrance's shack until he went into Randy's Convenience Store about 4:00 am."

"Buddy at Randy's told me that Greg was being more of a jerk than usual and seemed to be in a hurry," Sam said.

Sam explained that he found out that Greg spent the night before at Terrance Fisher's drinking and talking about Dawn and what he thought she was doing. Greg also told Terrance that he had gambled away most of their life savings and he was taking off to go home to Missouri.

Sam said, "I found out that he did live near Camdenton, Missouri, by the Lakes of the Ozarks, so that might be where he is heading. I've put a call into the police department down there and am waiting to hear back. Terrence said that he talked to Greg on the phone most of the way there, so I am pretty sure that is where he is."

Sam looked at his notes. As Murphy Dam stood up, Sam held a finger up and said, "Just a minute. I called Camden County and Camdenton PD and neither officer I spoke to knew of a Greg Pearl, but both would talk to their supervisors and have them call me back. What do you got Murph?"

"You are not going to find Greg Pearl down there. In fact, they have been looking for him, he is missing." Murphy looked at his notes and said, "When Sam told me that Greg Pearl had not been seen since before Jason's murder, I decided to do some checking. I ran Greg's information and well, there was nothing for the last six years when his Illinois driver's license expired. Greg Pearl, with that date of birth, was from Cicero, Illinois and went missing 10 years ago, while, get this, on a hunt for wild boar by the Lake of the Ozarks." Murphy walked to the white board and began write, but instead said "Anyway, I knew something was up, and I remembered that our Greg Pearl applied to be a fireman here several years ago. I was helping when they started the hiring process and fingerprinted the applicants. I remembered Pearl asking why we were taking his fingerprints, and he seemed nervous. I told him then that if he got through the physical and written tests, we would run a background check. At the time, I thought it strange because he asked if we ran everyone and I told him, 'No, only ones who go on to the next step.' I should have known something was up because he never showed up for the testing, but that was a little after he had married Dawn, so I thought he must be ok."

Murphy paused for a minute, got out some papers, saying, "So, his prints were never ran at that time. Luckily, they have been sitting in an envelope in the file boxes upstairs at the firehouse."

Sam was thinking to himself, as he often did with Murphy, "Come on what do ya got." But he also knew Murphy was never one to be short on words, so he just sat back and listened as Murphy when on.

Murphy held up a fingerprint card, and said, "I took these to the State Police Post and had them run the prints through the AFIS System- and low and behold, he is not Greg Pearl, but Winfred Shaland of Mack's Creek Missouri. His date of birth is 09/11/1961, he is 5'9," 255, red hair and green eyes. That sounds like our Greg, or now to be known as Winfred."

Sam was dumbfounded, as he thought probably everyone in the room was. What the hell was Dawn going to think or do? The man she married and lived with for the last 10 years was not who he said it was.

Murphy finished up saying, "Winfred Shaland has an extensive criminal record: thefts, domestic violence, burglary and also has an outstanding warrant. I could not find out what for yet, but I will. I just got this information late last night and didn't have time to call back today. I am just wondering if it is not for the murder of the real Greg Pearl."

Murphy looked over at Sam, and Sam said, "Well, that kind of explains a lot... in a way."

Buckman stood up from where he was taking notes, saying, "That information certainly moves Greg...uh...Shaland to the top of the list. If he killed once he is surely capable of doing it again and had a motive and the opportunity."

Detective Buckman asked Murphy Dam if he had any more information. Murphy looked at his notes and said "Not at this time but, there will be more this afternoon and tomorrow when they get some of the interviews over. These are bound to bring out more information... and probably more questions."

John Buckman, being the good detective he was had every report from every officer and deputy involved in the investigation, all in a file box in front of him. He was searching through and pulled out some papers then said, "Just so you know what has been covered, Kent Phillips and I went all through Jason's house. We didn't find much. There were some files from his most urgent cases that are going to be gone over by States Attorney's Office and FBI. There were some notes from Dawn and some notes he had on Greg Pearl, but not much there. That's about it from... Yeah, Reb?"

Reb Main stood up and said, "I started to tell Murphy at Jason's murder scene but...er, I couldn't then, and haven't had a chance to tell anyone till now. Jason called me early on the morning of his death, about 5:30 am. Jason had just talked to Dawn, and she was worried about Greg... Shaland being missing and he wanted to meet me around noon to talk to me about looking into him and..." He stopped, looked at B.J. Peeks, then said, "She thought that Aaron Peeks was following her." Reb could see B.J.'s face go from anger to worry as he thought about what was happening.

B.J. Peeks knew his son was a little odd, might be what they called "Goth" but was never mean or hateful. B.J. didn't think Aaron could hurt anything, let alone kill a person. He knew that Aaron liked Jason, he would go out and talk to Jason about horses. Aaron loved horses, even though he never had any, and would probably be scared to ride one. B.J. also knew how death investigations went, and that the detectives had to cover all the bases and eliminate all possible suspects. As for Aaron being out early in the morning, that was not unusual, Aaron did a lot of work around the funeral home when other people were not around. Aaron then liked to go out and drive around and listen to music to relax. He was sure that this would all come out and someone could vouch for Aaron's whereabouts during the time of the murder.

Detective Buckman looked at the schedule and said, "Aaron Peeks is scheduled for his interview at one o'clock pm this afternoon, Dawn is first at noon. Getting these interviews out of the way should clear up a lot of things." Looking back at the notes, Buckman said, "We are also going to talk to the people we have in jail from the raid the other night. We know that Shorty Walker and Joe Kerchak were there. We've marked Joe off the list, but he still might know something. Has anyone seen Shorty?"

Looking around the room, no one answered. Sam knew Shorty Walker did not live in McCracken's Bluff, but anytime trouble happened, he always seemed to be around. Shorty lived somewhere near Cave in Rock, but no one in the room was sure where. Most thought he was a "floater" as they called people who didn't really have a permanent residence, but live with friends or family most of the time. Cave in Rock, Illinois, was a town on the Ohio River. It used to be a thriving little community, but now was almost a ghost town. About the only thing that kept the town going was the ferry that crossed the Ohio River to Kentucky, and Cave in Rock State Park. The park was some beautiful woods with camping and hiking. The park had a little restaurant at the top of the bluff, which Sam thought made the best cheesecake in the world. Sam had taken the 30-minute drive, many times, just to get a piece of the delicious dessert. The park also had "The Cave." It was known as a hideout for Jesse James, and before that was used by river pirates to attack settlers coming down the river. The cave had also been used in several movies and was a neat place to explore. Sam and friends had camped there many times, and played outlaws and explorers.

John Buckman spoke again, interrupting Sam's thoughts, "Ok, does anyone else have any more information?' Again, no one spoke up. "Buckman said. It's ok, we are still early in the investigation, we still have a lot of work to do, and people to talk to. If you have free time or want something to do, contact Murphy or me. I'm sure there will be plenty of work to go around. Well... I guess we can go, keep in touch and updated."

B.J. Peeks quickly stood up and spoke before anyone had a chance to leave. "The M.E. is done with Jason's body, and I have talked with his family. The funeral will be on Wednesday, showing at our funeral home at 8:00 am up to the funeral at 1:00 pm. He will be buried alongside his parents at The Shawnee Hills Cemetery out on Route One. Hope you all can attend."

Sam thought how badly he hated funerals, and this was going to be a tough one for everyone. He wanted to find the person or persons who had done this so bad, he could taste it. Every time Sam thought about Jason and his family, and the good times he had with them, his eyes welled up with tears.

On the way out of the training room, Sam stopped Murphy and asked, "Did you get a chance to ask Buckman about me setting in on Dawn's interview?"

"Yeah," Murphy replied. "He said if it will make her feel better, he thought it would be ok. She doesn't have a lawyer, does she?"

"No, she said she hasn't done anything wrong and doesn't need one," Sam said.

Murphy shook his head and said, "I hope not."

"OK, well it's only nine thirty and I am going to get something to eat, then I will go pick Dawn up and drive her back here," Sam said.

"You're not going to church?" Murphy said with a laugh.

"I'd be struck by lightning if I walked into the church, it has been so long… Lilly is always on to me to go, and I really should, but seems like I'm always either working or trying to get some sleep. Do ya think God will understand?" Sam said smiling.

"Hey, you know what they say… "Blessed are the peacemakers, and you're a hell of a peacemaker Sam!" Murphy answered, thinking he was hilarious. "Catch up with ya later."

"I'll be back," Sam said in his best *Terminator* voice.

Chapter 15

Sam walked out of the sheriff's office. He looked up and saw the clouds building up, thinking, "Hmmm…, might storm, it pretty warm, but the humidity is bad." Sam could already notice the sweat building up on his forehead. As Sam pulled out of the parking lot, he noticed a big maple tree turning its leaves over. "Yep, it's going to rain," Sam said to himself.

Sam went to the Purple Lotus to get some breakfast. As he was walking in, Sherrie Hall was walking out. "Hey Sherrie, I got some time to talk if you do." Sam said, thinking this would be a safe place for them to talk. "Sorry Sam, I have got to run, going to ten o'clock Mass, but I am going to catch you… maybe when you least expect it!" Sherrie replied with a laugh. Sam watched her walk away and thought, "She's going to church in that dress, with those legs and that…" Sam shook his head and walked in the café.

Sam decided on the "Big Breakfast:" three eggs, bacon, ham, and sausage. It also had hash browns, toast, and three pancakes. Sam knew Lilly would have a fit if he ordered this much "unhealthy" food. She tried to watch his diet, but it was hard because of where Sam ate during work, and because Sam loved to cook and eat.

The waitress brought Sam his coffee and asked: "Are you ready to order, Hun?" Sam said, "Yeah, the Big Breakfast, eggs over easy."

Sam looked up and was getting the evil eye from Tilly, the waitress. "Sam! Do you think Lilly would approve?"

Uh… a uh… a guy needs real food once in a while." Sam said thinking that sometimes he hated living in a small town. She kept looking down at him, tapping her foot. Sam looked up and said, "Just bring me my food, ok?"

"Ok, but this won't help your diet," Tilly said as she walked away.

"How does she know I'm on a diet?" Sam thought as he stirred the sweetener and cream into his coffee. He then laughed at himself, "low-calorie sweetener, huh."

Sam enjoyed his meal, talked to four or five people who came by and asked questions, paid his check, and probably should have left a bigger tip, but he didn't like Tilly's comments.

It was almost 11:00 am when Sam left the Purple Lotus. He thought he could go on over to Dawn's and talk to her and Jenna for a bit before he took Dawn back to the Sheriff's office.

Sam drove through the streets slowly, one of the parts of police work Sam really enjoyed was patrolling, or like today, just slowly driving through the streets and watching and talking to the people. That was another reason Sam always drove with his window down. He felt it made him more accessible to the people. Sam liked the sights and sounds of the town.

When he was a kid, he liked to "cruise the strip." In McCracken's Bluff, the strip was mostly the downtown area. It went from the Dog in Suds drive-in on the east side of town to the Bowling Alley on the North-West side of the city. It was about a two-and-a-half-mile trip, but on a busy night it would take about an hour to make a whole loop, driving and talking to friends. Sam and his buddies hung out at the Dog and Suds. The Coney Dogs were good, but the root beer was the best. Back then, Sam and his friends could find a dozen pop bottles and cash them in for a nickel each and buy gas at 25 cents a gallon. They could cruise all night on a few bottles each.

Even back then Sam drove a police car, it was a dark blue 1965 Ford Custom, 4 door sedan that he could squeeze 8 people in the seats and 4 in the trunk if they were going to the drive-in. It looked a little ratty, had some rust, and he had his buddy Joseph Francis who always liked working on it. It had a good radio, which was real important and he had installed an 8 track tape player and additional speakers. Sam had only paid $700 for the car, and you couldn't tell by the way it looked, she ran like a cheetah: fast, very fast.

Sam thought that the kids don't know what they are missing today-cruising around, meeting friends, new girls and actually spending time talking to each other, not just texting one another. Sam's favorite thing to do was play practical jokes on unexpecting friends they would see on those nights. People learned really quick to never leave their car unlocked when Sam was around.

"Damn," Sam said as he noticed he had just driven past Dawn's house. He had his mind in the past, daydreaming. He put the car in reverse and drove back and parked beside Dawn's house. Again, Dawn and Jenna were sitting on the screened-in porch, but his time there was a man with them, Sam thought it was probably Cappy.

As he walked in, Jenna introduced Sam to Ural Wallace, or Cappy, as everyone called him. Cappy was not at all what he expected. He was a tall, soft-spoken man, with a full head of black hair, and darkly hued, weathered skin. Sam found out talking to him that his mother was full-blooded Osage Indian and his father a first-generation Belgian immigrant who taught on the reservation in Oklahoma. Sam thought, with a name like Cappy, he would be a short, stocky man with a gray beard, like the guy from the Gordon's fish stick box.

They sat and talked for a bit. Jenna tried to ask several questions about the case, which Sam deflected, saying he really couldn't talk about it at this point. He told her her, "As soon as we get Dawn cleared as a suspect, I can tell you more." He did explain there would be some details that they would not put out until they had a good case on someone. Jenna said that she understood, but Sam could tell she was not happy about it.

The conversation then turned to the funeral. Jenna asked Sam to be a pall bearer. Sam said he would be honored and asked who else she had chosen. Jenna said, "Well, since I haven't been around for a while it was hard, but I know he had 2 good friends at the State's Attorney's office in Chicago, and they agreed. Thomas Jay and Bill Houston where his best friends growing up and they said yes…Do you think Reb Main will be at the Sheriff's Office when we get there? I was going to ask him; they were pretty close."

Sam said, "He was there when I left, I think he was working on something. If not, I have his number."

"Can't I just go with you and Dawn and talk to him there?" Jenna asked.

"Probably not a good idea, I don't know how long we will be, and there is not a good place to sit and wait. Especially on Sunday, visiting day, it will be crowded with all kinds of…" Sam said, with Jenna interrupting him mid-sentence.

"I'm a big girl Sam, and Cappy can come too," Jenna said.

I just think it would be better for you to stay here. If I see Reb, I will tell him to come see you…oh, where are you two staying?" Sam asked.

"They are staying here Sam, I wouldn't have it any other way, and they can keep me company," Dawn answered.

"And I will be here in case Greg comes back," Cappy said.

"Ok right, Dawn we better get going, and get this over with… we'll be back in a little while. Everything will be ok," Sam said.

Dawn grabbed her purse and some Kleenex and headed out the screen door towards Sam's patrol car. Sam turned as he left, towards Jenna and Cappy, and gave the thumbs up.

As they drove to the sheriff's office they sat in silence for the first few minutes, then Dawn started to cry. Sam was never comfortable with crying women and didn't know what to say. He asked if she was ok, and if she wanted him to stop. Dawn shook her head, no, saying she would be ok in a minute.

"You know Sam; I haven't done anything wrong."

She started to say more but, Sam said, "I know that Dawn, you couldn't have killed him."

"No, it's not that, I've lost so much, and don't know why," she said, with her voice quivering. "I know seeing Jason was wrong, but Greg was so mean, I couldn't take it anymore. Now I don't have Jason, Greg, and he took my life savings. I just hope I can keep my job."

"There's no reason for you to lose your job. You haven't done anything legally wrong, and Wallow doesn't want to bring up the affair. I've got that covered for you," Sam told her.

Sam thought, "yeah, I got the poop on Chief Wallow," he had been notorious for sleeping around ever since he got on the department. Sam remembered, even when Wallow was a rookie and was late for midnight shift, and was supposed to be riding with Sam. Sam was calling Wallow while driving to his house. While en route Sam saw Wallow run out of the neighbor's house with his pants in hand and into his back door. Sam covered for him that night, even though he was almost 25 minutes late before he got in the car. Sam asked him where his wife was and Wallow told him since she was pregnant, she went to bed early. Sam just shook his head.

Dawn gave Sam a half smile, and wiped the tears from her eyes, "Ok, I've got this, Sam. I'm ready for anything, thanks for being here." They finished the rest of the drive with Sam telling her a funny story about Clifford Duggs. He even got a little chuckle out of her but could tell she was still nervous.

As they pulled into the sheriff's office, the parking lot was full. "Yep, Visitor Day," Sam said. He pulled around back to go in through the kitchen. He radioed on the jail frequency that there would be two coming in kitchen door so that when they got there, the officer in the control room could see them on the cameras and buzz the door open.

Sam and Dawn walked through the halls of the sheriff's office. Several people wanted to talk to them, but they kept it to a simple hello. That was, until Brandon Teasdale ran up to Dawn, and hugged her, telling her that everything would be ok. The look on Dawn's face was priceless, and Sam could not help laughing. Dawn pulled away thanking him and saying she needed to get to the interview room. Brandon apologized, and Dawn thanked him again while turning to go.

Sam patted Brandon on the back, saying "Settle down, kid," and followed Dawn.

Murphy met them at the door of the interview room and told them to come on in. The interview room at the jail was really a multi-purpose room. It had a large table for smaller meetings of about eight or ten people. It was wired for sound, and at one end was a one-way mirror that could be used to record through and also to do lineups, so the victim could not be seen.

Murphy told them to have a seat. He said, "Buckman is just getting the cameras set up and checking on the sound recorder, he will be here in a minute." Dawn sat in a seat that was across from where Murphy and Buckman would be sitting. Murphy had pointed at a chair at the other end of the table for Sam. Sam would be close enough to hear, but not really in the interview. Sam looked over at Dawn and smiled and winked.

"While we are waiting, we might as well get some of the preliminaries out of the way. Dawn, you know I have to read you your rights."

"Of course," she said. "Go ahead."

Murphy read them from the document, having Dawn initial each part as read and then sign at the bottom. Murphy said he should have looked them up, but while they were there, he asked Dawn her general information: full name, date of birth, address and so on, until Buckman entered the room.

"Ok, we are all set up. I got you reading Dawn her rights on video and the sound checks," Buckman said as he sat down next to Murphy. Buckman then bounced back up, turning on the light switch, that told people outside that there was an interview going on. Sam could tell Dawn was nervous. He wished he could help, but now was just the time to sit and listen.

Buckman started, "Ok, Dawn, just tell us in your own words what happened in the hours before Jason Kelly was found dead?"

Dawn looked at Sam, "When do you want me to start?"

Murphy said, "Well we know you were at the drug raid, so after that."

"Hum... ok but first I got to say, that while I was getting ready for the raid, Greg and I got into a big fight, and he accused me of seeing someone, he twisted my arm and threw me against the wall. I had had enough. He started to come at me again, and I, I ... pulled my Glock and threatened to shoot him. I could see fear in his eyes, it, it... was the first time I have ever stood up to him. I don't think he knew what to do." Dawn rattled the words out quickly.

"Ok," Murphy said, "but slow down... what happened next?"

"Greg grabbed his keys and left, saying, 'You'll never see me again, bitch!' He just walked out the door." Dawn thought for a moment and continued, "I finished getting ready, went out to my car, and called Jason, saying I wanted to see him… I needed to talk to him. He said he was home and for me to stop by. I told him I couldn't then, because of the raid, and it might be early in the morning. He just told me to text him before I came and he would be waiting."

"Um," Murphy said holding up a finger. "How long had you and Jason seen each other?"

"It actually just started out as friends. We would talk at his office, or on the telephone, for hours. This lasted for months. We were both just lonely and neither had a lot of friends. Then one morning he asked me out to his house for dinner, and…well it got romantic from there. That was about 2 months ago," Dawn replied.

"Do you think Greg knew who you were seeing?" Buckman asked.

"No, I don't think so. In fact, I'm not sure he really thought I was, but… when he accused me, I said, 'Yeah, and he is a real man, not a fat drunk slob like you that can't even find his penis!'" Dawn stated.

Everyone, even Dawn, laughed a little, and Murphy interjected, "Yeah, I think he probably thinks something now."

"Alright, Dawn, what happened after the raid?" Buckman asked.

"I texted Jason, and he said that he would meet me in the barn, so I drove there." Dawn paused for a moment and thought. "We talked for about a half an hour. He told me he had talked to an attorney friend that would handle a divorce for me, and file a restraining order if need be. I didn't like the idea of a restraining order...so he told me he wanted me to move in with him."

Dawn stopped, her lip was quivering, but she continued, "I said I needed time to think about all of this. Jason said he just wanted me to be safe and happy. Jason gave me a hug, then kissed me, I stopped him and told him I had to go and think. I started to leave, but went back, kissed him and told him I loved him, he said he loved me too. I ran and got in my car... as I was pulling out, Jason said he was going for a ride and to text him if I needed anything." Dawn broke down and started crying.

Everyone sat there silent, Dawn gathered herself and said, "I'm sorry guys, I just loved him so much."

Murphy took her hand and said, "It's ok, take all the time you need." Dawn looked up in surprise, not expecting compassion from Murphy Dam. Maybe she had thought wrong about him.

She wiped her eyes with a tissue and blew her nose. She looked up and all around the room, "Alright," she said, "I backed out of the driveway and drove to City Park and parked behind the old barn where I could not be seen, and just sat there for about an hour."

"Do you know what time that was?" Buckman asked.

"No... not really... oh, wait... just a few minutes after I got there, dispatch gave 5 o'clock time check, I almost answered it, but realized I wasn't on the clock."

"Did you see anyone, or notice any other cars, talk to anyone? Buckman asked.

"I did have to stop as I was backing out of Jason's driveway for a car going into town, but I really didn't pay much attention to it. I couldn't tell you anything about it. Sorry." Dawn thought a minute and went on to say, "There was a car, you know… I believe it was that big Caddy that that creepy Aaron drives… it pulled into the far end of the park as I was backing in behind the barn."

She paused, "Now that I think about it I know it was his car because it was there when I left, and I thought, 'What the hell is he doing here this time of the morning?' I had told Jason that I thought Aaron was stalking me, and gave me the creeps, but hadn't really seen him enough to confront him yet."

"That's ok, Dawn," Murphy said, "How long did you stay at the park?"

"I was there until I signed on duty at seven am. I had sent Jason a text message about…" Dawn pulled out her phone and looked at her sent messages and said, "It was five forty-nine am, then sent another at six ten and another at six twenty-eight, but he never texted me back." Dawn stared at her phone for a minute, as in a trance, unknown to the detectives, she had scrolled up to the last time that Jason had texted her and told her he loved her.

Dawn looked back up at Murphy and Buckman and said, "I left the park and drove to Randy's to get a tea and something to eat. I was there for a little while talking to some tourists. Buddy had told me that Greg was in there, and I asked what time. He said about 4 am, which made me wonder more what was he doing." Dawn thought for a moment, then said, "That's when you called me, Sam," looking over at Sam. Sam nodded yes, and she continued, "I drove back to the park and Sam and I talked for a little while until dispatch told me to go to Jason's office at about eight o'clock."

Dawn looked at Murphy, trying to see if he believed what she was saying. Murphy was hard to read. He seemed to be able to turn off his emotions while in an interview, maybe that what made him good at it. It was kind of spooky. Dawn went on, saying, "I went straight to Jason's office, which only took a couple minutes. Jill gave me some reports that Teasdale needed to work on because they didn't make any sense. I asked if Jason was in, and she said she had not seen him yet, but she didn't seem too concerned about it." Dawn sat and thought a moment and finished up saying, "I stayed at the office for a while hoping Jason would come it. I then heard Sam get the call about the horse, didn't sound serious, so I kept talking to Jill. After a while, I wondered why Sam was still there, so I decided to check on him, and drove to the school." She paused, "That's when…I …found out…about Jason." She broke down crying again.

A minute went by, and Buckman said: "Ok, I think we have heard enough." Murphy nodded. Dawn and Sam both looked at him with a shocked look on their faces. Murphy said, "You're good to go, Dawn, we have enough, all is good." Dawn looked at Buckman, then at Murphy, they both had smiles on their faces. Sam just sat there confused. "You mean, I'm not a suspect anymore?" asked Dawn.

"You were never really a suspect. We knew you didn't kill Jason, but we had to get your side of the story and do everything by the book, you know how it is." replied Buckman.

"Ok, but I'm still a little confused, you're just taking my word for everything?" Dawn asked.

"I probably would take your word for it, but we have collaborating evidence to your timeline," Buckman said. Dawn gave him an inquiring look, and Buckman continued. "After the meeting this morning, Murphy and I went to my office and were going through the video from Randy's store and it showed you there for the time you said you were there. But, here is the good, and a little creepy part."

Buckman stopped, and started walking out of the room saying, "It's stuffy in here let's step outside."

Everyone knew that meant he wanted a cigarette, and so did Sam. Outside, while they were lighting up, Dawn pulled out a pack of Marlboros and joined them. Sam gave her a look, and she said, "It been a tough few days, I've only had a few. I had to get a pack because I can't stand those Camels you smoke."

The cigarette break seemed to relax everyone and Buckman continued, "Anyway, after the meeting, B.J. was mad that Aaron was a suspect. He wanted him cleared as soon as possible, so he called him and had him come straight to the office. After we had finished with the videos, B.J. and Aaron were waiting for us in the hallway, and B.J. wanted Aaron interviewed right then... Well, Murphy and I had a little time, so we did. B.J.'s pissed because we didn't let him in the interview, but he will just have to be mad."

Buckman could tell Murphy was itching to talk since Murphy didn't smoke. He was just standing there, so Buckman said, "Go ahead Murphy, you finish it up."

Murphy jumped at the chance to talk and said, Yeah Dawn, you're right- that boy is a strange one. It was like pulling teeth getting information out of him, he would never look up at us, and he spoke so low we could hardly hear him. Hell, I had to get up and get a microphone and put it right in front of him. I was afraid the other one would not pick up what he was saying. He actually wasn't giving us much information until we asked him if he had seen you, then he got real nervous then and almost shut down completely. That's when I told him that his statement might help you as well as himself. When he thought, he could help you is when he really opened up."

Murphy laughed, "I guess the boy really has it bad for you. Aaron said he would do anything for you. He thought you were beautiful, smart and tough and had always wanted to get to know you. Aaron admitted that he was shy around women and knew you were married, so he just admired you from afar," Murphy said with flair, circling his arms and hugging himself. Dawn was not amused but didn't say anything, just listened.

"Finally, he told us," continued Buckman. "He saw Greg at Randy's that morning and wondered what Greg was doing out that time of night, so he followed him. Aaron said Greg drove out of town and he followed him for a while, but turned around about five miles past the city limits and came back in town by the back roads, then came down Cotton Mill Road to town. Aaron told us as he got near to Jason's house, he saw you back out of the horse barn and back down the lane. Aaron also saw Jason waving at you as you left. Aaron explained how you stopped for him to go by and he drove into town, parking beside the co-op until you passed and then followed you to the park. Aaron was there all the time, he sat there till you left. Following you, Aaron saw you go into Randy's and wanted to go in but chickened out. He said he looked at the time and knew he better get home and help with Mr. Straw's funeral, and B.J. verified those times."

"Aaron even admitted to us," Murphy said joyfully, "that he had sat outside your house on several occasions." But then Murphy got serious saying, "He heard the arguments between you and Greg and heard thing breaking and you screaming. He said he wanted to help, but was afraid of Greg." Murphy stopped, then said, "Why didn't you say something to us?" Dawn just bowed and shook her head.

Buckman looked at his notes, and said, "With Aaron's statements, the video, and we had run your and Jason's text messages and got a timeline from them, and asked Jill about when you were at the office, all the times were covered. You're free to go…Oh, the reason Jason didn't text you back that night, he left his house and jumped his horse over the back fence and lost his cell phone, we found it yesterday."

Dawn looked up and gave a little smile, she hugged Buckman then Murphy, which Sam could tell made Murphy uncomfortable. She said, "I can't thank you guys enough, I feel so much better, you are the best." As she said that, she looked at Sam and smiled, he gave her a big smile back.

Dawn even had a bounce in her step as she and Sam walked to Sam's car. She told Sam, "You were right, just let the system play out, and the truth be known." But then she stopped and said, "We still don't know who killed Jason."

When they got in the car, Dawn turned her investigator's mind on, saying, "Ok Sam, what other suspects do we have, Joe Kerchak?" Sam told her about Joe's alibi from Miss Val, Dawn saying that was one of the craziest storied she had ever heard, but knew Miss Val wouldn't lie for anyone. They discussed the case all the way to her house, and, for several minutes sitting in the car outside the house. Dawn asked Sam in for a piece of pie, but he said, he better get out and about, he had hardly patrolled at all. Dawn gave Sam a hug, thanking him.

Sam was thankful for a nice quiet afternoon, he just leisurely patrolled listening to the radio. About ten to three, evening shift signed on, and Sam signed off duty.

Sam drove home and went inside to find Lilly sitting on the couch crocheting. She looked up and asked how his day went. "Really great," Sam said with a smile. "We cleared Dawn and Aaron, but we still don't know who killed Jason."

"You will find out, Sam." Lilly said with a reassuring smile.

"Where are the kids?" Sam asked.

"Midg went back to school, but she will be back for the funeral, and Jeb just left to play some football with some friends," Lilly told him.

Sam looked at Lilly with a smile, and said, "So we have the house to ourselves...shall we retire to the boudoir?" "Oh Sam, I love it when you try to speak French!" They walked down the hall to the bedroom and almost got knocked down by Boo trying to get there first to get his favorite place at Sam's feet.

Chapter 16

Sam was in a deep sleep when his phone blared. He bolted up in bed, looking at the alarm clock, "Two eleven am, what the hell." Sam thought. Sam was trying to answer the phone when Lilly said, "I hate that damn ringtone, Sam." She rolled over and went back to sleep. Sam looked at the caller ID, and got out of bed and walked down the hall to the living room. "Hey Dawn, what's the matter?" He could tell she was crying as she tried to say to him, "Sam…Greg called…he sounded mad and drunk!"

Sam told her, "Ok, calm down, take a breath, I can barely understand you."

Dawn was just saying "Ok, ok give me a minute… He threatened me, Sam. He said he knew about Jason and me, and that he was not going to divorce me, and he will make sure Jason and I will be happy, in hell!"

"Dawn, did he say where he was? Did he call on his cell phone? Sam asked.

"No, no I blocked his cell number on my phone, I didn't want to talk to him, but this was a number I didn't know so I answered it. Sam, he said such hateful things, and then just hung up, what am I going to do?" Frantically she said.

"Is Jenna or Cappy awake? Sam asked.

"No I knew they couldn't help me, so I didn't wake them," Dawn said.

"Ok, I can get dressed and come over, I can be there in ten minutes," Sam said trying to calm her.

"Really? Oh Sam, would you please? I need to talk to someone," Dawn said crying.

"Yeah, give me a few minutes, I will be there," Sam said hanging up.

Dawn said, "You're the greatest!" But Sam didn't hear it, he had hung up and was getting dressed.

Sam put on a pair of jeans and a t-shirt, slipped into his tennis shoes, and stuck his Ruger in the back of the waist of his pants. He got into his patrol car and drove straight to Dawn's. As he pulled up a car pulled beside him, "What up Sam, is everything ok?" asked Tom Clifford.

"Yeah, Dawn just got a call from Greg, or Shaland or whoever he is, and I'm just going to see what I can find out," Sam said, getting out of his car.

"Does she know where he is?" asked Tom.

"No, but I got to get in there, she is really upset," Sam said walking towards the house.

"If you need anything, Sam, call me! Tom yelled out the window of the car.

Dawn was waiting at the door of her screened porch as he walked across the lawn.

"Thanks again for coming Sam. I have coffee on, or would you like something stronger?" Dawn asked.

Sam pointed over his shoulder with his thumb at his patrol car. "Oh, never mind, I guess coffee will have to do, come on in, I still have some pie left too,." said Dawn.

Sam thought, "Pie and coffee- that alone makes this trip worth it."

Sam was one of those people who can eat anything, anytime, day or night, never bothered him. That probably was the reason for his expanding waistline. He loved to get a can of tamales and cover them with hot sauce while working a midnight shift, then drink coffee up to time to go home, and then sleep like a baby.

"I'll get the pie, want ice cream?" asked Dawn.

"Nope, just pie, and your phone…can I use your computer?"

Dawn yelled, "Catch," throwing the cell phone to Sam. "The computer is right there."

Sam almost missed the phone, watching Dawn he thought, "Wow, she is wound up. I need to get her calmed down."

Sam looked at the phone and did a reverse look up on the number Greg had called from. "Wow, the Three Winds Lodge, I've been there. It's on The Lake of the Ozarks, real fancy place!"

"Oh, yeah sure, I bet he is enjoying himself, spending our life's saving, or at least what he didn't gamble away. Now, how am I going to send Brit to college? I had $22,000 dollars in that account, and he took it all." Dawn rattled out.

"We'll work on that. At least we know he is not around here," Sam told her, and that seemed to relieve her somewhat. "Did Murphy or Buckman let you know any more about Greg after the interview?"

"No, I left with you, remember?" Dawn said, "What about him?"

"Damn." Sam said, "I wish they had told you. Sit down, this is going to be a shocker."

Sam explained how Murphy tried to run Greg, but could not get any recent information. He told her about using some old fingerprints and found out his real name was Winfred Shaland, from Missouri. Sam said they have called down there and found out that Greg/Winfred had a long record. He told her that Greg Pearl came up missing from that area several years ago, and has never been found.

Dawn was dumbstruck. She couldn't believe her whole marriage had been a sham, and she didn't have any idea who she was married to. He might have been a murderer.

"Sam, what am I going to do?" Dawn asked.

"Hopefully nothing, if he is that bad of a guy, they will put him in jail. You can get a divorce and will be rid of him, and won't have to worry about him," Sam said, trying to calm her.

Sam looked at Dawn, she wasn't convinced. She was pacing as Jenna walked in.

"Dawn, what are you doing... up?" Jenna said stopping in her tracks, "Oh Sam, what are you doing here?"

"Jenna, Greg...Winfred or whatever called me while ago." Dawn blurted out.

"What is she talking about?" Jenna asked.

Sam again explained about Greg Pearl, and said, "Listen, Dawn, I will call down there right now and see if I can talk to someone if that will make you feel better."

"Would you please Sam? That would be great, to know where he is at." She asked.

Sam looked up the number for the Camden County Sheriff's Office and called.

"Candem County Jail, David Jones speaking."

"Hehehe." Sam thought to himself, "Davey Jones."

Regaining his thoughts, Sam said, "This is Sam Nickles with the McCrackin, Illinois Police Department. I need some information, how long have you worked there?"

"About three years, but I grew up here," replied David.

"Do you know a Wilbur Shaland from those parts?" Sam asked.

"I went to school with some Shalands, but not a Winfred, never heard that name. They live way back in the hills… huh… oh ok… hang on. My uncle Jimmy Jones from the Camdenton Police Department wants to talk to you."

"His uncle," Sam thought, "And James Jones, I wonder if his middle name is Earl." Sam chuckled, thinking, "Man, I'm up way to early."

A deep voice with a thick southern draw came on the phone, "You askin about Iggy Shaland."

"Well, Winfred Shaland is who…"

"Yep, Winfred Ignace Shaland, white male, he would be a little over 50 now, we always called him Iggy, I've arrested him dozens of times. A real asshole, we've been looking for him for years. You got him up there?"

"No, but he may be down there, at the Three Winds Resort," said Sam.

"No shit, hot dog, I hope we can get him before the Smith Brothers find him. They'll kill him- which wouldn't altogether be a bad thing, but we would like to talk to him first." Jimmy Jones said.

In his mind, Sam said to himself "The Smiths and Joneses, no one is going to believe this shit, but I got to ask." So, Sam asked, "Why do the Smiths want to kill him?"

"Well, several years ago, Iggy knocked up Rebel…er, Tammy Lee Smith, we called her Rebel because she was always a wild child. "Anyway, the Smiths, old Horace, her daddy, made him marry her, but a couple weeks later, he just disappeared. We looked for him for a while, but we also had an ole boy from up north comes up missing."

Sam broke in, "Greg Pearl, and Greg… uh, Winfred is married down there?"

"Greg?" Jimmy asked.

"Greg Pearl was the name he used up here, and he may have used it to check into the hotel, but he would have used a credit card with the name Dawn Pearl, that's his wife up here," Sam told Jimmy.

"He's married up there too? This is getting better all the time. I'll get some other guys, and we'll see if we can find him," Jimmy said, excitedly. "I'd love cuffing up that sum-bitch, maybe he'll resist."

Sam smiled thinking, "I like this guy, my kind of cop." He looked over at Dawn and Jenna, and they were both giving him that, "What?" look. Sam held up a finger, as to say give him a minute.

"Hey. Listen, Jimmy, if he is not using Pearl's name, he is driving an older red and white Chevy pickup with a yellow "Cat" sticker in the back window, he was an equipment operator up here. He is about 5'9" 280 with bushy brown hair and a beard."

Jimmy told Sam that he would get right on it. Sam and Jimmy

exchanged cell phone numbers and email addresses. Sam then asked that Jimmy call him back, as soon as he knew something.

"Oh wait, Sam," Jimmy said. "Can you send me a mug shot of him and a copy of that marriage license?"

"I don't think he was arrested up here," Sam said looking around the room, seeing a big picture of Dawn and Greg on the wall. "But I think I have a photograph and can get the license."

"Dandy, talk to you soon there, Sammy boy," Jimmy said and hung up.

As soon as Sam hung up the phone, both of the women, said: "What?"

Sam said, "You are not going to believe this."

Sam told them everything that Jimmy had related to him, finishing up the story he told Dawn, "I don't think you will ever have to worry about Greg Pearl again, or whoever he is, sounds like he will be in jail for a long time. This Jimmy Jones really wants him."

Sam thought for a minute and said, "Unless the Smith brothers, the brothers of Wife One get a hold of him first, Jimmy was sure they would kill him. Oh, and if we can prove he was still married down there, you won't have to divorce him, you can get it annulled. Can you email that picture of Greg and a copy of your marriage certificate to him down there?"

Dawn smiled shaking her head yes, but then started to cry, "If he killed the real Greg, so do you think he is the one who killed Jason?"

"Sounds possible, but we will still have to prove it," Sam said.

They sat and talked for a while, Sam gave Jenna a few more details of Jason's death that he couldn't tell her while Dawn was on the suspect list. Sam's text message alert sounded, he looked at his phone. It was Lilly asking where he was. Sam texted her back, saying he was at Dawn's and would be home in a few minutes and explain what was going on.

The time on Sam's phone was 7:22 am. He was glad it was his day off. He told Jenna and Dawn that he better get home, that they were safe from Greg, or whoever, he would let them know of any news. As Sam was walking, out Cappy came out of the hallway and said, "Howdy all, boy it's hard to rest without the sea rocking me to sleep. Leaving so quick, Sam?"

Jenna was explaining that Sam had been there most of the night, and about the phone call. Sam waved as he walked out.

Walking out to his car, Sam noticed the morning heat and humidity had instantly made him start to sweat. From outside, Sam reached in and started the cruiser. Pulling a pack out of his sock, Sam got out a cigarette, lit it, and waited for the car to cool down. While standing there, he got a page from Lilly saying she was going to work and would see him that night. She finished with a kissing emoji. Sam texted back an emoji heart.

With Lilly gone, Sam decided to get some breakfast at the Purple Lotus. Texting Murphy to see if he could meet him at her restaurant, Sam drove off. Thinking how many twists and turns this case was taking: Greg's not Greg but is a bigamist from Missouri named Iggy, who could have killed

Greg. Dawn's having an affair with a guy that Iggy might have murdered, and Aaron the creep is in love with Dawn. Sam just shook his head, took a long draw off of his Camel and drove down the street.

Sam was ordering a Spanish omelet and coffee as Murphy walked in. Murphy told Tilly, "Just my regular," and sat down. "What's up, Sam?" Murphy asked.

Sam proceeded to tell Murphy the whole story of Greg Pearl. Murphy just sat there the whole time in shaking his head in disbelief, which Sam thought funny. To get Murphy Dam to be quiet was hard to do.

"This case is getting nuts, what does your gut say about Greg being our guy, Sam?" Murphy asked.

"I'm not sure, we have him leaving Randy's a little after 4 am, and Aaron followed him way out of town, we know that the time of death is after 5 am, do you think he turned around and killed him, then went to Missouri? I guess it's possible. What do you make of it?" Sam replied.

The both stopped talking when Tilly brought them their breakfast. Sam looked over and thought, Murphy never changes." He had a bowl of oatmeal, with a little brown sugar, milk, and orange juice. "That must be how he keeps that boyish figure," Sam thought. Tilly asked if they needed anything else. Sam said, "What no commentary today?" and Tilly replied, "You two should switch meals," and she turned and left.

Murphy looked at Sam's plate, kind of shook his head with a smile then said, "I think we have a lot more investigating to do. We need a better timeline on Greg, we have several other suspects to question and find. The ones we had in the jail from the raid gave good stories, but we need to corroborate them too. We gotta do this right, Sam."

Sam shook his head in agreement. The two finished the food and was drinking their drinks when Sam said, "I wanted to thank you for how you treated Dawn. I think you shocked her."

"Well, I never did think she did it. I don't know if she has it in her to kill anyone. But, I'm glad it worked out the way it did. What do you think she will do about that creep, Aaron?" Murphy asked.

"I don't know, I think she should get a restraining order on him. That would be the best for now." Both men paid for their breakfasts. This time, Sam left a better tip, feeling sorry for the last time he shorted Tilly, she was an excellent waitress and usually served them quickly when they came in.

Murphy told Sam that he was headed to the jail to talk to Buckman and told Sam to call if he heard anything. Sam said, "I will, I think I'm going home for a nap, it's been a long night."

Chapter 17

Sam did get a nap in, but a short one. He woke at 11:10 am to someone banging around in the kitchen. Sam got off of his recliner and found Jeb piling food on the counter. "What's going on, Jeb?" Sam asked.

"Oh, hi Dad, I forgot my lunch and Harvey stopped by here in between jobs so I could get something." Jeb said while cramming some fried chicken, a few pieces of bread, 2 bananas and a whole box of Pop Tarts in a plastic bag. He said goodbye and left, slamming the door. Sam looked at the mess on the counter and just shook his head as he put things away.

When he got done, Sam figured, since he was up he might as well get some things done around the house. He checked his phone- no messages. He was really hoping he would hear something from someone.

Sam went into his office where his closet was and put on an old t-shirt, pair of bib overalls and a red bandanna on his head. He filled his pockets with the essentials: his favorite knife, a multi-tool, keys, his wallet, pencil and notebook in the bib, and a spare bandanna for cleaning his glasses. Sam also grabbed his iPod and ear plugs. Sam like listing to music when he was mowing, the music and the sound of the mower seemed to block out the world.

Before Sam went out and got on the mower, he grabbed his Glock and Ruger from the closet, then went out and got his 870 Remington shotgun and AR-15 out of the trunk. Sam tore all of the guns down, laying them on some old rags and sprayed them with cleaning solvent to let them soak. It was hot outside but even hotter in the garage so Sam turned on the big fan that he had built and stood in front of it for a few minutes.

After checking the oil and filled the mower with gas, Sam started the mower up and turned up the volume on the iPod. Putting the mower in gear, Sam then drove out of the garage into the sun. The summer had been so dry that the grass almost turned to dust as Sam drove over it. On the first turn a slight breeze blew the cuttings right in Sam's face, making him spit some grass pieces out. Sam could feel the sweat rolling down his back as he mowed. It was hot and miserable, but Sam still enjoyed this time away singing along with the Beach Boys: "I wish they all could be California girls..."

While Sam was finishing up cutting the grass, he noticed some low hanging tree limbs that need trimming. He thought he would get the chainsaw out when he finished mowing. When done, he let Boo out of the house and went back into the garage to get the chainsaw. Sam walked into the breeze that the big fan was making. Then, he stopped and decided to work on the guns for a few minutes and cool down in front of the fan.

Sam had just got done finishing up cleaning the parts of the Ruger as Clifford Duggs rode into his driveway. "Heeey Tam, whatca doin?" Clifford said while getting off of his bike letting fall to the ground.

"Hi Cliff, still out, huh?" replied Sam.

"Yep, washin cars and mowing lawns for Misser Wasson."

Sam grabbed his chain saw, and Clifford followed him around the side of the house.

"Tam, you be carefo cutting those twee limbs, don't be wike me." With that, Clifford fell to the ground with a big thump and started laughing.

Sam remembered that incident very well. Sam thought back, he was just leaving the jail one day a few years back and heard Dispatch send an ambulance to 14 Ohio Street. Sam knew that address well; he had arrested Clifford Duggs at his home many times. You just never knew what you were dealing with when you got a call on him. If he was sober he was usually ok, but drunk or on something, Clifford was dangerous, and at his house, Cliff would have more weapons, so he was more dangerous.

The jail was close to Clifford's house so Sam informed dispatch he would also respond. Jim, one of the paramedics, radioed, "Thanks" to Sam and said they were on their way. When Sam arrived he looked in Clifford's yard, there were chickens, turkeys, and pigs running around. Sam could see Clifford sitting on the ground, leaning against a tree. Clifford was holding his side moaning, lying beside him was a big tree limb, a chainsaw, and a ladder. Sam could imagine what happened, but it was Clifford who verified it, saying, "Oh Tam I hurt, so bad."

Sam told him that the ambulance was on the way, and to relax. "What happened, Cliff?" Sam asked, as he was checking him out.

"Tam, it hurts! I just climbed up the wadder with the taw, and when I cut it, boom! Down we came, and I landed on the limb," Clifford explained. Sam shook his head, trying to hold back a laugh, it was just like he had seen in cartoons as a kid so many times. "You're lucky the chainsaw didn't land you," Sam said, as the ambulance pulled up.

Sam explained what happened, as they all tried not to laugh. They got Clifford loaded up, and off they went to the hospital. A couple hours later, Sam saw the ambulance coming back into town and flagged them down. Sam found out from the medics that Clifford had broken his arm and three ribs. The hospital was going to keep him a couple days. They all had a laugh about it, but Sam thought, "At least he will get a few good meals and cleaned up."

"Yeah, I got hoyt bad dat day Tam, but you resoued me," Clifford said bringing Sam out of his thoughts.

"Yeah, well, Cliff, I'm not climbing any trees today," Sam said. Sam cut off several tree limbs, put the saw down, and was dragging some of them towards his wood pile. As Sam looked behind him, Clifford had gathered the other limbs and was dragging them to the pile, also. Sam thought to himself, "Cliff sure doesn't mind working and helping." Sam stopped and got a long cold drink of water out of the hose. He asked Clifford if he wanted some, and he took a drink and also ran it over his head. Sam was watching, and when Clifford was done, did the same thing, then cleaned his glasses with his bandanna, and soaked it in the cool water and tied it around his neck.

Sam walked back into the garage with Clifford at his heals talking a mile a minute. Sam started wiping down the parts of his 870 Remington with Clifford asking questions all the time, as Sam put the shotgun back together. Sam put the gun to his shoulder and pointed it like he was shooting something in the sky. Doing an action check, Sam shucked the slide and pulled the trigger. "All good," he thought to himself.

Clifford was mocking Sam, acting like he had a gun also, he said, "You got a big boomer Tam, but not tas big as Daddy Hooton. BOOM." Clifford shouted as he threw himself on the ground laughing again. "Daddy Hooton," Sam laughed, he never did know why Clifford called all of the sheriffs, "Daddy." You just never knew what he would come up with. Sam reached down to give Clifford a hand up, off of the garage floor.

Just as Clifford got off the floor, still laughing, Sam heard Willy Fogerty call out a pursuit from the scanner in his garage. Sam grabbed his Ruger, put a magazine in and racked the slide. He stuffed the pistol in the back of his pants, shoved six shells into the magazine of the 870, then shooed Clifford out of the garage. Clifford kept talking, asking questions as he left, heading for his bike. Sam got into his car, hit the garage door opener to close the door, and took off.

Willy had said that he was chasing a four-wheeler by the school. Sam radioed dispatch that he was heading that way. Chief Deputy Oldam radioed he was southbound on Deerhead Road about two miles from the school area. Just as Sam pulled into the school yard, he saw the four-wheeler cut through the woods at the far south end of the field with Fogerty hot on his trail. Fogerty radioed that they were now northbound on Deerhead.

Sam thought if he could get parked fast enough and run through the small trail he had been through just a few days earlier, he could maybe cut the four-wheeler off. Sam could hear the four-wheeler rev up as he started through the small patch of woods. Running through the water in the bottom of the ditch, Sam slipped as he went up the other side. As Sam came out of the woods, the four-wheeler flew by, kicking up dust and gravel.

Sam looked up to the north and saw Oldam coming towards him and the four-wheeler, from the south, Fogerty, was coming up fast. The four-wheeler locked its breaks up right in front of Oldam, who was trying to get shut down. As the four-wheeler slid to a stop, the rider cut it hard to the left and then gunned, it causing the back end to spin around. He headed back to the south. As he did this, the front tires came up off the ground, and the rider tried to hold on, but as he was sliding off of the back end, he just kept cranking on the throttle. Sam watched as the rider fell off of the back of the four-wheeler about twenty yards north of him and as the machine flew past him on the back wheels and crashed into the trees along the side of the road.

Sam had just stood there up till this point, not knowing where any of the vehicles were going to go. The four-wheeler almost hit him, but now he was moving towards the suspect, as was Oldam, who had jumped out of his car.

The rider was trying to get up, but Oldam jumped on his back and was giving him orders to give him his hands. Sam ran up and got there just as Fogerty did, they both pulled an arm out, and they got the suspect cuffed up. Oldam pinned the suspect against the car, and Fogerty pulled off his helmet.

"Well, Well, look who we have here, Wayne Little, I somehow knew you would show up to check on your brother's drug business. Were you at the raid the other night, Wayne?" Fogerty asked.

"There was no reason for you to come back, we took everything. You lost a lot in that raid, didn't you? Hope you weren't being fronted by someone with some power," Oldam added.

Sam asked Wayne, "What were you doing in the school yard, what were you looking for?"

"You haven't got anything on me, I haven't done anything, and you're not even a cop, you're a farmer pirate," said Wayne, looking at Sam.

"Fleeing and reckless is good enough for now," said Oldam.

"No big deal, I'll be out before you can get your paperwork done," Wayne said, laughing.

Oldam searched Wayne, then put him in the back of the car.

"Sam, do you think he could have dumped stuff in the school yard?"

"I don't know. Hey, Willy, you were closer. Did he dump anything?" yelled Sam to Willy, who was calling for a tow truck.

Willy walked back to them, and said, "You know Sam, I don't think Wayne dumped anything. I believe he was looking for something, it's until he saw me, then he rabbited."

"Ok, well I guess you're taking Wayne to the jail. Oldam and I will meet over in the school yard and look it over again," replied Sam.

The other two got back into their cars, and Sam had to search for a minute to find the little trail. As Sam got to the bottom of the ditch, he jumped the water. But, his foot slipped and he reached for something to grab on to. When he did he raked the palm of his left hand on a broken tree limb. "Damn, you have got to be kidding me, now the palms of both of my hands are screwed up," Sam yelled at himself.

He pulled the bandana out of his pocket and wrapped it around his hand. Aggravated with himself, Sam stomped up the little hill and on towards his car. He had left the car running when he got out, it was nice and cold. Sam sat down for a moment, steaming inside, lit a cigarette, opened the window and relaxed. Sam looked over and saw Oldam coming around the woods and drove towards the middle of the field.

As Sam got out of the car, a sad feeling came over him. It had only been a couple of days ago, but so much had happened.

Oldam was getting out of his car and looked at Sam and said, "You ok, Sam?"

"Yeah, but it was such a waste. Hard to believe he is gone… and I hate having found the body. I'll never get that picture out of my mind," Sam said.

"I was talking about your hands; what did you do?" asked Olden.

"Oh, it's nothing, I'm just seeing how much I can bleed this week," Sam said shaking his head.

They both look around for a while, and Oldam saw something glisten in the sun. Yelling to Sam, he said, "Look here Sam, looks like someone did lose something!"

Oldam pointed out a glassine baggie with what looked to be an 8 ball of meth. This was about 30 yards west of where Jason's body had been. Sam guessed they just didn't search far enough out. Sam also noticed a Black Jack Gum wrapper lying near it.

Sam said, "I found a Black Jack wrapper by Jason's body, Black Jack gum on Joe Kerchak, and now this wrapper. There has to be some kind of connection. Maybe I need to go talk to Joe again, and maybe Randy at the store."

Oldam tagged and bagged the evidence, and they walked the area again but found nothing. Sam asked Oldam if he wanted him to come to the jail with him, but Oldam told Sam, "Try to enjoy the rest of your day off, farmer pirate."

"Yo ho ho and a bottle of moonshine," said Sam, with a smile.

Sam got back in his car and looked down at his hands. He still had bandages on the left one from the other day, and the blood was soaking through the bandana on his right. He thought to himself, "If I keep this up, I won't be able to drive by the end of the week." Sam could also feel the pain from running through the woods, and wrestling with Wayne. "Who said these would be the golden years?" he thought. Sam drove home slowly, enjoying one last cigarette and watching the world go by.

Chapter 18

Sam noticed Midg's car in the driveway as he pulled up to home, and figured she must have left school early. She met him at the door with a hug, as Boo circled around his feet. "He can hear you coming from a block away. He jumped down off of your chair a minute ago, and has been by the door ever since."

"Yeah, my little buddy is always here to greet me, then wants to go out." Sam said as he walked to the back patio door letting Boo out. Boo ran around the yard barking at the birds, until there was none still the yard.

"Hey Dad, do you have plans for dinner?" Midg asked.

"Hum, no... you want to take me out?" Sam retorted, smiling.

Midg said, "If I had any money I would, but I was thinking a big pot of your special spaghetti."

"Ohhhh... you want me to cook dinner, I see... I guess I can do that, just for my favorite daughter." Sam joked.

"Well, it's not just for me. When I got back to school, my roommates wanted to know if I brought sauce back. They really loved it last time you sent some back with me. So, when I told them I was coming back, they told me I had to get some more, and I looked in the freezer, and there wasn't any there," Midg said.

"Ok, but hey, how did you get back here so early?" Sam asked.

"My afternoon class got canceled, the professor ran off with the lady who cleans his office, and no one has heard from them in a couple days. So, no class until they find someone to take his place. I got Shelly to take notes in tomorrow's sociology class, so I'm good," Midg reassured Sam.

Sam was going through the cabinets as they spoke, and making a list of things he needed. "Well Midg, I have most of the things, I just need some mild ground sausage and parmesan cheese. But also pick up the makings for a good salad, and some garlic bread," Sam said.

"I'll be back in a few," Midg said turning towards Sam, holding out her hand. "Cash or card, please."

Sam got his debit card out of his wallet and started to give her the pin number, but she said she knew it, and off she went.

Sam went to his office and changed clothes, let Boo back in and fed him, then started getting everything out to make the sauce. He was chopping up the onions as Lilly came in and put her arms around him and gave him a hug.

"What 'cha doin?" Lilly asked.

"Making spaghetti sauce per request of our daughter," Sam said.

"Mmmmm, that sounds good, with a salad too?" Lilly asked.

"Of course, nothing but the best for you," Sam replied.

Lilly asked if Sam needed any help, but he told her he had it handled, so she went off to get changed. Sam continued by dicing tomatoes, banana peppers, mincing some garlic and putting water on to boil.

Sam had everything prepped, but he could not continue until Midg got back. He just then remembered the guns in the garage. He went out, and the heat in the garage was awful, so he gathered everything up and brought it to the kitchen table. He was working on putting his Glock back together when Lilly walked back in and said, "Sam, you know how I feel about those things in the house, but on my antique kitchen table, really?"

"It was so hot in the garage, and I've got rags down. I won't get anything on the table," Sam said. "Besides, they are tore down and unloaded, they can't hurt anything."

"I still don't like them; they make me nervous," Lilly said.

"Ok, I'm almost done, just give me a minute," Sam said.

Sam got the AR-15 back together, put it in the case, packed up his cleaning box and took both of them to the closet in his office.

Midg came back in with several plastic grocery bags. Sam was thinking there was a lot of bags for what he had sent her for when she said, "I have a few more bags in the car."

Sam went looking through the bags looking for the sausage, but mostly found quick prepare meals and snack foods. "Typical college student, stocking up while at home," Sam thought.

When Midg game back in, Sam asked her if she had enough to last a while. She said, "It's just a few things to snack on while studying."

Sam just smiled, found the sausage and parmesan cheese, and started to cook. Spending time in the kitchen was one of Sam's other favorite things, just after being on the shooting range. Sam did most of the cooking at the house. Lilly didn't really like to cook but was a good at it, and Sam had insisted that both of the kids help him cook as they were growing up so they could at least make basic things when they became adults.

Lilly finished up making the salad, and Midg set the table. Jeb came in the front door and said, sniffing the air, "Mmmmm spaghetti, when do we eat?"

They all sat down to dinner. It had been a few weeks since they had all sat down and eaten together. Everyone wanted to know what Sam knew about Jason's murder, but Sam was hesitant on saying much. First of all, he didn't want much information to get out to the public, and second Sam really didn't like mixing his job and home life. The less they knew, the better.

Sam tried to get more information about how Midg was doing in school, but all he got was "Got a 3.5 GPA." Then it went to boys and ballgames, not what Sam wanted to know about.

So Sam asked Jeb if he had any idea if what he wanted to do after high school. Suddenly Jeb got excited. "I forgot to tell you, I met Cappy uh… you know Jenna Kelly's, no, what is her name now, Dad?"

"You know, I keep meaning to ask her, but forget when I talk to her." Sam Said.

"Anyway," Jeb continued. "Cappy said he could use some help on his boat this summer, and if I worked out it could be full time. Wouldn't that be great?!"

"Wouldn't that be dangerous?!" Lilly said.

"What about college?" Sam asked.

"Now wait…" Jeb continued. "It will be a trial run at first, but if I like it, he said if I did well, and studied online, I could work my way up to an officer position or even a captain. There is good money in it."

"But really, Jeb, at sea, being gone all the time…" Lilly started.

"Hold on Lilly, let's look into this a little before we get too far into it. He doesn't even graduate till spring. We could have Cappy and Jenna over and talk to them about it," Sam said.

"Ok," Lilly said with a huff. "But I don't like it."

Sam just smiled at Jeb and continued eating. The rest of the meal was small talk, with Lilly making barbs about her children running off with the circus.

Jeb thought it would be a good idea to volunteer to do the dishes, and Midg put the extra sauce in some containers to freeze. Sam went to his office to check his e-mail and surf the web, Lilly came in and sat down.

"Sam do you think I'm wrong?" Lilly asked.

"Wrong, no. No parent is wrong wanting to protect their child, but we also have to let them find their own path. We didn't stop Jenna from wanting to go to law school just because it would be hard, did we?"

"No, but that's different," Lilly said.

"Not enjoying what you do for a living can be a hard way to go through life. He might try it for a summer and find out it's not as romantic as it sounds," Sam said smiling at her and giving her a hug and a kiss. They just sat there for a long while Lilly snuggled into Sam's arm. Lilly looked down at Sam left hand, and said, "Now what have you done? What am I going to do with you?"

Sam said, "I know, I'm a walking bandage."

"You think you would learn to be a little more careful. Can you even drive like this?" Lilly asked.

"Yeah, drive, shoot, cuff, stuff, all of those cop things. Now, it might be hard to do some Lilly stuff," Sam said laughing, "Anyway I wouldn't feel right if something on me wasn't cut or bruised."

Lilly bandaged Sam's left hand, then looked at the other and rebandaged it. She looked at him and asked, "While I got the first aid kit out, do you have any more boo boos that need to be taken care of?"

"Hmmm if I do, will you kiss it and make it better?" Sam asked.

Lilly poked him a few times with her finger, saying "I'll give you something that hurts." Sam grabbed her and kissed her, and she stopped. They got ready and went to bed, Sam reading and Lilly playing solitaire on her cell phone.

Lilly broke the silence, "Sam, what do you want to do when you retire? It's not that far away."

"I really don't know. I don't think much about it. Wouldn't know what to do if I didn't work." Sam said.

"Well, you like to read, how about writing a book?" Lilly replied.

"A book! Me write a book- my English skills are bad enough, but my typing is hunt and peck. I'd be forever writing a book," Sam said back, shaking his head.

"I think you would be good at it. I listen to you tell all of those police stories when you and your buddies are out at the fire pit. Put those together, and that would be a great book. You have a great sense of humor," Lilly stated.

Sam said, "I don't know, Lilly. Anyway, I still have a few good years in me."

She snuggled up to Sam saying, "Yes you do, Mister, you sure do," and kissing him on the cheek. Sam turned the light off.

Chapter 19

It was 6:00 am and Sam's cell alarm was going off. He reached over with a groan and shut it off. Sam was thinking it was probably going to be a long day, so he might as well get up and going. Lilly rolled over and said, "Wake me before you leave, please, Sam."

"Ok darlin, will do," Sam answered.

Sam headed to the bathroom, and as he was brushing his teeth, he looked in the mirror. "Ugg, I'm looking old," he said under his breath. He felt old that morning. The last few days had been stressful, and he wasn't sleeping well. Twice, he woke up seeing Jason's dead body. Sam had seen a lot of death in the years as a police officer, but never someone that was murdered and was so close to him. His parents had died a few years back, but of natural causes. This was different.

Sam got dressed, did a weapons check as he did every day before going on duty. Sam had a routine that he had done almost every day for the last twenty-seven years. He did it now without even thinking: checking his pockets to see if he had everything, then his gun belt, doing a weapons check, handcuffs, lastly jumping up and down a couple times to make sure he didn't make too much noise when he moved. These were things he read about in an article in a police magazine, and that he had done it since he was a rookie. It was probably the only thing Sam did by habit. His brain usually didn't work that way.

Sam went back into the bedroom, kissed Lilly on the cheek and told her it was 6:45, time to get up. Lilly stretched and said "Ok, love you." Sam, walking out the bedroom door, said, "More."

Sam stepped outside noticing it didn't feel so hot, and there were clouds and a breeze. He hadn't checked the weather this morning, but didn't care what the forecast was as long as it felt this good. Getting into his patrol car, Sam started his daily log then signed on, "Dispatch, City four is ten forty one."

"City four, a Jenna Wallace request you meet her at the Purple Lotus," returned Dispatch.

"Wallace! That's her last name!" Sam said to himself, the answered, "Uh, Clear Dispatch, go ahead and show me out there."

It was just a short drive to the Purple Lotus. Sam parked and went in. He looked around but didn't see Jenna, so he took a seat by the window. As soon as he sat down, he heard a voice behind him say, "Got ya!" It was

Sherri Hall, she started to say something else, but Tilly walked up and asked Sam what he wanted.

Sam said, "Just coffee right now, Tilly."

Again Sherri started to say something and Jenna walked up and sat down. Jenna looked up at Sherri, who had an aggravated look on her face and said, "Oh, I'm sorry, am I interrupting something?"

"No," Sherri snipped as she turned around. She said, "I'll catch you later Sam," as she walked out the door.

"Was that something important, Sam?" Jenna asked.

"No, it will be ok, what's up?" Sam asked.

"I'm just really worried about Dawn. She goes from worrying about one thing to another, but then she is really grieving over Jason. I think if this didn't happen, they would have got married, but now I'm afraid she is going to make herself sick," Jenna said.

Sam thought and said, "You know she is stronger than you might believe she is She just needs to get through this funeral and get back to work… to get her mind occupied."

"Speaking of funerals, Sam, I… well, Dawn and I would like it if you would do the eulogy. Jenna said as a tear rolled down her cheek.

"I would be honored. I think I can do Jason right. He was a great guy, thank you," Sam said handing her his bandana.

They spoke for quite a while, until Sam got a call to go to the station.

"I've got to go, Jenna, but I'll come by and see Dawn a little later Thanks for all you have done for her," Sam said, and turned to go. But then, he turned around and asked, "Hey Jenna, Lilly is worried, how dangerous is it out on a boat like yours?"

"It's safe. Cappy is an excellent seaman, and we are a research ship. We try to stay out of the foul weather, but it is an exciting life. I know your son seemed really interested, we would be glad to have him," Jenna answered.

"Ok, I'll see you later." Sam waved.

Sam drove to the station, thinking about Dawn and everything they had been through and how well she handled bad situations. She seemed to be able to smile through hard times, but this was real personal, and she still didn't have any closure.

Sam pulled up in front of the station and went on in, not expecting Chief Wallow to start yelling at him even before he got into the door. Wallow got into Sam's face and was yelling about the case, the paperwork and never being told what is going on. Sam didn't like people in his personal space, and this included Chiefs of Police. Sam took two fingers and stuck them in Wallow's solar plexus, pushing him backward, and by the look on Wallow's face, causing pain. It was a bad few days, and Sam had had enough! As the first words came out of Sam's mouth and Sam tied verbally into the younger Wallow, Winnie's eyes get bigger. Winnie then decided to disappear into the back room. She didn't want to be a witness if

Sam decked him.

Sam told him, "Listen, I'm tired of your crap. Strutting around here like you're something, but you've never even paid your dues, let alone learned your job. If you had, you would have known where the paperwork was, and how we file cases like this. We not only have our paperwork in order, but we have copies from the Corner's Office and the Sheriff's Department, and everyone else involved. All of us out here have been busting our asses tracking down every lead, and I worked both of my days off. What the hell have you done? And don't tell me you were dealing with the news, this isn't even our case. You should be letting the sheriff's office deal with them, but nooo, you have to be a big man for your little reporter girlfriend!"

Wallow stepped farther back saying, "I don't…"

"Don't even deny it. You don't think I haven't seen you two leaving the bed and breakfast on 5th street early in the morning? You better wise up, a lot of people in town know it, and it won't be long before your wife finds out," Sam stated positively. He was starting to cool down as he watched Wallow's expression go from arrogance to fear.

"I should bring you up on insubordination char…" Wallow tried to get out.

"Insubordination… try it, I'd love it, remember what I told you as a rookie." Wallow just stood and stared at Sam. "A good cop sees everything and knows what is happening in their town," Sam said smiling. "Now if you have a real question for me, go ahead and ask, if not I have work to do!" Sam said.

Wallow looked at Sam, then back at Winnie's desk, but she wasn't there. He turned and went to his office.

Sam went back to his car, huffed and puffed for a few minutes cooling down, then he started laughing. "Damn, that felt good!" Sam said to himself, lighting up a cigarette.

Sam thought back to when Seth Wallow was a rookie. Sam was his training officer, and one night, they were working a midnight shift. Wallow had only been out of the Academy a few days, and Sam was driving. As the night grew longer, Wallow's eyes get heavier, and he finally nodded off about 5:00 am. Sam drove slowly down to the river front, and turned on his red/blue lights and yelled as getting out of the car, "They're getting away, come on let go get them!" Well, the river front at that time of night was pitch black, and Wallow jumped out of the car, into about 4 foot of river water, causing him to go completely under water. Wallow splashed around awhile then finally stood up. He could hear Sam laughing. Sam pulled the car away from the river, and Wallow yelled, "What the hell was that!"

"Just a little rookie initiation, and a reminder not to fall asleep on duty," a lesson Wallow never did learn. He got caught a couple time sleeping on duty while a patrolman, but having his family ties, nothing happened. Sam did understand Wallow being so mad. Max Peters did the same thing to

Sam when Sam was a rookie, so Sam laid a blanket on the seat and took Wallow home so he could change. Sam had had to walk home when it had happened to him.

Three days unpaid leave was what that prank cost Sam. Even though it had been done to every rookie since Sam could remember and before, it had never been pulled on a whinny grandson of the mayor. Thinking back, Sam knew he should have known better, but it was well worth it. The thought made Sam smile.

After dealing with Wallow at the station, Sam needed a drink. He headed to Randy's for a thirty-two-ounce Coke. While there Sam talked to Randy to see if he had heard any scuttlebutt about the murder. Randy said, people were asking a lot of questions, but no one saying anything about a suspect. Sam asked Randy who regularly bought Black Jack Gum. Randy thought a minute, "The only ones can think of Sam is Joe Kerchak, Alvin Clapp, and Greg Pearl, it's not a big seller."

"Alvin Clapp, you mean the old hermit that lives in that shack by the creek?" Sam asked.

"Yeah, he will come in and buy a whole box at a time, probably the only reason I even carry it," said Randy.

"Ok, thanks," Sam said, while thinking. Sam knew Alvin was a strange guy, a real hermit, but he was always roaming around at night, picking up junk and scraps of food. He was about 6-foot-tall and 100 pounds, always looked feeble and a hundred years old with his foot-long gray beard and hair. Then Sam thought, "Well if he snuck up on someone, maybe."

Sam send a text to Murphy and Buckman about Alvin Clapp, and Murphy texted him back that they were close to Clapp's cabin and they would check him out. Sam was glad about that. Alvin probably had not had a bath since the last time he fell in the creek and his, "cabin" was disgusting.

It was about noon, and Sam decided to go check on Dawn. Jenna had seen Sam pull up and yelled at Sam, "Come on in, lunch is ready!"

Sam said he wasn't expecting to be fed, but when he saw fried chicken and freshly picked sweet corn and tomatoes he couldn't resist.

Sam sat down and ate while talking to Dawn, Jenna, and Cappy. Dawn even ate a chicken leg, which he thought strange, he thought she was a vegetarian, but he didn't say anything. Dawn asked if Sam had heard anything back for Missouri, he told her he hadn't, but it had only been a day. She was still worried that Greg was going to come back and cause trouble. Sam hadn't noticed it before, but he looked down and saw that Dawn was wearing her off duty gun. Sam thought that as soon as he left he would call down to Camden County. Dawn didn't need these worries.

Sam heard, through his his walkie radio, Murphy and Buckman sign out of their car on River Road at Little Creek, Alvin Clapp's cabin was under the bridge.

Dawn asked, "What's going on there?" Sam told her that they were just following up on a lead. Dawn said, "Alvin Clapp?"

Sam replied, "No stone unturned."

Sam was getting ready to leave when his phone rang, he answered, pulled out his pen and notepad. Sam sat back down at the table and was writing. Dawn was trying to read Sam's terrible writing, and every time, Sam would say, "Ok," Dawn would say, "What?" This went on for about twenty minutes, and Sam hung up and had a big smile on his face. This time, Dawn, Jenna, and Cappy all said, "What?"

Sam told them, "You are not going to believe all of this!"

"What, Sam?" they shouted.

Sam continued, "The cops down there went to the Three Winds Resort. They didn't have anyone registered by Greg Pearl. When they showed his picture to them, the girl at the desk said, "Oh yeah, that jerk, he tried to proposition me when he checked in. He's in room 324. I hope he's wanted for something."

Sam continued with the story, "They went to the room and knocked, but no one answered, and the desk clerk let them in."

Sam started to laugh, and all three again, said, "What?"

"Well, Greg was whacked out of his mind, on drug or alcohol or both, and for some reason, he was only wearing a thong and his body was covered with Vaseline and baby powder."

Everyone burst out in laughter. "The room was trashed and..." Sam stopped to listen to a call on the radio.

"City three to dispatch, have the coroner signal 8 this location," Sam heard Murphy say. Sam got a perplexed look on his face and stopped with his story.

Sam asked everyone to hold on a minute, and he called Murphy on his cell. "Hey Murph, you need me to come down there?"

"No, hell I don't want to be here, it's disgusting!" Murphy said, and continued, "But, I think you can take old man Clapp off of the suspect list, he's been toast for several days."

"Do ya need any Vicks or a cigar?" Sam asked.

"No, I had some Vicks in the car, and you know Buckman with his stogies," Murphy replied.

"Ok, but if you need anything just call me, I'm at Dawn's. Oh and they picked up Greg in Missouri," Sam said.

"Good to hear, do we have a timeline on him yet?" asked Murphy.

"No, but more information. I'll get with you later," said Sam.

Sam looked over at the group. He could tell they couldn't wait to hear the rest of the story, but what he liked best was he could see Dawn's face with a smile.

"Ok. Greg did try to fight them, hitting one of the officers with a lamp, but then he turned and ran out to the balcony and took a dive right off it. He landed on a limo parked out front of the hotel and smashed through the sunroof, breaking both legs, his shoulder, and several ribs. The worst part for him, he ripped his balls almost completely off. The doctors told Officer Jones that they may not be able to re-attach them," Sam said, trying to hold back from laughing.

Jenna and Cappy were also trying not to laugh, but not doing a god job of it. Dawn just had this huge smile on her face. Sam then said, "And guess whose car it was?" Everyone was laughing too hard to ask, they just looked at him. "The Chief Justice of Missouri's Supreme Court, he and his wife," Sam said, laughing "… were covered in Greg's blood, before officers could get them out. It must have been a mess."

Dawn said, "He deserves everything he gets, Sam. Do you still think he could have killed Jason?" Dawn looked saddened.

"Doesn't look like it, he checked into the resort at ten forty-two am, and I don't think he could have killed Jason and got down there that quick. But, I still have to run the times and check a few other things," Sam said, reluctantly.

Dawn's eyes were welling up again, so Sam said, "But I might have some more good news from down there. In the room they found several pieces of the real Greg Pearl's identification including a class ring from Cicero High School with Greg Pearl's name engraved in it. So, they think they may have enough to make a case on murder, kidnapping or maybe both. And, in Greg's… hell, I don't know what to call him, anyway…in his truck was a handgun and $37,000 dollars in cash."

Dawn perked up and said, "My money, is it my money Sam?"

"I don't know Dawn, but we will try to get it back for you," Sam said patting her on her hand.

Jenna asked, "What else did he say, Sam?"

"That's about it, they did say it would be a few days before they could even talk to him at the hospital, but they have him under guard. It's not like he's going to run off, but more to protect him from the Smith Brothers if they find out he's there. Oh… Lee Smith never filed for divorce from him, so they are legally married, so he is a bigamist too! They are going to try to get all the paperwork ready before he can be arraigned in court and hit him with everything at once. Those people down there really don't like him, but they are going to keep him for a long time!" Sam told all of them.

Sam noticed himself nibbling on another chicken leg, which he really didn't need, but was so good. He looked at his phone, and it was almost 1:30 pm. He thought he'd probably been there long enough, he had better get back on the street. He asked Dawn if she needed anything else. She just shook her head no. He could tell she was in deep thought, so he had just started towards the door when Jenna said, "I'll walk you out."

"Sam, thanks. Knowing that Greg is not coming back is going to take a lot of worry off of her mind. I never met him, but he must have been a piece of work. Now if we can just get her through the funeral tomorrow, I think she will be ok," Jenna said.

"Yeah, she's tough, but tomorrow will be a long and rough day," Sam stated with a nod.

"How is the eulogy coming along, Sam? Oh… did I tell you that the governor is coming?" Jenna added.

Sam coughed, "It was going ok, till now! The governor… anyone else?"

"Just some lawyers and business people from Chicago, I'm not really sure, oh the Illinois State Police are sending their Honor Guard," Jenna said.

"Well the honor guard is great. He deserves it, but I have to talk in front of all those people. I thought it was just going to be a little local funeral," Sam said, shaking his head.

"I'm sorry Sam, I couldn't tell them they couldn't come. Anyway, our little church will only hold so many. You aren't going to back out on me are you, Sam?" Jenna asked.

"No, Jason deserves his life remembered right, and I guess I know more about him than most anyone, besides you…well, maybe Dawn," Sam said with a smile. "I won't let you down, I'll see you tomorrow."

Sam took a tour around town, trying to get some thoughts together for the eulogy. He wondered if he should make notes, "No," Sam said to himself, "This has to come from the heart." He decided he would pick out four or five points that made Jason the man he was and that should be long enough to show respect, but not so long to get boring.

Turning the car down River Road, Sam thought he would check out what was happening there with Alvin Clapp. He pulled up and stopped on the bridge when he got out of the car he got a whiff of a terrible smell. "What the hell is that!" he asked himself.

The only vehicles there was Murphy's car and one of the fire trucks. The truck had its generator going, and several power cords were running under the bridge where the cabin was. Sam figured they needed some lighting because he knew Alvin didn't have electricity there.

Murphy came out from under the bridge and walked up to where Sam was standing. As soon as Murphy came closer, Sam almost gagged, "Oh Murph, you reek, that's disgusting!"

"You think it's bad out here you should be down there, it's bad, really bad. You wouldn't believe it!" Murphy said.

"I smelled some bad dead bodies, but...WOW!" said Sam, moving upwind from Murphy.

"The body is gone, it's everything else. He has buckets of crap, and I mean crap, milk jugs full of urine. I don't know why he didn't just go in the woods. There is rotten food everywhere, and you know when a possum or a coon gets ran over and sits on the road long enough to look like a furry pizza?" Murphy asked.

"Uh... yeah," Sam said.

"He has stacks of them, probably a few hundred. Why? I don't know, but this is the day from hell. Did they tell you about the body?"

"No," Sam answered, trying not to breathe.

"It was almost like a mummy. You know, like the one we had on 3rd street, maggots everywhere, and I think something chewed his foot off… (Murphy shivered) …anyway, we figured we would just lift him with the blanket and put him in the body bag, no problem right? Oh no! When we lifted him, the blanket ripped, and his spine come through and what was left of his organs spilled all over the bed. (Murphy shivers again and gags.) Everyone lost it, even B.J., and I've never seen anything bother him!"

"That's crazy, what are you going to do?" Sam asked.

"The fire department is in there now with their breathing tanks. B.J. and Buckman are directing from the door. I had all I can stand. We all agreed from the body position that it was a massive heart attack, so that will be the cause of death. The cabin and stuff inside will have to be bulldozed."

"I'd do something before you get home, you will never get the smell out of those clothes," Sam said, sidestepping Murphy.

"Oh, you can bet on it," Murphy replied. "Anything new in the real world?"

Sam filled Murphy in on the conversation with Jimmy Jones in Missouri. They both laughed at the antics of Greg Pearl and was glad he was in custody with several charges pending.

"Do you think he is still a suspect?" Murphy asked.

"I doubt it, I don't think he could have killed Jason and got to Missouri when he did. I hate to say it, but I think we can mark him off the list," Sam said.

"There's not much left on the list. We talked to the ones from the raid, this morning before we got this call, and it looks like nothing good there," Murphy said.

"Did you talk to Wayne Little?" Sam asked.

"You mean Tommy? No, he lawyered up, and we know where he was at the time of the murder. Do you think he had something to do with it?" Murphy asked.

"No I mean Wayne, Tommy's brother. We arrested him yesterday, close by where we found Jason's body, and we also found an eight ball of meth near there. We figured he was looking for it," Sam told Murphy.

"I don't think Buckman has talked to him. I'll check, but this is the first I've heard of it," Murphy said, shaking his head. "You know this case has gotten completely crazy We have paperwork coming from everyone, I can't even keep up reading all of it. At least the feds are going to take over the case from the raid on Tommy Little, I guess several of the guns were stolen from out of state, and the big bottles of Sudafed came from an Indiana pharmaceutical warehouse burglary. That will free Buckman and Main up some."

"That's good, but I just wish we could get a really solid lead in Jason's murder. I feel so sorry for Dawn and Jenna, I know the not knowing is killing them," Sam said.

"Yeah, I heard you are going to do the eulogy. That's going to be tough," Murphy said.

"In a way, it will, but… Jason did so many good things, it actually won't, if I can just get through it without breaking down," Sam replied.

Murphy started to pat his friend on the back, Sam's eyes got wide, and he stepped away, Murphy looked at his hand, and they both got a little laugh.

"Ok…well I will see you tomorrow morning. Bring any new paperwork with you. I think since everyone will be there, we are going to get together after the wake," Murphy said as he started back down into the creek.

Getting back in the cruiser, Sam began to drive away, but his phone rang. It was Jimmy Jones from Missouri, so he pulled back over and put the car in park.

Jones told Sam that they found a long suicide in Winfred/Greg's room. In the note, he said that he knew about his wife having an affair. Greg was sure she was checking up on him and was afraid she knew his real name. In the note, he also wrote that 10 years ago, he had heard about a wealthy tourist that wanted to go hunting and fishing and needed a guide, so he devised a plan to get the guide job, kidnap him and get a ransom. After he had got Greg Pearl out to a backwoods cabin, Pearl died. He didn't say how, and he couldn't find anyone to contact in Cicero. Winfred wrote that he cut the body up into small pieces and dropped the parts in different areas of the lake. Winfred then became Greg Pearl and used all of his identification and property. That's when he moved to Illinois.

Sam said, "That's great, you have a real kidnapping case and at least manslaughter case."

"Yeah, he's pretty much toast here, but I think I have some bad news for you. We found a receipt from a McDonald's in Sikeston, Missouri and it looks like he went through the drive through at 6:42 am. That puts him out of your timeline, doesn't it?" Jimmy asked.

"Sure does, damn it! I've driven there many a time, and there is no way he could have been here at the time of death. Well, back to the square one," Sam said.

Jones told Sam he would send him the receipt and also keep him up on what the judge did with Winfred's marriage down there.

Sam thanked him, saying, "Talk to ya soon, maybe I'll bring Lilly down there on vacation."

"That you wife? We would be glad to have ya, I got a cabin you can stay in," Jimmy Jones said.

"That sound great," Sam said thinking. "It would be great to get away now."

Sam took another pass through town waiting for evening shift to sign on. When he got home, Sam went to his office, took off his clothes, and got out his dress uniform. He tried it on to make sure it still fit, as he had not had it on in a couple years. The uniform was a little snug but would be ok. The worst parts were going to be the neck and getting that top button, buttoned for a tie.

Sam sat down at his desk and polished his brass and shined his leather gun belt. Sam hesitated about putting all the awards and accomplishment metals on, but he figured everyone else would, so he should. The eulogy was on Sam's mind as he was putting the uniform together and he decided he would stop and make some notes on what he wanted to say.

Sam hung the uniform back up, then reached up to the top of his closet and got his dress hat and shoes. He brushed the dust off of them and sat them on the desk. Sam was glad he didn't have to wear those patent leather shoes too much, they always hurt his feet, but they always had a shine.

After he had everything together, Sam opened a window and enjoyed a cigarette, well at least till he heard Lilly come in. "Sam, are you smoking in the house?!"

Chapter 20

Sleep escaped Sam that night. Between thinking about the case, and thinking about what he wanted to say in the eulogy, he could not turn his mind off. Sam gave up at 4:30 am, he got a cup of coffee and when out on the front porch to smoke. It was still in the 80's even at this time of the morning, but there was a good breeze. Checking the weather app on his phone, Sam saw it was going to be near 100 degrees during the day and cloudless. He just hoped the wind would keep blowing. "Not a good day for an outside funeral," Sam thought.

They had to move the funeral to the riverfront park when they realized that the guests were going to be too many for the little church. Sam thought that Jason would approve of the change. He would often see Jason eating his lunch sitting in his car, watching the river go by. There was some shade at the park. The service would be in the bandstand, which had a roof, and there were several old trees in the park, but it still would be hot.

Pulling up the Peeks' Funeral Home website, Sam looked at Jason's Memorial page. He could not believe how many people had posted sympathy notes in the comment section. While going down different messages, one caught Sam's eye. He couldn't believe what he was reading. It was posted by someone who said his name is Mack Knife and read "It's good when bad things happen to people who use their power to hurt ordinary citizens. BIH!"

"Well, we have another suspect if we can figure out who he is," Sam thought. Sam thought it must be someone older, due to the use of "Mack the Knife" reference, and since the writing was pretty good.

As Sam was thinking about the comment, he noticed a police car go by. They must have seen him sitting on the porch also because its brake lights lit up, then backup lights. The car pulled to the curb and parked, Brandon Teasdale stepped out, and yelled, "What are ya doing up so early?!"

"Shhhhh! Brandon, people, are sleeping," said Sam in a loud whisper.

Brandon walked up to the porch and took a seat next to Sam. "What are you doing Sam?" Brandon whispered.

"Smokin and thinkin, just smokin and thinkin," Sam said.

"Do ya think that there is any way the horse…" Brandon started.

"No!" Sam yelled, but then caught himself and whispered, "Brandon, get the horse out of your mind." Sam thought for a minute. "You are kind of good with this computer stuff aren't ya?" Sam asked.

"Yeah, I know some stuff. Why?" asked Teasdale.

"There is this post on Peeks' website. Is there any way to find out who wrote it?" Sam asked.

"It will be easy. I can get the IP address of people who register and post if Mr. Peeks will let me into his website dashboard," Teasdale told Sam.

"Great. Tomorrow after the funeral, ask B.J. and see what you can find. This might be the break we need," Sam said excitedly.

"Do you want me to ask him now?" Teasdale asked.

"No, no, B.J. will be sleeping, and he will have a long day tomorrow, or today. In fact, so will I. I'm going to try to get a nap now," Sam said getting up, heading for the door.

Teasdale got up, and said, "Ok Sam, I'll see you at the funeral."

"Goodnight, Brandon," Sam replied.

Sam went back inside. He knew he still would not be able to sleep, but he wanted to jot a few notes down. He went into his office and sat back in his chair as he wrote. He was excited that he might actually have a suspect. All of the rest fell away so quickly, and the list was almost down to nothing.

Sam wrote down several questions he had for Murphy and Buckman. He needed to know how to get a warrant for a computer case. Did they need to get a computer expert from the state police or would Brandon be able to do what they needed and testify on it?

As Sam was thinking, he felt his stomach growl. The sandwich he had

had for dinner was not holding him over. He looked at the time on his phone. It was 6:42 am, and Sam figured Lilly would be up in about 30 minutes, so he would fix some pancakes for both of them. He walked into the kitchen as Boo came running out of the bedroom. Sam opened the porch door, letting Boo out. Sam got everything out and started cooking.

Lilly came out of the bedroom and asked, "What are you doing Sam?"

"Just making us a hearty breakfast, it's going to be a long day."

"Yes, it will be, a long, sad day. I know you are going to be busy. If it's ok, I will stay close to Dawn and Jenna, just in case they need something," Lilly said.

"That would be great," Sam said, kissing Lilly. "You are the best."

They ate their breakfast together, talking about the eulogy. Lilly thought Sam should have some notes, but Sam thought it would seem too impersonal. After eating, Sam went to his office and Lilly to their bedroom to get dressed.

Sam put on all the extras, including white gloves he had on his belt. The only problem was he could not get the button at his neck fastened. He walked into the bedroom to ask for Lilly's help, but when he saw her he stopped and just said, "WOW! I haven't seen you in that black dress for a long time… Still fits you, as it should." He went up behind her, giving her a hug.

He showed Lilly his button problem, and she dug into her jewelry box and found a little button extender. She put it on him and fixed his collar and tie, then stood back and said, "Looking sharp, Sam."

"I'm glad I don't have to wear all this brass and tie every day," Sam replied. They both took turns with the lint roller, getting Boo's fur off of them, which was a regular habit at their house.

There was already a crowd when Lilly and Sam got to the river park. Several limousines parked nearby, which was unusual in their small town. Lilly went off to find Dawn, Jenna, and Cappy. Sam went to find the other pallbearers. Sam was impressed with the number of people in attendance. B.J. had done a good job arranging everything. He almost had enough seats for everyone and had arranged the chairs so most of them were in the shade. Besides the heat, it was a beautiful day on the riverfront.

B.J. Peeks called everyone together and waited until the last few people filed past the casket. Reverend Chapman started off with a prayer, then a reading from Romans. Sam was up next. As he stood up he saw Lilly, then looked at Dawn, who looked back up at him with tear-filled eyes. A lump grew in Sam's throat. He glanced at Jenna, but then looked over the crowd to the river before he started crying himself. Sam kept his message upbeat, focusing first on childhood memories, then on all of the good Jason had done in his career and his personal life. When Sam mentioned the loss of Jason's parents is when almost lost it, he had to clear his throat and take a drink of water. Sam ended by saying "I hope that the spirit of Jason Kelly would stay with all of you, and you will remember the way he has touched each of us."

There was a moment of silence and another prayer by Reverend Chapman. Sam stepped down from the bandstand and met up with the other pallbearers. The Color Guard took the flag off of coffin, folded it ceremoniously, and presented it to Jenna. The casket was closed, and they carried it back to the hearse. Jason had in his will that he be cremated, so there was no trip to the cemetery. However, B.J. announced that there was food set up by several civic groups in town at the south end of the park, and everyone was welcome to stay, eat and celebrate Jason's life.

Sam went to find Lilly, and she was still with Dawn and Jenna, who were surrounded by people giving their condolences. Dawn had asked Sam and Lilly to come by her house after everything was over, she said she wanted to spend the evening with close friends.

Sam was surprised when the Governor came up to him and commended him on the eulogy. After he had left, Lilly hugged him and whispered in his ear, "You did good Sam, you made everyone laugh and cry." To Sam's surprise, he didn't remember any of it, only the river flowing by.

Lilly told Sam to go eat, she was going to stay close to Dawn and Jenna, and she would meet him at Dawn's house. Sam got a heaping plate full of all kinds of food. He had never seen so much food. He found Murphy and Buckman and several other officers already eating and sat at the end of the table, listening to an update on the case. Teasdale had already told them about the message on the funeral home site. Buckman was sure that B.J. would have no problem letting them have access but thought they should get a warrant just in case. Buckman said, "We have time, the State's Attorney is here. I'm sure he can type something up pretty quick, and the judge is here too so we can have it in no time."

The rest of the conversations went to the lack of local suspects. Murphy said, "We have gone through the whole list, talked to everyone and verified their alibis. John and I have reviewed every video we can find on that morning. What we did see is the movement of all of us... going to and from the raid. The question that brings up is, did someone know about the raid and decide it would be a good time to kill Jason since so many of us were busy, but then how would they know where Jason would be and how did they get to him?"

Sam sat and listened to the conversation, and got more depressed as the morning drew on. By noon, almost everyone was gone. Sam and Murphy went down and sat on some stairs that led to the dock. Both of them had a handful of pebbles and were trying to hit a leaf that was floating in the river. "Murph, we need to find the bastard who did this," Sam said.

"I know... I've been racking my brain, over every part of this case. I've walked that field so many times...thought about the metal...Hey Sam, was there any copper pipe at those oil tanks at the other side of the field?"

"I don't know, never thought to check," Sam said as they looked at each other and got up. As they walked to their cars, Sam looked over and saw a single figure sitting underneath one of the trees by the river bank.

Sam said, "I'll meet you out there, Murph."

Sam could see it was Clifford Duggs under the tree. As he walked up, he could see Clifford was crying. "What's wrong Cliff?" Sam asked.

"I mist Jason, he always helped me." Sam sat down and put his arm around Clifford and Clifford leaned into Sam like a little boy would with his dad when he was upset. "He would bring me horse poop for my garden and help me fix things around my house, now who will?"

"Jason was good to a lot of people," Sam said.

"Who will write letters to my sister in Tincity?" Clifford continued.

Sam smiled. he knew that Clifford's sister was in a nursing home in Cincinnati, Ohio. "I could always help you write them, Cliff," Sam said trying to comfort him.

"And help me fix my house, pay for my lectric and water?" Clifford said excitedly.

"Yeah, Cliff, I can probably do that, but right now I need to go meet Murphy. Will you be ok?" asked Sam.

"Yeah, I'm otay, just going to tit here for a while," Clifford said.

"Ok, I'll talk to you later in the week. No drinking, now," Sam told Clifford.

"Hehehe, Dats what Jason would always tay," Clifford answered.

Sam drove to the school grounds and across the dusty field where he had found Jason Kelly's body. He shivered as he drove through the area. He pulled off his tie and unbuttoned the top button of his shirt. Murphy was already out of his car around the concrete slab in front of the oil tanks.

"Hey Sam, come look at this," Murphy said holding up a pipe. Sam looked at an old looking copper pipe that had its end crushed and gnarled up. "What do you think?" Murphy said pointing to some fibers in the breaks on the end of the pipe.

Sam touched the fibers, looked at Murphy and said, "Steel wool, I've used it when doing some plumbing at my house."

"There's also something else on the end of the pipe, do you think it could be blood, Sam?" Murphy asked.

"I don't know, but we need to get it to the lab," replied Sam.

Murphy bagged the piece of pipe and locked it in his trunk. "Ok, at least we still have something to work on."

They talked for a minute, and Murphy got a text from Buckman saying he had the warrant in hand. They had spoken to B.J. after the funeral, and he gave them the username and password, saying he would do anything to find the murderer. Murphy told Sam that he would let him know if anything came up, or he would see him in the morning.

Sam drove to Dawn's. Lilly met him at the screen door and gave him a big hug and kiss. They went inside. Dawn was curled up on a big chair, Jenna and Cappy on the couch. Reb Main was at the kitchen table that was piled with food. Other close friends mingled around the house. Jenna asked Sam if he was hungry, but Sam couldn't think of eating anymore after the lunch at the park.

As soon as Sam sat down the questions started, Sam filled them in on what he knew. When Reb learned about the pipe, it peaked his interest. Reb said his goodbyes and went off to find Murphy. They sat for a long time telling stories about Jason, laughing some and crying a lot. Dawn fell asleep in the chair. Jenna covered her up and asked everyone to go outside. Outside, hugs and goodbyes went on for several minutes until it was just Sam and Lilly left. Sam asked Jenna how long she and Cappy would be staying. She told them that Cappy had to go back in a few days, but she was going to stay for a while and try to take care of Jason's estate. "The house is in both of our names, so I may just keep it, I'll have to think this out," Jenna said.

Sam and Lilly drove home, neither saying anything on the way. Once home, Sam took off his clothes and put on a robe, even though it was still daylight. He sat down on the couch, and Lilly also came into the living room, and lay on the sofa with her head on Sam's lap. They both just sat there in silence with Boo at their feet.

Chapter 21

Sam slept hard that night, and was awoken by Boo breathing in his face. Boo didn't bark or scratch to wake up Sam, he would just stand next to his head and stare him in the eye, his hot breath right in Sam's mouth. Sam said, "Ok Boo, I'll let you out." With that, Boo would jump off of the bed and head straight for the patio door and dance around until Sam could get there. Sam pushed the start button on the coffee maker and sat at the kitchen table, watching Boo chasing and barking at birds.

After all the birds were gone, and Boo had done his business, Boo would want to come in, unless, like this morning, Sam took his coffee and went to the patio. Boo would sit next to Sam so Sam could pet him and they would enjoy the quiet time. Sam finished his coffee, went inside and got dressed.

Sam left home and drove straight to the station. Dawn was still off, and he would be the only one working day shift. He unlocked the door because

Winnie didn't come in until 8 am. He went through the door and down the hall to the squad room and almost bumped into Chief Wallow who was going across the corridor. "Good Morning Sam," Wallow said and continued into his office.

Sam smiled, thinking, "I guess our little talk had an effect." Sam didn't want to press his luck, so he grabbed the paperwork from the day before and headed back out.

Sam had a little time to kill until the State's Attorney's office opened. He decided he would go to the Purple Lotus for a cup of coffee and a bite to eat. He walked in and sat down at his favorite table by the window. Outside, Sam saw Sherrie Hall walking across the street. She turned to go down the sidewalk, passing by the window where Sam was sitting. Sam knocked as Sherrie walked by. She looked up with a start and Sam motioned for her to come in. Sherrie smiled and turned around, hurrying in. Sam pointed to the seat across from him, but she sat next to him, grabbing him by the arm saying, "Finally I got you all to myself!"

Sam looked around at all of the people in the diner and thought that this may not have been a very good idea. Sherri asked, "Are you still as good as you use to be?"

Sam thought to himself, "How does she remember/know how I use to be?" But he said, "Yeah...I guess so."

"Remember the time down by the lake?" Sherri asked.

Now Sam was racking his brain, thinking, "Was we drinking?" But he replied, "Uh, yeah that was fun."

"Sam I need you…" Sherrie started when Miss Val walked by and asked Sam how Joe was doing. Sam told her he was in jail, and was having some withdrawal, but they were taking care of him. Miss Val, thinking Sherri was Sam wife said, "You two make such a pretty couple. You got a catch, Sam." Both of them laughed but didn't try to correct her, because she said she was in a hurry and walked off.

Sam just sat the dumbfounded at what was going on, Sherri turned to him, this time, she got her mouth real close to his ear and said, Sam, I want you to…" Boom! Brandon Teasdale plopped in the chair across from Sherri. He blurted out, "Hi Sam, Hi Lil-ly, oops you're not Lilly."

"No Brandon, this is Sherri Hall, a friend from high school, she just came into town to visit. Sam said.

"Oh, I see," Brandon said with a smile.

Sam asked, "Brandon what do you want?"

"Oh, Sam we found out who posted that message, it was…" Sam held up his hand.

"A lot of ears around here Brandon, that's not for everyone to hear, I'll talk to you later," Sam said sternly.

Brandon gave that sad puppy look again, and got up saying, "Ok, sorry." He started to walk away but turned and said, "Oh, nice to meet you." Then he walked out of the diner.

"Ok, Sam I'm just going to come out and say it," Sherri stated in a louder and stern voice.

Sam got embarrassed, and said, "Can you keep it down a little? There's a lot of people here."

"Oh yeah, some people still get upset about it," Sherrie said.

Sam just looked at her and said, "Yeah!"

"It just that it's been so long…" Sherrie started to continue, when Tilly asked if they were ready to order.

Sherri just asked for some toast, Sam said, "I think I've lost my appetite." His head was spinning at this point.

Sherrie reached over and grabbed Sam's face in both of hands and said, "Before we get interrupted again, Sam, I need to learn to shoot." She let go of his face, looked down and continued, "My ex-husband is acting a little nuts. I don't think he would come here, but I want to be able to protect myself."

Sam looked at her, breathed a sigh of relief and said, "Shoot… a gun…sure no problem, we can go out to the range some afternoon."

"Can we go alone, I don't want anyone to know," Sherrie said, squeezing Sam's arm again.

"Sure," Sam said, thinking, "Unless Lilly wants to go."

"Oh thank you, Sam, I feel better already," Sherrie said, putting her arm around him and kissing him on the cheek.

Sam turned bright read, gulped down his coffee, then his whole glass of water, Sherrie laughed at him a bit, then they discussed guns, which made Sam more comfortable. Sherrie told Sam that her father had several guns, rifles, shotguns, and pistols. Sam told her he would come by and look at them, and that she should learn at least the pistols and shotguns.

Sam watched Sherri finish her toast, and wished he had ordered something to eat, he was hungry now. When Sherrie was done, Sam told her he had better get back to work. She gave Sam her cell phone number and said he could call her anytime.

Sam got back in his car, and when he started it up, "Baby I want you," by Bread was playing on the radio. Sam thought about Sherrie, and how he never knew how she felt about him, even when they were younger was she just teasing him. And now? Sam just shook the thoughts out of his mind, and got his mind into the case at hand, well mostly.

Sam drove around for a while. As he was going by the police station, he noticed Murphy coming out, so he quickly turned in and pulled up next to him. He yelled out, "Hey Murph, got time to take a turn around town."

"Yeah, I got a few minutes." Murphy said while getting into the car.

Sam pulled off, not wanting to stay at the station, when Murphy started in, "Winnie said Wallow and you got into it, what happened?"

"He started in on me the night before the funeral, I guess I had too much on my mind, and hell, just snapped and let him have it. I even told him I knew about him and that reporter. Well anyway that shut him down. What does Winnie know? She unassed the area when we started."

"Oh no, you know Winnie she doesn't miss a beat. She was just outside the room. She heard everything, and heard Wallow on the phone to Rhonda, telling her that they had been caught and they needed to talk." Murphy was laughing, and followed up with, "Shoot, I guess he has taken off the rest of the day. He told Winnie he may not be in tomorrow either. She was supposed to let McDollin know he is in charge until further notice, you must have really rattled his cage."

"Yeah, I guess so. Anyway, what's going on with Jason's case?" Sam asked.

"Wait, speaking of rattling cages, wasn't that the Sherrie girl that you said rattled yours when you were younger, that you were having breakfast with this morning?" Murphy teased.

"Yes it was, but no big deal, she just wants me to teach her to shoot," Sam said.

"Are you sure she just doesn't want to get your weapon…?" Murphy continued.

"Stop, it's nothing, back to business. What's going on? Sam demanded.

Murphy explained that they found out it was Harold Mookie who left that message, and they were going to get a warrant to search his computer today. Sam knew Mookie, but could not ever remember arresting him. He was an old hippie who never seemed to grow up. Mookie lived off of his parents until they died, and even since then he lived in his parents' house. Living off of his inheritance until he blew all of it, Mookie then got himself on disability, somehow. No one ever remembered him working and the beautiful old craftsman house they lived in, he had let just crumble around him.

He hardly ever ventured outside, but most people knew him from his Facebook page and Blog where he was always complaining about how the government mistreated the people. He called himself an anarchist, but Sam though he didn't have enough gumption to actually do anything. Sam understood that Mookie didn't like the government in general, but he didn't think he even knew Jason and didn't know why he would write something like that.

"What do you think is going on there Murph?" Sam asked.

"I don't know Sam, with a weirdo like Mookie, you never know. But, we are about to find out!" Murphy said.

Buckman called Murphy to say that the warrant was ready to search Harold Mookie's house and seize his computer. Sam drove Murphy back to the station to get his car. Murphy got out, came around the car and said, "You coming to help?"

"I'll drive over there, but I better stay close to my car, I'm the only one on today," Sam said.

"See ya there… oh, Buckman and I are driving to Chicago tonight to do some interviews with the feds. If anything comes up, call me," replied Murphy.

At 738 Pine Street, Murphy and Buckman pulled up along with Sam and Deputy Kent Phillips, who went to the back of the house. Buckman knocked and announced that they were police serving a search warrant. A voice came from inside the house, "This is a sovereign nation, I don't recognize your warrant or your court." With that Buckman kicked in the old door almost taking it off of the hinges.

As soon as he stepped inside, both Murphy and Buckman were hit by a strong odor of marijuana. They found Mookie hiding in the bathtub with a big blanket covering him. They cuffed Mookie up, and Buckman told him, "You are not under arrest at this point, we are just securing you for your and our safety." To which Mookie replied, "Gestapo, you have nothing on me. I am not a citizen of your country. You can't arrest me; I have immunity."

Buckman had Deputy Phillips come around front and sit with Mookie on the front porch. Sam sat with them for a few minutes, but had enough of listening to Mookie's ramblings. Sam said, "I got to go. Either he has lost it, or he is really, really high…. or both."

As Sam was pulling away, Murphy and Buckman were already carrying the computer equipment out. Sam drove towards the town square and circled the area for a few minutes, checking on the shops. As he turned onto 2nd Street Sam noticed Dawn, Jenna, and Cappy going into the Fuwalda. He figured it was for lunch and beer, and it was good to see Dawn out. "Rhythm of my Heart" by Rod Stewart came on the radio. Sam drove to the side streets so he could sing along. So far this had been a nice quiet day for Sam. He wished he had clues to work on, but the leads in the case were wearing out, and the detectives had most things covered.

Sam was enjoying just cruising when he saw Tom Casey waving at Sam. Casey said, "Sam you need to do something. Those kids, they about gave me a heart attack."

"What happened, Tom?" Sam said stepping out of the car.

"They put a cat in my mailbox, when I opened it up, it jumped out, and I about came out of my skin," Casey said.

Trying hard to keep from laughing, Sam asked, "Do you know who it was?"

"No, but all of these kids just run the streets all the time, getting into things," Casey complained.

"Ok, I'll make a complaint on it and see if I can find some to talk to," Sam assured Casey.

"I hope so; a guy could die from a surprise like that," Casey said walking back towards his house.

Sam made a note on his daily log sheet and kept giggling, it brought back a funny incident from his youth.

Growing up, there were always cats around Sam's house. His mother loved cats, and said they kept the mice away. There were so many you could hardly walk across the porch without tripping over one trying to get in the house. Sam thought he could not have been much more than 6 or 7, and he was with his mother in their old 1946 Plymouth Coupe on her way to take him to school on a frigid morning.

On this morning, Sam's mother noticed they needed gas and pulled into the Sinclair Station. His mother pulled up to the pumps, and the attendant came out. His mother told him to fill it up. After getting the gas started the man went around to check the oil. When he popped the hood, there had been a cat trying to stay warm on the engine. It must have gotten really scared when the engine started running and couldn't get out. When the hood went up, the cat pounced out and wrapped itself around the attendant's face. He took off running and screaming around the lot, trying to get the cat off. Mom panicked, and Sam cracked up. This story was told at every family party for years.

Sam drove off, enjoying the rest of the afternoon. When the evening shift signed on, Sam was already in his driveway and signed off duty. He headed for the house and his recliner. He needed a break from the last few days.

Chapter 22

The next few days went on without much of any kind of event. In fact, Sam thought the lack of calls that they received was a little creepy. It was even quiet in the office. Chief Wallow had come in on Thursday morning, worked in his office all morning, came out a little after noon time, gave Winnie the next month's schedule and signed order saying Kent Phillips was in charge for the next two weeks. He told Winnie that he was talking vacation, and would be out of town. She had asked him where he was going. He said, "Not here," and walked out.

Sam and Winnie had sat and talked one afternoon at the office, she told him that after the incident with him and Wallow, the chief locked himself in his office. She said she could hear him on the phone and he was yelling several times, but didn't come out until the end of the day and walked out with a big box, not saying anything as he left. "I know he's not going home at night, I pass by his house all the time, and his car is never there," Winnie

said.

"He's not at the bed and breakfast or the inn, he must be staying at her house," Sam replied. "All I know is, it's nice not having him around."

Almost 2 weeks had passed. A lot had happened, unfortunately not on Jason's murder case. John Buckman had called a meeting on Saturday morning at the school yard near where Jason was found. All area officers were invited to catch up on the investigation, but also, they were going to do another walk of the crime scene and see if anyone could think of something new.

Sam arrived early to help Buckman and Murphy set up a couple tables and handouts. Buckman said the sheriff would not be coming because the jail inspector was coming on Monday and he was running around trying to get things up to par. Murphy said he doubted Chief Wallow would show up saying, "I haven't seen him forever, I don't even know when is vacation will be over."

Sam broke in, saying, "Did you guy see the news this morning? Wallow's news girlfriend has got a job in Kansas City and is leaving at the end of the week. He is probably going to help her move."

"What's he going to do when she leaves? His wife has filed for divorce and locked him out of the house. He is going to be hard to live with at the station!" Murphy said.

They were all surprised at the number of officers who were showing up and had not lost interest in the case. Almost all of the deputies and city officers, along with three State troopers and two State Police investigators were there. One of the local FBI agents came in. Buckman had told him about the meeting while they were in Chicago. Before they got started, he filled them in on the latest from there.

Buckman first explained that nothing came out of Murphy and his trip to Chicago. However, was just told by Agent Biker that they had a couple more people from Jason's past cases that they need to talk to.

Everyone got a laugh at the exploits of Greg Pearl, now known as Winfred Shaland. He had agreed to plead guilty to First Degree Murder and life without parole if they took the kidnapping charges off the table, along with the death penalty. Lee Smith and Dawn would be able to get their marriages annulled because he also pled guilty to the bigamy charge. There wasn't any extra sentence for that charge, but Winfred got his payback for what he did to Lee.

While he was recuperating, Lee's brothers snuck in the hospital and beat the crap out of him. At least that's who they think did it, but there were no witnesses and Winfred was not talking, he probably knew they could get him again at the jail.

The best of all of this was that Dawn would never have to worry about him again. He could not give any other excuse for where the money he had used had come from, so she would get her money back, plus his truck, which was in both of their names.

Next, came what was going on with Harold Mookie. Buckman said, "The State's Attorney is working up a warrant as we speak, and we will be arresting him this afternoon." Buckman paused, and everyone was hoping they had their killer. Continuing he said, "Unfortunately, not for the murder of Jason. Mookie was online during those hours, mostly having video sex, so we know he was there. However, while searching his computer we found file after file of pictures of underage girls. So, we are filing child porn charges."

"As for Alvin Clapp," Buckman almost gagged just thinking about it, but continued, "Well, I think we all know what happened with him."

Murphy took over, "Well the bad news is, there is really not anything new to report on the case. We found a copper and steel pipe at the tanks behind the school, and it did have blood on it, but after test and a few calls, it turned out to be snake's blood. The pumper used it to kill a copperhead that was on the steps and would not leave." Murphy looked at Buckman for more. Buckman said, "Look at the papers we passed out, the names of all the people we interviewed, and if you think there is someone we missed, speak up. Also, take a look around the area and see if you can find anything me missed."

Reb Main spoke up, reminding Buckman of Wayne Little, Tommy Little's brother. Buckman said, "Oh yeah, well, Jason cleared that one, himself. Wayne Little had been at the party, he was going across the school yard on a four-wheeler when he saw a car and cut it hard to turn around and flipped it. During the wreck, unknown to him, he lost an 8 ball of meth. After Wayne had got up, he headed back the other way and went out Cotton Mill Road. Jason was outside waiting for Dawn when he saw the four-wheeler go by and continue on the north for as far as he could see, which out there is a long way. Jason texted that information to Reb Main, but then lost his phone soon after. Anyway, Wayne's alibi matches this, and his sister said he came to his house about 4 which also matches to what he told us. The good part, to clear himself of the murder, he had to admit the meth was his."

Murphy spoke up again, "I have worked a lot of cases over the years, but I have never seen so many cases being cleared up or people arrested for just the investigation of one incident and I think that has to do with all of you. So far you all have followed up on everything that we have found out and dug even deeper, let's keep it up and get this thing solved."

Everyone hung around for a while, breaking up in groups, looking at the scene and the area, and discussing ideas with each other and with the investigators. Several theories were voiced, but all had been investigated. Teasdale even brought up the horse again and when he did everybody in unison said, "The horse didn't do it!"

Sam left after about a half hour and went back on patrol. About noon he was going by Dawn's house and saw her sitting on the back porch. Sam stopped and went up to talk to her. Dawn seemed to be in a good mood and even smiled when she first saw Sam. Sam asked, "Is Brittany back from your mom's?"

"Yep," said Dawn.

"Where is she... and Jenna and Cappy?" Sam asked.

Dawn told him, "Brittany went with Jenna to take Cappy to the airport, I needed a little me time. When they get back, we are going to go out and check out Jason's house."

Sam said, "That may be hard on both of you, you know."

"Yeah, but Jenna and I have become really close these last couple weeks, we can get through it together."

"You know you call always call me if you need anything. I mean that, Dawn," Sam said.

Dawn smiled, "Sam, you have been so great through all of this, I couldn't have done it without you. You find out who your friends are when hard times hit, and I have a lot of people to thank." Dawn paused, looked down, and smiled.

Sam said, "What?"

Then Dawn continued, "Guess who called me?" Sam shrugged his shoulders and shook his head.

Dawn then said, "Aaron Peeks... he wanted me to know that he wasn't being disrespectful following me and that he just admired me, but was too shy to say anything… I told him I wanted to do something to thank him for coming forward and telling the truth about what he was doing. I asked him if I could meet him for a cup of coffee so I could thank him in person."

"So you have a date with Aaron Peeks?" Sam said slyly.

"It's not a date… it's just coffee, you're bad, Sam," Dawn snapped back.

They both laughed and talked for a while, discussing Greg, how Karma came around and showed him the kind of bitch she can be. They were talking about Dawn coming back to work when Sam got a call of keys locked in a vehicle on the town square. Dawn said, "I think I'm ready, but I still have a couple personal things to take care of, probably a couple of days."

"Well you're not missing anything; it's been scary quiet," Sam replied.

As Sam was leaving, he told Dawn to call him when she and Jenna got some time, and they would go out for a drink. Sam called out from the car, "Let me know how your coffee date goes?"

Dawn yelled across the yard, "It's not a date!"

About a week later, Jenna stopped by Sam's house early in the evening. Sam invited her in and told Lilly she was there. Lilly came out of the kitchen with her usual big smile and said, "Jenna, what a pleasure to see you! Can I get you some coffee?"

Jenna held up a bottle of wine and said, "No, but I'll share this with you if you like."

"Sounds better," Lilly said, turning to get some wine glasses out of the antique china cabinet.

"What's going on Jenna? I haven't seen a lot of you lately." Sam asked.

Jenna replied, "I've been finishing up some business, and getting ready to go back to California in the morning. I've found an excellent caretaker for the house, and they know how to take care of the horses too. They are going to live in the stable house, so now I don't have to worry about selling it or the horses."

"That's great," Both Lilly and Sam said, and Sam asked, "Well who is it, anyone we know?"

"Yep," Jenna paused and smiled at them and said, "Dawn!"

"Dawn." They again both said at the same time.

"Sam, you didn't tell…" Lilly started.

"I didn't know… I've talked to Dawn all week and she never even mentioned anything about it."

"We hadn't even considered it until this morning, I was talking to Dawn, and she was upset that she was going to probably have to move, because without Greg's…er…Waldo, or… whatever his name is, paycheck, she couldn't afford the rent where she was living. I got thinking about the stable house. It's small, but has 2 bedrooms and is really nice. Dawn likes horses and knows how to take care of them, so it seemed like a perfect fit."

"And you two are so close, when you come back to visit, it will be like being with family," Lilly said.

"She really does seem like a sister I never had." Sam could see that Jenna almost choked up before continuing, "Anyway we went out to the house and checked everything out. She loved the stable house, and Brittany was already playing in the barn and picked out her bedroom. She can live there for free, for taking care of the place, and it will take a load of worries off of me, so it works out for everyone."

"That's great, but why are you leaving so quickly?" Sam asked.

"Cappy called a few day ago, saying that we had a scientific charter we can pick up because another ship had an accident and has to go into dry dock. But… we have to leave in a week, and he needs my help getting everything ready. It's time to get back to my real world."

"We are going to miss you," Sam said, and Lilly hugged her.

Jenna looked at both of them and said with a tear in her eye, "I want to thank you both, but Sam, you have been great, you have been so good to me…and Dawn. I know that Jason's killer will be found and that you won't give up until he is."

Now it was Sam who had a tear in his eye. He gave Jenna a big hug and told her that she needed to consider them as family and if there is anything she ever needed, she would just have to call.

They talked until late, Jenna inviting them to come on the ship and spend some time. It would be a great vacation for them. She also reminded them that Jeb had a job after he graduated from high school.

Parting was full of hugs and goodbyes. Sam would miss her, but also deep in his gut, he was also missing Jason.

Chapter 23

The turning of the leaves brought about many changes in McCracken County, but not in the investigation of the murder of Jason Kelly. The case was at a frustrating standstill for the investigators, officers, and friends. Hardly a day went by that Sam wasn't asked by one of the citizens about the case. An unsolved murder hangs heavy on a small community, but the seasons still turn.

Fall was Sam's favorite time of the year, the cooler air, gentle winds, and beautiful colors. Sam took Lilly to the Garden of the Gods to take a hike and enjoy the view. They walked to a spot just behind the Camel's Head, one of the rock formations overlooking the valley, and had a picnic. It was a perfect day with yellow and orange fall foliage, intermixed with a spattering green from the evergreen trees. The sun was bright and warm, but a steady breeze kept everything pleasant. Sam had fried chicken and

Lilly had made her wonderful potato salad. After lunch, they stretched out on the blankets basking in the sun.

The only down part of the day was that as they were leaving, Sam heard of a college student who got himself stuck on top of Devils Smoke Stack, a 30-foot rock tower, which Sam knew from experience, was a lot easier to get up than down. Luckily, Sam had seen some other climbers with ropes earlier and recruited them to help with a rope rescue. After they had got the "climber" down, Sam realized it had been a while since he had done any climbing and his knees, back, and shoulders hurt. Sam looked at his hand, which was rope burnt, and he remembered how badly they had been cut up in the summer time. But then with the bad comes the good and Lilly felt sorry for him and gave him a long back rub.

The hot summer temperature wasn't the only thing that was gone. Chief Wallow had resigned shortly after returning from vacation. In fact, he never actually came back after the day he and Sam had gotten into it.

Seth Wallow came in the office after his vacation was over, packed up another box, went to the mayor's office, turned in a resignation letter and left. He gave no two-week notice or even told the mayor why. Sam wasn't sure if it was him confronting Wallow that made him decide to leave or the threat of telling his wife about the newswoman. Sam found out a few days later, as fate usually has it, the day of the confrontation, Wallow's wife had found out, went to see an attorney, then went home and threw all of his clothes in the yard. It was not a good divorce. Luckily, no children were involved, but the police were. On two occasions, officers were called to her house when they were trying to divide up the property.

Soon, Wallow moved to Kansas City and in with the newswoman, but that didn't last for long. While job hunting, Seth Wallow falsified his employment and education records when applying for a job as the chief security officer with a bank. They ran an extensive background check and found out he had lied. This seemed to go through the security community in the city and Wallow couldn't beg a job. The high-profile newswoman wasn't having any of this, not only him not having a job, but his reputation being tarnished. When Wallow was unable to find another job, she was embarrassed. She kicked him out, and the last anyone heard, he was living near St. Louis, working as a rent-a-cop at a chemical plant in Granite City, Illinois.

One of the sights that fall that Sam was having a hard time believing was the sight of Dawn and Aaron Peeks horseback riding together on many an evening. On one shift that he and Dawn worked together, they met in the park and Sam asked, "Are you really going out with Aaron?"

"You know Sam, he is really a kind and gentle guy. I know he is soft spoken and a little strange acting, but it's because he is shy. He probably never got a word in around home with his dad," Dawn said.

"But what do you have in common? Isn't he into all those ghoulish things?" Sam asked.

"He is into alternative music and that steampunk stuff, but he also likes classic rock and classical music, we both like old black and white movies and he is teaching me to play guitar."

"Hmmm, I never would have thought it," Sam said, shaking his head.

"He loves those horses. He treats them like babies. He does most of the work around the stables," Dawn concluded.

"I never looked at him to be a hard worker either, just shows some people can fool you," Sam told her, and continued, "As long as he treats you well and you're happy, I'm happy."

"That's the other thing. He is a real gentleman. He treats me like a queen, always opening the door, pulling out my chair, bringing me flowers… I've never been treated so well, and Brittany adores him. He is teaching her to ride English style. I never knew it, but he took lessons while in college."

"Then I'm happy!" Sam said with a smile.

Aaron had cut and quit dying his hair black, and it went back to its natural red tint. Being out in the sun more and helping her take care of the horses, he almost looked normal, except he still had that creepy smile that weirded Sam out. Dawn and Aaron were seen together at many town events and at times he rode along with her on her shift. This caused a lot of talk around town for a while, but like everything in a small town, it became part of normal life after some time.

One of the best things that have happened as far as Sam was concerned was the naming of Kenny McDollin as Chief of Police. McDollin had been on McCracken's Bluff Police Department for 20 years and had a Bachelor's degree in police administration. Sam had thought Kenny should have been promoted to chief when Wallow was appointed, but politics got in the way. Not only was McDollin educated, but also had street smarts, and understood that a police department job was not only to arrest criminals, but to serve the public.

The town council was also happy about the appointment of McDollin and appropriated extra money for the police department to get some equipment, training, and even some more pay. McDollin called Sam into his office one afternoon, asked him to close the door and have a seat. Sam couldn't think of anything he had done wrong, so was clueless about why McDollin would want to talk to him. "Sam," McDollin started, "I'm trying to bring this department up to par…but I need help."

"You're doing a good job so far. What do you need with me?" Sam asked.

"I want you to be my Assistant Chief…Wait, before you say anything, I have put a lot of thought into this, and you are the logical choice, hell you probably should be Chief," McDollin said.

Sam sat there for a while, this was not what he was expecting, nor what he wanted. Trying to put the words together right, Sam said, "Thanks for asking, Chief, but you know I am getting close to having 30 years in and I'm thinking of retiring. I'm tired and don't have the energy that any of the younger guys could bring to the position. I believe that you are doing a good job, and I will help you in any way I can, but I just don't think I would be a good fit."

"But Sam, all the men respect you, on this department and the others around us. That and your knowledge would really help," McDollin replied.

"Why not Murphy? He would love the job," Sam said.

"I can't afford to lose Murphy as a detective; not now, with Jason's case still open, and Murphy's overall investigative knowledge. And you know as well as I do, he sometimes rubs people the wrong way," McDollin concluded.

"Sorry Chief, I just can't see it, what about Tom Clifford? He is smart, he would be great covering meeting for you and everyone likes Tom," Sam added.

"He was my second choice, but I wanted to talk to you first, are you sure?" McDollin asked.

"Positive," replied Sam.

Tom Clifford was appointed Assistant Chief and moved to the evening shift. He would be responsible for the busiest shift of the day, and would handle scheduling. In fact, all officers were given some sort of responsibility. Willy Fogerty was put over evidence, and even the rookie Brandon Teasdale was to work with school kids, even though he wanted to be special weapons.

Murphy did stay on as the detective. He was upset about the Assistant Chief job for a while, however after McDollin explained that he was irreplaceable. They made the position a sergeant's rank with a pay raise so Murphy learned to live with it, especially when he found out he would have an unmarked car and could work in plain clothes.

Sam saw Murphy the morning after McDollin had explained all of this to him. "Murph, where you going?" Sam asked.

"To work, where do you think?" Murphy answered.

"What's with the sports coat and tie?" Sam asked.

"Because I look so good in it," Murphy said, then sang, "Every girl's crazy bout a sharp dressed man."

"Oh, so now you're Inspector Sex Magnet!" Sam said laughing.

Murphy just smiled!

"Anything new on Jason?" Sam asked.

"No, I feel I am running around in circles. We have interviewed so many people, several for the second time. I have read every report, lab note, and autopsy over and over, I just cannot find anything that fits. I'm even having dreams about the case. I see Jason riding his horse, then just a big swoosh of something, then him lying on the ground. Someone had to be there, but how and why?" Murphy said.

"We'll find it, Murph, the answer is out there somewhere. We just have to keep looking," Sam replied.

A glimmer of hope did come in the late fall when Buckman got a call from Stateville Correctional Center, near Chicago. One of the snitches in prison told a guard that two of the other inmates were talking about they had done a hit on a State's Attorney in the Southern part of the state. The warden wanted someone familiar with the case to interview to them first. Buckman and Murphy dropped everything else they were doing and got ready to head north. Murphy had called Sam to give him the news, "Sam maybe we can break this case, finally!"

"When are you leaving?" Sam asked.

"Just as soon as we can get packed, we already have it cleared with the bosses," Murphy replied.

"I'll be off in two hours and have the next two days off. Can I ride up with you guys?" asked Sam.

"Don't see any reason why not," said Murphy. "Be like old times."

"Ok, will ya come by and pick me up?" asked Sam.

"See you about a quarter past 3 then," Murphy said.

Sam called Lilly to make sure there were no problems, and she thought it was great. She told Sam he needed a break, and all was ok at home, and for him not to worry. Sam thought to himself, "That woman knows me, what would I do without her."

The drive to Stateville Correctional Center in Joliet, Illinois was a good time, all three men were in a good mood, hoping that they might finally break Jason's case. They got to their hotel in Joliet about 9:00 pm. After taking their bags to their rooms, the three met in the hotel bar. They took a seat at the back of the bar, all three trying to sit in the two chairs against the wall. Finally, Sam took the outside seat when he noticed the mirrored wall, and he could see behind himself. The bar was full of business types, and Murphy said, "I should have worn my sports coat and tie, I feel underdressed." Since they were going to be on the road most of the day, all three men just wore jeans and a casual loose shirt that covered their guns.

"Hey at least we are comfortable," Sam said waving to the waitress and telling her, "three shots of Jack Daniels."

Buckman shouted, "A Coors for me!"

The waitress brought three shots and a Coors, so Sam took two of the shots and gave one to Murphy. Sam paid for the drinks and asked for a glass of ice water, and Murphy ordered a Black Russian. Sam and Murphy slammed down the first shot, and Murphy sipped on the second shot, chasing it with the water. The three nursed their drinks watching the people in the bar, telling stories and laughing. As the night got later, they noticed several scantily dressed women coming into the bar and making their rounds.

Sam got up to go to the restroom, and on his way back, one of the "Ladies" asked him if he wanted to buy her a drink. Sam looked at her and in his best Clifford voice said, "Do wan me to bwy you a dwink!" while crossing one eye and curling his mouth to one side. She looked at him like he had just grown horns on his head, and Sam walked back to the table laughing. Sam told the others, and they all started talking like Clifford and laughing.

Murphy got tired of waiting for the waitress and went to the bar while standing there another of the women came up and asked him if he was looking for a date? Murphy said, "Date, you mean like dinner and dancing? Ok, but first I got to see if you can dance." Murphy grabbed her hand and pulled her out onto the dance floor, spinning and dipping her as fast as he could, then stopped and looked her dead in the eye and said, "You no dance so good." He let go of her, and she almost dropped from being dizzy, and he went back to get his drink.

The group decided they had had enough fun, and that they better get some sleep because they had to be up early in the morning. They all went to their rooms. Sam, in his, turned on the TV and then the shower. About the only thing, Sam liked about staying in hotels was that he could take an almost endless shower. As soon as Sam got into the shower, his phone rang, it was Lilly. She just wanted to say good night. They talked for about twenty minutes, catching up on the day and the kids, Lilly could tell Sam had been drinking and teased him about it. Sam said he would let her know if they found anything out at the prison, told her he loved her and said good night.

Sam spent almost a half hour in the shower, the hot water felt so good after the long day. When he got out of the shower the bathroom was like a steam room, he dried off in the main room and lay back on the bed, to let the steam clear and mirror de-fog before shaving.

The next thing Sam knew was the alarm on his phone going off. It was morning, he didn't remember pulling the blankets over him, or getting a pillow. He got up realizing he still needed to shave his face and head, get dressed and go down to get some breakfast before they went to the prison.

Murphy and Buckman were already in the breakfast room when Sam arrived. Coffee was the first thing he wanted, he got a cup took a few long sips and sat it down at the table. Murphy said, "How's your head?"

"Not too bad...but then not too good," Sam said shaking his head.

Sam got himself a plate of pancakes and sausages, thinking that would set pretty good on his half queasy stomach. When he got back to the table he looked and Buckman who was just drinking coffee and large amounts of water. "I guess we're not the party animals we use to be," Sam said.

"I can't believe I lost it last night, I haven't puked in years," Buckman said.

"Well... none of us drink much anymore, seems like we are either coming from or going to work, then there is the kids and family, and face it we aren't twenty-five anymore," said Sam.

"Yeah, I got thinking, and it's been about a year since I have had any whiskey." Murphy chimed in while devouring a plate of biscuits and gravy.

After breakfast, they checked out of the hotel. On the way to the prison, they stopped at a convenience store and got some more coffee and some aspirin.

The trip to Stateville took them by the old Joliet Prison, a foreboding limestone structure that was built in the 1800's, housing prisoners until 2002. They stopped and took a couple quick pictures, wishing they could go inside.

Stateville was also a scary looking facility- old, with massive concrete walls topped with numerous guard towers, and the huge "Roundhouse" in the center. The prisoners that they needed to talk to were in the maximum security section of the prison, and it took some time for them to get through the security checks. Finally, after getting clearance and a Visitor's ID badge they were led down a long hallway to a set of several interview rooms. Hamish McLaughlin, the guard who accompanied them, was the largest human being that Sam had ever seen when he stepped into a doorway the light disappeared. They were given packets on both of the prisoner's background and criminal history and were asked if they were ready to talk to them. They asked for a little time, saying that they hadn't seen this information and would like to go over it. Murphy and Buckman read through the records, then swapped them, Sam looked over them quickly as they talked to Hamish about interviewing them separately. He said they were in a holding cell together now but didn't know why they had been pulled out of general population.

Both prisoners were in for an armed robbery/murder. They held up a small liquor store in Coal City, Illinois. The robbery went smoothly until the 86-year-old mother of the owner came out of the back room and spooked Dan Greenmile who turned and shot her, point blank, with a shotgun.

Buckman didn't think that was a problem and asked to talk to Emanuel Bent first. Bent was the smaller of the two but seemed to be the alpha male. He was a wiry guy, about 5'9", with a shaved head and tatted all up. Bent put up a cocky attitude from the moment they talked to him and read him his rights. Buckman and Murphy sat on one side of the table with Bent handcuffed and shackled on the other side. Sam sat in the corner of the room watching. Bent asked Murphy, "Why you wasting time talking to us? We're lifers already, what do you think you can do to us?" Bent went on and on, but at the end signed the Maranda warning paper. Bent then returned in, throwing barbs at the officers, calling them stupid for wasting his time.

After the formalities were over, and Buckman got tired of hearing Bent's mouth he said, "Would you shut up for a minute, seems like all you like to do is talk."

"What do you mean by that?" Bent asked.

"We hear you have been bragging about killing a State's Attorney down state. What do you want to tell us about that?"

"Maybe I did, or not, what if I told ya, what's in it for me?" Bent asked.

Bam! Sam came out of his chair, and his fists hit the desk yelling, "What's in it for you, you son of a bitch! Jason Kelly was our friend, and you killed him you bastard!" Bent laughed. Sam started around the table, Murphy and Buckman grabbed him as Bent fell over backward off his chair and scooted to the far corner of the room.

Murphy took Sam out of the room, "Sam…chill, we have got to keep cool to get what we need from him," Murphy said.

"I know, I know, I'm sorry Murph, you know I'm not good at these things when they act like that. I'll just stay out here and let you guys do your job."

Sam had a seat in the hallway as Murphy went back into the room. Hamish looked over at Sam and smiled. Sam shrugged his shoulders and smiled back.

Murphy and Buckman were in the room for about an hour and a half with Bent. He was not quite as cocky when he left as he was when he went in, but he did stop and smirk at Sam. Sam just smiled and said, "See ya, never!"

Hamish brought in Dan Greenmile. Sam looked at Murphy as he was going back in the room for a hint of how it was going. Murphy just shook his head and closed the door. It was quiet in the room and in just over thirty minutes they came back out with the prisoner, who was crying. Hamish locked him in the holding cell. Buckman went over and discussed something with Hamish when he had them secured.

"What did you find out Murph? Do we have them, are they our killers?" Sam asked.

"Let's wait till we get to the car, too many ears around here," Murphy answered.

They all were quiet walking out of the facility. Sam was glad to be leaving, he felt claustrophobic all the time they were in there. They thanked Hamish for helping them, Sam felt like when he was a little boy shaking Bear Kelly's hand for the first time when shaking Hamish's big paw.

Sam was anxious to get to the car and find out what happened. Murphy was the first to speak, "I can't believe we wasted all this time on those two Bozos."

"Yeah, it was pretty worthless, but I think I fixed Bent," Buckman said.

"What?" asked Sam.

"I told Hamish about Bent implicating the leader of that gang, saying he hired them to do the hit on Jason," Buckman said.

Murphy laughed, and Sam said, "It was a gang hit job?"

"No, there was no hit, but there might be if the word gets out about Bent's big mouth," Buckman said laughing along with Murphy.

Sam was more confused, asking. "What the hell is going on? Did they do it or not."

"No, no, Sam they didn't do it, they are just a couple second rate punks that were looking for some prison cred," Murphy said, pissed off.

"What did they say?" Sam asked.

"Well Bent, the little guy you wanted to throttle, said right away that they did it, but when we asked him how they did it, the story all fell apart. They must have read the newspaper reports and decided they could be a lot bigger men in the yard, than just killing a little old woman. It was good we didn't release a lot of the facts, so they guessed at them," Buckman said.

"What did they say happened?" Sam asked.

"Bent said that they were hired by this Montoya guy who is the leader of some Chicago gang, and who is also in prison. He said It was that Jason convicted Montoya and he wanted revenge," Buckman continued.

"So it was a hit?" Sam asked.

"NO Sam, they didn't do it," Murphy said. "Bent had all of the facts wrong. He said they hid behind some trees, and when Jason walked by, Greenmile grabbed Jason and he cut his throat."

"We noticed that Bent was left handed and when asked what side Greenmile grabbed Jason from, he said the right. Well that didn't make since, and the biggest thing was neither of them ever mentioned the horse. Bent kept up the story even when we pointed out the lies, so we decided to talk to Greenmile instead," Buckman added.

"When we talked to Greenmile, it didn't take long to break him down. When we mentioned that there were no trees in the area and that Jason was on horseback, he just started stuttering and said it was Bent's idea to make the story up. Greenmile said that they were catching hell from the other prisoners for killing an old lady, so after Bent read the story in the paper and that it was unsolved, he made the tale up. It was all to get some prison yard credibility." Murphy said, "And a waste of our time!"

"Wow, I guess we are back at square one... Oh, why was Greenmile crying?" Sam asked.

"He felt bad about killing the woman, kept saying he didn't mean to, he just started crying and wouldn't stop," Murphy said.

"So now what?" Sam asked.

"We drive home," Murphy said, putting the car in gear.

"Hey wait a minute Murph," Buckman said, "We got a little time, let's run up to White Fence Farm. It's a restaurant in Romeoville, about ten miles from here, they have killer fried chicken and great pie."

"Hey, might as well get a good meal out of the trip, the rest was a bust," Murphy said.

"Did someone say pie?" Sam said from the back seat.

They all laughed as they left the parking lot. But after the meal, they were miserable, not just from overeating at the restaurant, but Jason's murder was just as far from being solved as before, and they didn't have anything else to put their hopes on.

Chapter 24

By mid-December the first snow had fallen but was already gone. The nights were cold but the days pleasant. Sam liked the winter. He enjoyed the colder weather, and hardly ever wore a coat. If he did get out of the car for extended periods of time, he would put on his sock cap and gloves, but it had to get below zero degrees for him to put on his big bulky police jacket. Sam always laughed at Murphy, who, once the temperature got under forty, he would put on his long johns and probably wear them all winter.

It was Saturday morning and time for the monthly update meeting on Jason's murder. The meeting was a little less attended than the first few, but most of the local officers still showed up. There wasn't a lot of information to share, so the meeting didn't last long.

After the meeting was over, Sam left the building and went straight to his car. Murphy tried to wave him over to see if he wanted breakfast, but

Sam sped off. Murphy just figured Sam was in a hurry to get home to do something with the family, but as Murphy passed by Sam's home on the way to his own house, he noticed Sam's car wasn't there.

On Monday morning, Sam was leaving the station when Murphy pulled into the parking lot. Murphy caught Sam before he got into his car and asked, "Where did you go after the meeting Saturday?"

"Nowhere," Sam said, getting some paperwork off of his clipboard.

"Nowhere, you had to be going somewhere, you took off so quick and you didn't go home," Murphy said.

Neither of them had seen Dawn walk up until she said, "Yeah Sam where were you going? I saw you drive by the house, and you didn't even wave.

"What are you two doing, spying on me?" Sam said, trying to look like he was busy.

"No, but what are you hiding?" asked Murphy.

"Nothing, I went to the range, Ok?" Sam replied.

"You went to the range by yourself? You would chew us out if we did that." Dawn said.

"I wasn't by myself," said Sam.

"Who were you shooting with?" Murphy asked.

"Just a friend," Sam replied.

"We're your friends Sam, Who was it?," Dawn said.

"Sherrie Hall," Sam said, ducking his head back into his car getting a cigarette.

"Woo hoo Sam, you and Sherrie out on the range alone, I know how your testosterone gets while you're out there! So, what happened?" teased Murphy.

"Yeah, Sam, tell us all." Dawn chimed in.

"Really ya'll, she has been after me to teach her to shoot, so I dropped by to see her at her mother's house on Friday, because she said he father had some guns that she might be able to use. I couldn't believe it; he must have been as big a Ruger fan as I am. He had almost every model of pistol they make, from the Blackhawk and Vaquero to the Semi autos, several shotguns and mini-14's. I was in heaven. He even had a P-89, just like I carry, but it was still in the box and had never been shot," Sam told them.

"Dang Sam, marry that girl!" Murphy said, laughing. Dawn was giggling too.

"Quit! It's not funny. I told her I would meet her at the range at 8:30 on Saturday morning, I had forgotten about the meeting, so when I remembered…I was hoping to get out early. So when we did, I headed straight out there. When I got there, she looked at her watch and said, 'What's the matter Sam, wouldn't Lilly let you out of bed?' I told her about the meeting, but she said she didn't believe me."

"You got her on the hook Sam, she knows you are a stud," Dawn said.

Sam shook his head. Dawn said, "Go on, tell us more?"

"Well, we shot for a while, she is a very natural shooter, she handled everything I gave to her," Sam said.

"I bet she did," quipped Murphy.

"NO... I mean she shot .22 pistols, the 9's and .357 magnum. She also did well with the 12 gauge shotguns and the mini 14's. She handled them all really well and wasn't scared of any of them. We shot the LC9 quite a bit because that's what she wanted to carry. We were out there about two hours and that was that."

"Come on Sam you can't fool your partner; you wouldn't be so nervous about that," Dawn said.

"Or your old partner, give it up pal." Murphy agreed.

"Well...when we got done, she thanked me...then she gave me the P-89 that her dad had, saying she wanted me to have it. I tried to tell her it was too much, but she then just reached up and gave me a big kiss...right on the lips." Sam was blushing as he finished saying. "I couldn't say anything more, she said thanks again and got in her car and left."

"That's it, that's no big deal, I thought you were going to say you did her on the 50-yard line and..." Murphy said.

Both Sam and Dawn said, "Stop!" Dawn continued saying "I don't need that mental picture; I'll never be able to shoot out there again without laughing."

"But what do I do now, what do I tell Lilly?" Sam asked.

"Don't tell her anything," Murphy said.

"No, you haven't done anything wrong, and you don't want to, do you Sam?" Dawn said.

"No!" Sam answered.

"Then just tell her," Dawn said, punching him on the shoulder. "Ya, big lug."

"Maybe Lilly will buy you a bigger gun," joked Murphy.

Sam gave Murphy a raspberry and took the paperwork back into the station.

When Sam came back out, Dawn and Murphy were still talking. Sam just got into his car and left, thinking wonders never cease.

Enjoying the crisp air coming through his car window as he drove down the street, it seemed to Sam that all was good in his world. All of the leaves were off of the trees, the fields were barren, and the sky was clear with a bright sun. He was glad the snow was gone. He could never understand that people live in an area where it snows every year, but at the first snow of the year, they lose their minds, sliding into ditches and bumping into each other. Other than the accidents, Sam liked the snow. It brought back memories of good times from his youth: sledding, snowball fights, and his mom's snow ice cream.

Sam's happy thoughts were broken by a call on the radio, Deputy Reb

Main was making a vehicle stop on Deerhead Lane. Sam was close, and there wasn't anything going on in town, so he thought he would back him up.

Reb had an old red and white pickup pulled over on the left side of the gravel road. Sam turned his lights on and pulled in behind Reb. As Sam was walking up to the passenger's side of Reb's car, Reb was walking back from the pickup. Reb got into his car and rolled down the passenger window so he could talk to Sam. "Hey, Reb, what made him pull over on this side of the road?" Sam asked.

"He was already stopped here as I was coming down the road, when I got close he came running out of the woods, jumped in the truck and started to take off. That's when I lit him up. This guy is a real squirrel. Can you watch him, while I run him?"

"Sure no problem," said Sam. Reb was calling in the suspect's information and asked that the vehicle plate is also checked. While waiting, Sam was watching the driver, but something in the woods caught his attention.

Reb got back out of his car and said, "He's clean, he had said that he had just stopped to take a leak in the woods, maybe he was telling the truth, I'll just be a minute Sam."

When Reb came back, Sam was looking over the top of Reb's patrol car, through the woods to the school. Reb said, "What are you staring at, Sam?"

"I'm not sure," Sam looked at his hands, "but it could be something, will you meet me in the school yard?" said Sam.

"Sure Sam, be right behind ya," Reb replied.

Chapter 25

The first of April was one of Sam's favorite days. It was April Fool's Day and everyone who knew Sam was leery around him and about what he might do to them. Sam has loved playing tricks on people since he was a kid, and he was a professional at it. Sam was in a great mood as he started his day, even though it was a little warm for his taste. All was well in McCracken's Bluff since the case involving the death of Jason Kelly had been solved.

Sam had planned his tricks carefully and knew who was going to be the subjects of his trickery. The only person Sam no longer pulled a trick on was Lilly, she almost left him over the one time he did, a year after they got married. Sam had taped a rubber snake under the toilet lid so it would pop up when she lifted the lid. Lilly went screaming from the bathroom, and when she saw Sam laughing she started hitting him, which made Sam laugh more. This just made her madder, and she left and got in her car and drove off. She didn't talk to him for 3 days afterward, and it took flowers, candy and dinner and dancing to make up. That was the last trick he ever played on her. Now the kids were a different thing. Lilly even helped play tricks on them.

Sam radioed Dawn to meet him in the park, she had just got back from her vacation with Aaron, and he was curious to see how the trip went. This was the first time Dawn and Sam had worked together since she got back. When Dawn pulled in, she pulled next to Sam's car, but was a couple of arm lengths away. Dawn was excited and told Sam that she and Aaron went to Gatlinburg, Tennessee and got married and tattooed. "Married!" Sam said, "Really already?!"

She showed him her hand and instead of traditional wedding rings, they got each other's names tattooed on their ring finger with a black rose. Sam wasn't a big fan of tattoos but each to his own. Sam didn't have any tattoos, but Lilly did, and Sam teased her about it because she did it in her college days and it seemed so far out of character since he had known her.

Sam couldn't see the tattoo very well, so he got out of his car and had a paper bag in his hand. This made Dawn very nervous, and she started to roll up her window. Sam said, "What are you doing, I just want to see your tat." Pushing the bag in front of her, he said, "Here I picked you up a blueberry muffin at the bakery."

"Uh... you didn't have to do that," Dawn said, trying to lean away from the bag and taking it with just her finger and thumb, then setting on the seat next to her.

"Let me see that ring," Sam asked, and Dawn stuck her hand out the window towards him. He looked it over, and Said, "Well, that's different."

"So are we, Sam," Dawn said smiling.

They sat and talked awhile, Dawn asked, "Are you going to the courthouse to hear the big plea deal today?" During that time, she never touched or even looked at the sack sitting next to her.

"No, I'm not going to get mixed up in that media circus," Sam replied.

"Aren't you going to say anything at the hearing Sam? You pretty much broke the case."

"No I didn't. It was a team effort, and Cliff's testimony really helped," said Sam.

At the park, Sam told Dawn that he had talked to Jimmy Jones down at Ozark Police Department while she was away. He told her that her ex-husband got put into the jail after he got out of the hospital. Jones said that they call the former Greg Pearl, "No-Balls Shaland: now. Not only did he go through that but Rebel Pearl's two brothers got themselves arrested on purpose, and caught Shaland in the jail's exercise area and beat the crap out of him, again, so he was back in the hospital. Dawn just shook her head, she was just glad that part of her life was over.

While at the park, Sam got a call to the sheriff's office. He congratulated

Dawn and drove off, smiling. As he was driving to the sheriff's office listening to Bohemian Rhapsody by Queen on the radio, he was thinking "This is going to be a great day."

Sam walked into the sheriff's office with a large box from the bakery with, "From Sam, thanks for all you do!" written on the top. He sat it down on the counter as he walked in not saying a word. Karla DeCarla just looked at the box with suspicion.

Sam went on to the new Sheriff Mike Oldam's office. "Good to see ya, Sam, thanks for coming by," Oldam said. "We will probably need a little more security at the courthouse, some people are really riled up over this plea deal."

"Damn, I was trying to avoid going down there. I'm one of those riled up people, the stupidity of it all," Sam said.

"Aren't you going to say anything at the hearing?" asked Oldam.

"Nope, I'm afraid I might lose it and shoot that son-of-a-bitch," said Sam. "But anyway...I'll be outside and I'll tell Dawn. She came back to work today. We got your back." Sam stuck out his hand to shake Oldam's. Oldam started to shake Sam's hand but hesitated.

Sam showed Oldam he didn't have anything in his hand and turned to walk away, smiling and thinking to himself, "This is so much fun." He walked out of the sheriff's office without saying anything about the box of donuts, just leaving them laying on the counter. "A plan working perfectly,"

Sam thought.

Sam called Dawn and told her that Sheriff Olden was asking for extra security at the courthouse at one o'clock. The hearing was at two o'clock, but they wanted to keep any crowd clear of the door.

Dawn said, "I didn't think you were going."

"Hey the job is the job, ya gotta do it even if you don't like it. I am going to try to stay back and watch the perimeter, though, I don't want anything to do with the news," said Sam.

After Sam hung up, he just took a slow turn around town. As he turned onto Shawnee Street, he saw a female figure jogging in front of him with her ponytail swinging and in dark blue yoga pants. "Oh my goodness," Sam thought.

As he got closer, he realized it was Sherrie Hall. Sam had not actually talked to Sherrie since that day on the range. In fact, he had tried to avoid her. Now he was too close to just stop, and there was nowhere to turn. As he got near, she turned and stopped waving him over. "Hey Sam, where have you been?" She said leaning into his passenger side window with her low cut top, Sam could feel his face getting red.

"It's been busy around here lately," Sam replied.

"I heard. Great work, but I knew you would figure it out, you're so smart," Sherri said.

"It was a team effort, I just kept my eyes open," Sam replied.

"Anyway, when are we going to go back to the range again?" Sherrie asked.

"I think you are familiar enough with the guns for what you need,." quipped Sam back to her.

"I'll bet there is a lot more you could teach me, Sam," Sherrie said, while jiggling back and forth in the window.

Sam was thinking, "Why does she do this to me?" He started to saying to her, "Sherrie …I." He looked up the street and saw Clifford Duggs crossing the street ahead of him. Sam finished saying, "I need to talk to that guy, I'll have to get back to ya?" Sam pointed ahead and pulled off.

Sam looked in his rearview mirror and could see Sherrie standing feet spread with her hands on her hips, he could tell she was not happy. "C'est la vie," Sam thought.

Sam caught up with Clifford a few blocks away and waved him over saying, "Hold up Cliff." Clifford pulled next to Sam's door on the patrol car.

"Hey Tam, what'ca doin?" "I wanted to thank you for your help and tell you that I am proud of you for staying off of the hooch water for the last couple months. You are doing great." Sam said smiling at Clifford.

"Yeah, Tam, no more bwain busters in the morning, since I haven't had any hooch." Clifford giggled.

"So, Cliff, I got it set up for you to go to the co-op and they are going get you a new pair of bib overalls, a couple new shirts, and a pair of boots. You can pick out the kind you want, my treat," Sam said.

"Wilwee Tam, Tan I get a stuwah hat too? Thummer comin," Clifford asked.

Sam laughed, "Yeah, you can get a hat too."

Clifford turned on his bike and took off towards the co-op as fast as he could, giving out a big Wooooop as he did. Sam smiled, thinking, "Just a big kid."

Sam looked at the time and thought he had better head towards the court house. Deputy Kent Philipps waved over Sam and told him to park blocking the courthouse parking lot's Western entrance. Sam got out of his car, and grabbed several white paper bags from the bakery. On each was written: "From Sam." Before the crowd got too big, Sam walked around to each officer's car, put a bag on the hood of their patrol cars and just waved and walked on.

Sam went back to his cruiser and stood by. All of the news outlets were now there. They had an area where they could set up across the street from the courthouse. Three reporters came by to talk to Sam and try to pry some information out of him. Sam just played dumb, claiming not to know anything, but in reality, Sam was one of the few people who knew everything.

He thought back to that afternoon on Deerhead Lane, while he was looking over the top of Reb Main's patrol car. Since the leaves had fallen off of the trees, Sam could see the school from this spot on Deerhead Road. He could see not only the school, but the broken tree limb, that he'd cut his hand on, the damaged metal hand rail that he'd cut his other hand on, and the area of the school near the air conditioner units, where the handle of the water spigot was broken. Not only could see all of these things from where he was, but they were in a straight line of each other. Sam couldn't be sure from there, but he bet that where Jason Kelly's body was found would also be in that line, between the broken handrail and the spigot.

Once Reb and Sam met behind the school, Sam went out to where there was still a small red flag that had been placed where the body was, along with other flags where evidence was picked up. Sam stood over the red flag and looked both ways, and he was in a direct line of both the points.

Now, over the radio, Sam heard that the sheriff was en route to the courthouse with the prisoner. Sam took a look around; everyone was getting ready to make sure the crowd stayed back. Sam could also see that no one had touched any of the seven sacks he had passed out. Sam smiled, this was going to be a great day!

Thinking back again; Sam had asked Reb to stand where he had been. Sam then went to the spigot. Getting down eye level with the spigot, Sam could see that the place on the handrail that had been broken was in a direct

311

line but about five feet above Reb's head. That is where Jason would have been, Sam knew it.

Sam started looking around on the ground as Reb was walking towards him. "Reb, bring a camera and an evidence bag!" Sam yelled excited. When Reb got back, Sam took several pictures of a piece of mangled metal laying in the corner or the school. "What is that?" Reb asked. "That is a bullet, a very big bullet," Sam said.

It was a big bullet, a .50 caliber, shot from a .50 caliber Barrett sniper rifle. After some lab work, the copper from the bullet matched the other bullets in a box, that was missing a single shell, that was in the sheriff's department evidence room. Sam was thinking of who shot that gun, and Clifford had given him that answer.

Sam looked up and across the courthouse parking lot and watch as the sheriff's car pulled in. Sam never cared much for Larry Dickens, when he was a jailor or the sheriff, but he really disliked him now. Sam did think there was a little bit of justice, considering how badly Dickens treated Clifford Duggs, and that it was Clifford that put it all together. Sam had remembered about Clifford talking about Daddy Larry, and his big boomer, back last summer in Sam's garage.

When Sam found the bullet, he went and hunted down Clifford. Sam took him back to that place it happened on Deer Head Lane. Clifford, spite everything else had a good memory; he told Sam, about the sheriff stopping to get the gun out, when Sam drove up and gave him a sandwich. Clifford said that after Sam left Larry Dickens got the big gun out, got 1 bullet out of a box and shot into the woods. Clifford laughed while he was telling Sam that the gun knocked Dickens on his ass with a big boom. He said that Dickens hopped up, put the gun in its case and told Clifford to get in the truck and they drove on to the jail.

Sam now watched the sheriff and three deputies lead Larry Dickens into the courthouse. All of the news people were trying to a good shot. No one was allowed in after Dickens went in. The judge was not allowing cameras in the courthouse, but a few reporters were allowed, along with a few Dickens family and anyone else involved. Dawn decided early on she didn't want to be in there. Buckman and Murphy, though, wanted to go.

The hearing only lasted about forty minutes, Sam knew what the plea was before it took place, but had not told anyone. Dickens was relieved from office as soon as he was arrested, he had no objection to that part, but after talking to his attorney, he pleads not guilty to involuntary manslaughter. It was not until all of the forensics came back from the lab, and he could not any longer give a decent defense that he took the State's Attorney plea deal: two years in jail, to be served locally, ten years' probation, and never being able to own a gun again.

Neither Dawn nor Jenna liked the plea, but both understood that you have to show intent for murder, and this was just an act of stupidity. For both of them, it was good to know that Jason was not dead because someone hated him. Sam hoped that Dickens moved out of town as soon he got out of jail, he never wanted to see his face again.

While waiting outside waiting for Dickens to be brought out, Chief Kenny McDollin pulled up behind Sam and got out with the department's new hire. Eric Daisy was twenty-three but looked fifteen. Sam liked him when he met him at the recruit testing, the kid always had a smile on his face. When they walked up, Sam reached into his car and pulled out two more bags from the bakery and gave one to Kenny and one to Eric. Kenny held his bag away from himself, but Eric stuck his hand right in.

All of the officers in the area were watching, with their bags still sitting on the hood of their cars. Many of them smiling and could not wait to see what kind of trick Sam was pulling on the kid, and which they had avoided. Eric pulled out a big blueberry muffin and took a big bite, then another and another. Everyone was waiting to see something happen, but it never did. Everyone was looking at Sam, and he smiled and pointed around at all of the officers in the courthouse lot and yelled, "Got ya!"

They all thought about it for a minute, and everyone started to laugh, they then opened their bag and ate their blueberry muffin, laughing at themselves. It was a good time for a laugh. The case of Jason Kelly was finally over, as Sheriff Oldam brought Dickens out and drove off to the jail with him.

Everyone wanted to get out of the courthouse area and get things downtown back to normal, plus the news people were looking for officers to put on camera, and nobody wanted to do that. Sam headed down towards the riverfront to finish out his daily log and kill a little time till the end of his shift. While sitting, watching the river go by, Sam thought about retirement and what he would... The radio broke in, "Dispatch to City four, we have a horse in Randy's parking."

"A horse," Sam said aloud. "Oh hell, no!"

ACKNOWLEDGMENTS

Many thanks to Dark Ink Press for bringing the second edition of this book to life, especially Emily Hakkinen who patiently edited the manuscript and opened even more doors in the small town of McCracken's Bluff. Thanks to John Gray who designed the new cover with a horse of a different color.

facebook.com/DarkInkPress
@DarkInk_Press
@darkinkpress

www.ingramcontent.com/pod-product-compliance
Lightning Source LLC
Chambersburg PA
CBHW030606180626
46816CB00005B/1691